MAGICAL MIDLIFE MEETING

Also by K.F. Breene

MAGICAL MIDLIFE MEETING

BY K.F. BREENE

Contact info:
www.kfbreene.com
books@kfbreene.com

CHAPTER 1

A ROUND FACE loomed over me and I screamed, clutching the bed covers and yanking them up to my chin. My magic boiled within me, nearly releasing. If I'd lost control, it would've blasted the intruder across the room.

"Good morning, Miss Ironheart." Cyra, the mythical phoenix who lived in Ivy House but wasn't officially a member of the team yet, clearly hadn't learned the rules of personal space. She smiled down on me, her silky black bob shining within the soft light from the windows, giving her hair a slightly blue sheen. It struck me that the light didn't reflect off the thick-rimmed glasses over her jade-green eyes.

I lifted my head and squinted at her. "Do you have any lenses in those glasses?"

She laughed and straightened up. Fire curled into the air from her shoulders and something like liquid magma dripped from her fingers onto the bed and floor.

"Oh, whoa." I scooted away, only then noticing the presence at the end of my king-sized bed, its little body standing on the corner of the mattress, its painted-on baby face turned down in sorrow. It held a glass of water. "No!" I kicked at the doll, but the bed was too long for me to reach. I scooted down and tried again. "No dolls on my bed. No dolls—"

A spot on my comforter blackened before a tendril of smoke rose into the air. Small thuds sounded across the floor, more dolls rushing forward. The one at the end of my bed skittered toward me.

Fear quickened my heart. I threw out a hand to blast it away, but it tossed the water at me before I could, glass and all. Water slapped my face, and the glass thunked down onto my ribcage. More liquid splashed up from the floor, hitting me crossways.

"I'm not the one on fire!" I hollered, patting at my bed, snuffing out the little flames the dolls had missed. My comforter slipped down, and I quickly hauled it back up to my chin. "Cyra, away. How many times have I told you not to come wake me up? Mr. Tom gets special privileges because he brings me coffee."

"Yes." She gestured to the nightstand beside the bed. "I have brought you coffee. It is scalding hot, just like you like it."

"No…" I groaned.

"What's going on?" Hollace sauntered through the open bedroom door, but at least he had the good grace to step to the side rather than approach the bed. Leaning against the wall, he crossed his large arms over his chest, the darkness of his skin contrasting with a crisp white dress shirt, the sleeves rolled up to expose his muscular forearms. He was another new addition, the third being a gargoyle and the last being dead.

A pang hit my heart as I thought about Sebastian, the odd mage who'd taught me so much in such a short period of time. Before Elliot Graves had killed him.

I pushed the thought away before any of the attached rage or guilt could drag me under. Elliot had only killed Sebastian because of me, something I couldn't seem to get past. Then, not long after, he'd amended his causal invite to meet for a drink. I was now invited to his residence, the exact location to come later, along with a collection of other mages, the number of total attendees and who they were not disclosed, to compete for his attention like some sort of dating show. The invite had been vague at best, and now Niamh was scrambling to find out more information, uncovering only bits and pieces at a time. For example, she'd found out that the residence seemed to be some sort of collection of tunnels within a mountain, possibly with limited entrances and escapes, but nothing beyond. To say I was on edge about it was a vast understatement.

Hollace kicked out, an almost lazy movement, clipping a doll and sending it rolling across the floor.

I smiled despite myself, the expression melting away immediately, not unlike the bedroom rug probably would beneath Cyra's lava-dripping elbows. "Cyra, stop shedding fire!"

"Oops." She laughed again and yanked her arms in tighter. Little droplets of fire sprayed out.

The doll on the bed ran for the glass next to my ribs.

"Gross, get—" I kicked, connecting with it this time and knocking it to the floor with a *thunk*. They were helpful when it came to Cyra's unconscious droplets of fire, but they were still animated murder dolls. I hated having them around all the time, especially when I first woke up.

The rest of the dolls ran to the bathroom with their glasses, going for more water.

"What's going on?" Ulric jogged in, his pink and blue hair spiked and his lithe frame shirtless. "We having a meeting? Oops. Those dolls are failing in their duty. Look at this—five spots of fire." He stamped on the nearest. "We're going to have to get the floor redone at this rate."

Hollace pushed forward, his focus on the ground, snuffing out another spot. "The miss needs to learn the spell for canceling fire so we can lock up the dolls."

"I know, I know." I pinched the bridge of my nose. "I just can't seem to get the elemental spells right. The root spell is super complex. It's at the very top of my power scale and there is literally no room for failure. I need help…"

The room fell silent, and I looked out the window, feeling a stronger rush of sadness chased by rage. Sure, Sebastian had been Elliot's employee, something I hadn't known until the end, but Elliot hadn't needed to *kill* him.

"Maybe send out another summons?" Ulric asked, stomping at the ground.

"And potentially get someone else killed?" I shook my head.

"If he could not defend himself, he wasn't good enough for this team anyway," Cyra said, something she repeated often. She wasn't just trying to make me feel better—she was speaking the truth as she knew it, and most of the team agreed with her. The magical world was cutthroat, and I was starting to wonder if I had what it took.

Not like it mattered. I'd taken a blood oath to protect this house and these people, and there would be no takebacks. I was in it to win/lose it regardless of what I might want.

"It's fine," I said, nearly sitting up before I remembered what I was wearing. I had put on a see-through lacy number last night, hoping Austin would eventually make it over. He hadn't, unfortunately, still kept insanely busy by his ever-growing pack. "I'll figure it out. Can you all leave now so that I can get up?"

"My, my. Busy morning, isn't it?" Mr. Tom bustled in carrying a silver tray laden with a steaming white mug, a thin white porcelain vase containing one red rose, and a plate with fruit and biscuits. His tuxedo was freshly pressed, his nose high, back straight, and loose jowls wobbling as he made his way to the table by the window. He'd clearly thought I'd want to take breakfast in my room, usually done in silence and with the door locked. Given everything I'd been pummeled with within minutes of waking up, he was correct. "To what do we owe the pleasure of so many loud personalities so early in the morning?" A question I hadn't thought to ask after the invasion of the dolls.

I reached over and tapped the screen of my phone. Half past nine, not early for Dicks and Janes—the non-magical—but an hour or so before I usually got up.

"I've been thinking..." Cyra scratched her eye through the rim of her glasses.

"What happened to the lenses?" I asked, bewildered.

"They made my vision blurry," she replied.

"So why wear glasses at all?"

"It makes me look more human."

"Our faces make us look human," Hollace drawled, back to leaning against the wall. "Our bodies. That's why we inhabit them."

I squinted my eyes and bit my lip, still struggling to understand the natures of our new houseguests—Cyra a phoenix and Hollace a thunderbird. Their souls lived on from body to body, through the eras, which wasn't like me, obviously. But they both had a magical shape, like a shifter or gargoyle (like me), and a human form. They looked human, at any rate. Yet they didn't think of themselves as human. I couldn't wrap my head around it. Was I not human anymore? Were any of us?

"It is too early for an existential crisis," I groaned, closing my eyes.

"If I may prompt the next phase of this conversation…" Mr. Tom transferred the coffee to the table, shooting a withering look at the cup on my nightstand, which had blackened fingerprints along the rim, before straightening up. "What is it you were thinking, Cyra?"

"Yes." She smiled. "When you practice, Miss Ironheart, you batter us with your magic, and you stab at us, but you are doing so against the protective shield you have on us."

"Otherwise I'd kill you," I said, eyes still closed, will-

7

ing patience.

"And you also keep a layer of defense over yourself, since the defensive spells applied to us reflect magic in some cases."

"Yep."

"So that's not good."

I peeled an eye open, trying to read her face. The supportive expression didn't relay any additional meaning.

"Why?" I asked.

"Oh yes, I see." Hollace nodded. "If she's wasting all that energy trying to keep us and her safe, she's not putting all her power into the kill shots."

Cyra bobbed her head. "When this Elliot Graves accepts your rose and is finally in your sights"—she'd watched one too many episodes of *The Bachelor*—"you won't be accustomed to working with full power, and you will hold back. It might make the difference between success and failure."

"Right, except I can't practice kill shots on people who aren't protected from them." I finally sat up, holding the sheets over my chest. "I feel like that's pretty obvious."

"Agreed," Mr. Tom said, crossing behind Cyra and lifting the still-simmering cup of coffee. "We only have two weeks before we go to Elliot's...residence, or tunnels, or whatever he calls his lair. The time for experimentation is over, if there ever was one. Instead of waking the miss for these types of musings, maybe your time would be better spent harassing the rock-throwing old crone next door into learning more about Elliot's dwelling. Surely she should've uncovered something useful by now."

I pulled up my knees and dropped my forehead on-to them. "Mr. Tom, leave Niamh alone. She has to learn a few decades' worth of magical politics in a month. She's doing the best she can. We know roughly the type of...dwelling we're going into."

"The inside of a mountain isn't a great place for a team of fliers," Hollace said.

"Which is likely the point," I replied. "As Niamh pointed out. But it's fine. We'll bring some of Austin's people. We'll be fine."

"Ah yes, the dreaded *fine*." Mr. Tom stepped away. "We will be *fine*."

What else was I supposed to say? *We're almost certainly heading to our doom because I'll only get one chance to take out Elliot, and it's not going to work because he has decades more experience with just as much or more power.* "Fine" would have to do.

"For the first part of training, you should practice your magic on us like usual," Cyra said. "You'll need that ability to protect us in battles with mages." She stepped back. In the process, her boot heel clunked against a glass of water held by a doll with porcelain hands. The doll, knocked off balance, fumbled and spilled the water down its side. More fire shed from Cyra, liquid magma plopping onto the doll's head. Its plastic brown hair started to melt before its whole head caught fire. It squealed, something I hadn't known they could do, and then tottered around the floor, flailing its hands.

Great. The last thing I'd needed was more night-mare fuel.

Hollace kicked out as the doll ran by, catching its melting head and sending it rolling across the floor. The rest of the dolls chased after it, water glasses full, slopping most of the water onto themselves before they saved the half of a head it had left.

"This has been a very bad start to the day," I mur-mured.

"When you are nearing the end of your training," Cyra continued, not at all bothered by the pandemoni-um she had caused, "you will strip all your defenses and attack me with everything you have. You will not give me any kind of alert before you do this. You will attempt to kill me."

I rubbed my face with my palms. "Except Elliot

might be able to block my magic, and then he'll fight back with power I probably can't defend against. So it still won't be like the real thing."

"I can likely consume a dose of your magic without falling, and my self-preservation instincts will kick in. I will fight back just as fiercely as Elliot Graves would. Either you will be burned half to death before I relent, or I will die."

"Oh no, Cyra, you mustn't ask the miss to kill you." Mr. Tom shook his head gravely. "If Edgar catches wind of this, he'll start asking her to retire him again. Though after that sunflower debacle last week, I think she should've finally given in and shown him mercy."

"Shown *him* mercy?" Ulric said with a laugh. "He gave consciousness to a giant sunflower with razor-sharp leaves. Which would have been great if he'd bothered to teach it the difference between friend and foe. That thing cut me up something good. Thank all that could fly that the basajaun was on hand and hungry. I'm not up for messing with weaponized plants. Killing Edgar would've been a mercy to *us*."

"Yes," Mr. Tom said. "That has always been a given."

My phone buzzed on the nightstand. I glanced over and caught Austin's name on the screen.

A thrill of excitement stole my breath.

"Get out," I said, reaching for it. "*Everyone get out of here!*"

People and dolls alike spun and headed for the door. They knew the score. I was officially dating the town's alpha, and the taking-it-slow act was just that: an act. I felt like I was going to combust every time I so much as heard his name.

I was pretty sure the only person I was fooling was myself.

I snatched the phone up like a grinning fool, waited long enough for Mr. Tom to close the door behind him, and swiped to answer the phone.

"Hey," I said with a gush of breath, my stomach flipping.

"Hey, babe," he responded, his tone smooth and deep and the term of endearment completely nonchalant. Which was a little crazy considering the guy had planned on being a bachelor for the rest of his life. He'd even resisted the growing attraction between us in the beginning.

But he'd pulled a complete one-eighty one day, and now he had no doubt that forever was knocking on his door. There was no more resisting. No anxiety. He hadn't had a single freak-out!

He probably figured I'd have enough of them for the both of us.

The shifters were convinced Austin and I were sliding into mating, a sort of permanent bond that magically connected two people, somewhat like the one I had with Ivy House but deeper. And they were probably onto something: with each passing day, my depth of feeling for him increased, my desire ballooned, and my happiness grew.

But I was newly divorced, dang it! New to magic, new to solo home ownership, and new to being the reluctant master of creepy dolls. I couldn't just hop into another lifelong romantic commitment willy-nilly. I hadn't even played the field! Austin was technically a rebound, for criminy's sake. I had to approach all of this logically, which required at least a little freaking out. It required brakes, and if I had to bear down on them for a while, so be it. His infallible confidence could take it. He'd said as much a few times over.

Take as long as you need, Jess. I'll wait. You will *be mine.*

I shivered and suddenly couldn't stand the distance between us. I couldn't stand to hear his voice but not feel his touch. He needed to be closer. *We* needed to be closer.

"Do you have a second to FaceTime?" I asked. If I couldn't do it physically, I'd do it through the Ivy House bond. It would have to be enough.

"Yeah, sure. I'll call you back."

I hung up, bounced around in the bed organizing my pillows, and then lay down, splaying my hair out around my head. His heart throbbed in my chest, next to mine, something that had happened for the first time a couple of weeks ago. It should have felt strange, especially since I'd started life as a non-magical person, a Jane. But it didn't. It was intimate and comforting.

The phone rang for FaceTime, and I answered, unable to help the excited smile. His handsome face filled the screen, his eyes hooded with fatigue and his hair standing every which way. His head rested against leather, and I imagined he was probably on his couch.

"Did you just get in?" I asked, feasting my eyes on him and enhancing Ivy House's magical link between us, feeling the answer for myself. I immediately launched into healing his fatigue.

His little grin said that my magical touch was appreciated. "Long night. I had a few direct challenges, one from a very strong shifter, and then a raiding party came through."

I furrowed my brow. "A raiding party? Like a bunch of Vikings?"

He sighed and scrubbed his fingers through his hair. I loved seeing him like this. At home and on his own (or with me), he was able to be so expressive, unlike when he was in public and donning his "alpha" mask of non-emotion.

"Basically, yeah," he said. "They roll through and try to grab whatever they can. Or kill whoever they can. Or just create mayhem. It's pretty standard for a newly established pack to suffer raiding parties. I'd thought I'd be immune, since my brother helped me set this place up and everyone knows I took down a phoenix, but no such luck."

"Oh. You should've let me know—I could've helped."

"Thanks, but it's good. I used it as a training exercise. It cut into sleep time, though. I have a pretty packed day today. That's the reason I called." Frustration bled through the link. "Can you push off training for a few hours so I can stop by before I hit the bar?"

"Or maybe you should use those few hours to get some rest, and I'll try to kill the phoenix on my own?"

He paused for a moment, and wariness trickled through our link. "Kill the phoenix? Did Cyra do something to piss you off?"

I told him what she'd suggested. "It won't set us back too much. Apparently her magic is like the gargoyles'—it responds differently when she has an alpha who calls her, and through the link I've figured out how to call her. So there won't be much of a delay training-wise if I'm able to kill her. She'll regrow to her adult size pretty quick."

"And if you aren't?"

"It'll hurt like the blazes, and I'll need to drink a half-dozen protein shakes for all the energy I'll need to heal myself…"

He issued a soft sigh. "If you think you're up for it… I'd prefer to be there when you try, but…"

"When I succeed, you mean."

His smile made my heart flutter. "Obviously. I'd prefer if you'd put it off until I can be there. I trust that she won't go too far, but just in case."

"You'd prefer it, but you'll defer to your alpha's decision?"

Hunger flashed in his eyes. I was the only person in the world who wouldn't turn him rage-y if I talked about dominating him. Quite the opposite, actually. Bedtime wrestling was sexy as all hell, and I didn't mind losing. Neither did he.

His voice was low and rough. "If I must…"

I ran my tongue along my bottom lip, catching his gaze.

"Do you have a few minutes?" I asked, then panned the camera down my body, red lace barely covering my flesh. Pushing the covers down more, I dipped my hand between my spreading thighs.

Desire flooded the link. My moan matched his.

"An hour, at least…" His hand drifted south, and through the now extremely sensitive link I could feel our combined passion building higher.

A few moments later, pleasure swept me away, pulsing hard and hot, leaving me wondering how long I could possibly resist the mating bond, and what sort of ritual a female gargoyle enacted once she'd finally chosen a mate.

CHAPTER 2

"HEY, MISS IRONHEART." Kace nodded as he entered the clearing, jet-black five o'clock shadow on his square face to match his hard onyx eyes. He'd come to town with Austin's brother and stayed on as Austin's second, his beta. Five grim-faced men and women followed behind him. "Alpha told us to report to you."

I nodded and glanced over at my team. The gargoyles had shifted into their flying forms—they were stronger like this, in the air or not—but they hadn't taken to the skies. Elliot's place seemed to be a collection of tunnels running through a mountain. Any fighting would be ground-bound, so my team had been practicing that way in preparation.

"Just you guys?" I asked, wearing basketball sweats with buttons down the sides in case I had to change shape in a hurry. There were usually twice as many shifters.

"Yeah. He said you'd have plenty to deal with." Kace

stopped in the clearing I usually used for practicing, in the woods behind the house.

I glanced at Cyra, waiting patiently off to the side. I *would* have plenty to deal with, yes. The second I shot a spell at her, it was on.

I blew out a breath. Austin had barely managed to defeat Cyra, and he'd endured *incredible* pain. That guy could handle an awful lot without passing out.

I could not.

"Right, then. Let's do this." I clapped as Niamh skittered around to my back in her little gremlin form. She was a dirty fighter in any form, but this one, all teeth and claws, still haunted my nightmares. Didn't matter that she was on my side.

Kace and the shifters stripped with quick economy and changed into wolves, he the brawniest of the bunch. One sleek brown one—Isabelle—had been around a few times before, and she always managed to get through my defenses and tackle me. While my magical shield kept her claws and teeth from finding purchase, she always knocked the wind out of me, and it hurt like Hades when I hit the ground.

My crew and the shifters spread out around me, encircling me. Nervous flutters filled my belly and my small hairs stood on end. God, I hated this. Being surrounded by vicious predators, even though they were *my* vicious predators, freaked me out every time.

Breathing deeply, staying calm, I slipped a defensive spell on each of them before coating myself in magic twice as strong. Every spell I did would bounce off them and fly back at me, stronger and more potent. My shield would soak it in and store it up. When it came time to knock out Cyra, I'd let loose all of that stored-up energy and hope for the best.

Who was I kidding? I'd probably let it loose and then run like hell. Maybe I should've waited for Austin…

Hollace, in his human form, wearing battle leathers and really handy at hand-to-hand combat, offered me a slight nod. Now or never.

I gritted my teeth and hit Kace with a laser beam of magic, using a punch of force that would have blasted a hole through his body if he hadn't been protected. His fierce growl ran up my spine. My magic slapped off his shield, knocking him back. I didn't want to kill anyone (well, anyone other than Cyra), but I was fine with bashing them around.

The spell zipped back to me as I pushed out another one in an arc, curving it around from my position so it punched into everyone's shields. Hollace gritted his teeth and took one step back, fighting it, but Ulric flew off his feet and tumbled end over end through the air.

Jasper nearly followed, flapping his wings to stay put.

Niamh recovered the quickest, and she was mid-leap by the time I got my hands up again, creating a magical net in the air and spinning her into it. I weighted the spell and spun again, knowing it would drop straight down and she'd have to chew through it, or however she dealt with magic. I never got enough time to watch.

One of the big timber wolves lunged. And then another, and another. I slammed them out of the way, barely able to do spells fast enough to keep them off me. A jet of fire hit my shield from the side and heat bled through my world, so potent that it singed my hair.

I jogged away, sending a cooling blast at Cyra. But I had yet to master elemental magic, and the blast only neutralized her fire instead of countering it. A furry body hit me from the side. Freaking Isabelle!

I flexed my shield, using some of the accumulated magic to blast her off. Then I sent another repulsion spell at the shifters and a wall of blistering pain at the gargoyles, who were advancing much less gracefully than their shifter counterparts. Little clawed hands grabbed my leg, and I just barely caught sight of a gaping mouthful of razor-sharp teeth ready to chomp down before I quickly released more stored magic at Niamh.

Sweating now, I redoubled my efforts, blasting Kace away, keeping Hollace at bay, and knocking Nathanial, the newest gargoyle in our crew, backward. Isabelle slunk behind two of her crew, waiting for an opportunity. I spun to fling a bruiser of a spell at the wolves, but a weight banged into the center of my back, shoving me forward. Before I could regroup, a foot sped for my face. Hollace's.

I yanked my weight backward, seeing the dirt on his sole as it barely missed my face. That would've hurt.

I'd arched too far back, though. My bones groaned. My muscles couldn't hold the awkward position. I tumbled to the ground, and the shifters were on me immediately, pinning me, trying to get at my jugular.

Fear overwhelmed me, the primal part of me screaming that they were going for the kill. That if I allowed them at my throat, I was done for. That was the benefit to training like this: I *did* forget, and it allowed me to fight like I really was struggling for my life.

My gargoyle form exploded out, my wings snapping along the ground, one tweaking painfully against my sweats before the confining material ripped away. Magic ballooned from me, a nasty spell I'd learned from the second Ivy House training book rippling outward from my defensive layer. Furry bodies blasted off me. An acidic gale eroded their protective shields, bearing into them without mercy.

I sprang to my feet, fighting the lingering terror, knowing I had my salvation in my magical arsenal.

I pounded everyone with another nasty spell. The dangerous parts didn't make it through their shields, but the sheer power battered them around the field. Niamh was up first, never down for long, and I sent a magical explosion her way. I'd always been good at blowing things up. She zoomed sky-high from the concussion, her gremlin form almost comical as it zipped through the treetops. The shifters followed.

Cyra stepped forward, slipping out from behind a tree. I knew immediately that she was on the offensive. She must have decided I might not go for her plan unless she goaded me into it, because it was obvious she didn't intend to wait for a surprise attack.

So be it.

I yanked all of the others' protective shields away, leaving only mine. Power surged through me, like I was a ship freed from an anchor.

Cyra bent a little and brought her hands together, readying what I knew would be a thick stream of white-hot magma. She wasn't pulling any punches.

Watching Austin fight her, I'd worried for his life. I'd forged my blood bond with Ivy House after months of hesitating, in the hopes that it would make me powerful enough to intervene and help him. He hadn't needed me in the end, and although I'd thought it remarkable that he'd defeated such a strong adversary without any help, I hadn't realized *how* remarkable. It turned out Austin was the only shifter in recorded history to have dominated a phoenix. Learning he'd knowingly risked his life for me, again, had nearly made me throw up (I'd ignored the primal part of me that had been incredibly turned on).

Now it was my turn. Cyra was one of the most powerful beings in the magical world. Would I measure up?

She pushed her hands forward, sending forth a thin stream of glowing red and white flame that shed smoke as it cut through the air. I fortified my shield with everything I had, as much power as I could wrap around myself.

Her magic hit my shield like a Mack truck. The point of contact couldn't be larger than the head of a pin, but she'd condensed a staggering amount of power into it. Flame coughed out at the point of contact and black smoke drifted up.

I gritted my teeth and took a step forward, which seemed counterintuitive, but I felt the need to take some sort of action, and stepping back was not an option. Her magic burrowed into my defensive spell, incredibly potent. Cyra shook with the effort, her thin brows low and her jade eyes focused.

A surge of emotion welled up through the link. Austin clearly sensed what was happening and was sending his encouragement.

I held firm, taking another step forward. Ready for my turn. Ready to attack.

"Rip her magic away," Hollace yelled, watching from the sidelines, holding his injured arm. "Don't let her sap your strength—fight back!"

"I don't know how—"

Cyra tore away the magical magma and blasted a thick stream of fire at me, like a flamethrower. I sucked in a breath, ignoring my fatigue, and soaked in the magic. The flames looked terrifying, but they weren't anywhere close to touching me. A moment later the magical magma was back, the pinprick focus digging into my shield. She was mixing it up to throw me off guard. Apparently she thought I had enough versatility to do more than doggedly focus on my best shield. Joke was on her.

This blast didn't make it any deeper than the first. I could withstand her most powerful magic.

I would've rejoiced if she didn't rip the spell away and sprint at me.

"Oh crap—"

She slammed into me, flash-heating the air around

us and knocking me to the ground. I couldn't feel the heat on my skin, my defensive spell soaking it in, but I could definitely feel her fingers wrapping around my throat.

I supercharged my defensive layer, which was incredibly potent from all the power she'd fed me. The spell pulsed, turning red as it did, and zapped every square inch of her body where it was in contact with mine. She convulsed against me, but her hands were still wrapped around my throat, cutting off my air. I pulsed my power again, then fed a mini-explosion into my defensive layer, trying to force her off.

Her grip tightened around my neck, holding on. Black dots swam in my vision. Surely she wouldn't kill me on purpose, and yet... I wasn't sure she had a handle on herself. I wasn't sure she would remember to let go.

Fear kindled within me. Her focus on ignoring her pain was so acute that her eyes were closed. Air dried up in my lungs, no more coming through my closed-off throat.

No one was coming to help me.

With Austin across town, maybe no one could.

I released a hand from around her wrist and reached for my pocket, for my knife Cheryl, but claws raked across my side. I'd changed into my gargoyle

form and completely forgotten about it. I had claws!
Why wasn't I using my claws?

Blackness clouded my vision, my head light. A rush
of dark rage rose through me, fueling my resolve. I
punched my claws into her stomach, piercing flesh. She
groaned but didn't relent. I ripped down, opening thick,
messy gashes that spilled blood down on top of me. Still
she held on. This woman was tenacious. I punched into
her chest next, then her neck, ripping to one side. The
sickly gash that opened up would've killed a human. She
merely flinched, one hand losing strength and nearly
reaching for her neck.

It was all the leeway I'd get.

I knocked her weak hand off my throat, pried the
second one away, and then shoved her back. As I did, I
hit her with another punch of magic that blasted her up
and off.

Throat bruised, breathing ragged, I hopped onto my
feet. Pulling up every ounce of power I possessed, I sent
my own thin slice of magic, the nastiest spell in the Ivy
House library. It cut through the air, straight for her.
Her eyes widened and she *poofed* into her phoenix form
and spread her mouth wide to catch the spell. She
swallowed the spell, and I immediately sent another.
This one was weaker—exhaustion was setting in—but
hopefully still strong enough to beat her down.

But it didn't have the chance. Before the next spell could reach her, she squeaked and then burst into flames, falling into a pile of smoldering ash.

The second, and now unnecessary, blast of magic continued past her, heading straight for the basajaun, who'd snuck in at some point, as if taking in a matinee movie. He was hunkered down in the tree behind the phoenix, a terrible location to watch the fight.

He dove out of the way before I could do more than holler, "Loork oww-t!"

My spell crashed into the large pine and blasted a hole into the trunk. Wood crackled and the tree shivered. I held my breath, wondering if it was going to come down. Silence descended on us, everyone else clearly wondering the same thing. Loud pops and crackles preceded the tree shaking, starting to lean, gaining speed.

"Get out of the way!" Hollace yelled, running for me.

Nathanial got there first, wrapping his arms around my middle. His powerful wings beat at the air, and we darted skyward, gravity ripping at us, the speed thrilling. The pine fell, but we were already up over the treetops, still gaining altitude.

"Phoe-nix kii-llerr," Nathanial said in my ear, his speech within his gargoyle form amazing, his pride unmistakable.

I wanted to tell him that she'd nearly been the victor, to ask why they'd all sat watching while she nearly strangled me, but it would've been too arduous with my gargoyle mouth. I'd chastise everyone later. Instead, I relaxed in his grip, pointed at the open horizon, and said, "Fll-y."

He altered his hold to be more comfortable and then shot out into the big blue horizon, the others joining us in no time.

I had enough power and perseverance to take down a phoenix.

Cyra didn't fight dirty, though, and a lot of mages did. Elliot surely would. If I gave him the opportunity. Which was why I intended to hit him with my most powerful spell the second he was in my sights.

CHAPTER 3

"**A**NOTHER!" NIAMH PICKED up her glass without looking up from her laptop and rattled the ice cubes within it. The evening was coming on, and she sensed Jessie was on her way to the bar to check in. Niamh had to finish up before she got there. The name of the game was to keep all nonessential information from her until she could handle bad news.

Lately, Jessie could barely handle good news.

"Hey." Ulric stopped behind Jessie's open seat, recently evacuated by some tall and thick yoke who slobbered a lot. One of Austin's flunkies, no doubt. Some of the *eejits* who came to this town to join the pack were as useless as teats on a bull. "Any news?"

Niamh clicked a few keys on the laptop. "Like what, a call from Elliot with a detailed schedule, a map of his premises, and an explanation of his motives these last lock'a months?"

"In a good mood, then?"

"I'm always in a good mood until someone asks

stupid questions." She clicked through to another magical peon's social media page. Nothing was really secret these days. It had been so much harder to find information when all a body had to go on were newspapers and rumors from unreliable sources. Now younger people posted their whole lives on social media, desperate to share each fart. Niamh was making incredible progress getting back up to speed on the goings-on in the magical world, but some information remained elusive. And most of it centered on Elliot Graves.

"Did Jessie say anything about officially bringing the new people onto the Ivy House crew?" Ulric asked.

Niamh jotted down a vague post about "the snake" inviting new friends into its lair. That had to be about Elliot. Which meant the peon's boss might be another of the attendees.

"Yeah, she plans to make them official when Cyra regains her human form. In a couple days, probably."

"She going to ask them all?"

"Yeah. They'll all accept, too. It still leaves us with open slots, but Austin Steele can fill in the gaps for now. She's got enough good people to be gettin' on with. It's her that we need to keep our eye on. She is still very new to this world." Niamh dug through a few more posts before clicking onto the poster's profile. None of the other posts proved useful, so she clicked through to one of the eejit's other social media platforms, handily listed on his profile page.

"Yup." She shook her head, turned to the beginning of her notebook, and made a checkmark. "Rufus Fernsby has definitely been invited, and it sounds like he's accepted. That makes five mages I'm almost positive are going. Elliot Graves is making a party of it with some experienced, highly dangerous mages. He's planning on re-entering the magical world, I think, and he's working on his connections to do it."

"How does Jessie fit into that plan? She's powerful as hell, I think we can all agree on that, but even I can see she is…not where her power level says she should be."

"She doesn't know her ass from a hole in the ground, ye mean." Niamh glanced down at the robust list of mages. Once they would've shat themselves to get an audience with Elliot Graves. Now…

"Something I didn't expect…" Niamh said as she flipped through her notebook. "The Anal Repository, as a few people call the guild, is a full-fledged outfit now. Before I came here, they were nothing. Not even worthy of a name. It wasn't until Sebastian mentioned them that I pulled me head out of me arse and realized they've blundered into some power."

"The Mages' Guild?" Ulric leaned over the chair and

put up his hand for one of the bartenders to see him. Why they needed help noticing him, what with his crazy hair, Niamh did not know. She couldn't help but be sidetracked by that bright shade of pink every time he walked into the room. "Yeah," he said, "they've been corrupt for years. They heft their weight around to keep other operatives from getting off the ground. Austin Steele's brother, Kingsley, talked about his efforts to try to get the shifters to come together nationally. It seemed like every time he was close to making something happen, the guild or that nutsack crime boss Momar stepped in and hamstrung him. When he was here, he was trying to keep his hard-faced alpha thing going, but I could tell he was frustrated."

"Just as soon as Austin Steele is up and running, he'll make it happen, just ye wait," Niamh murmured, shutting down her laptop and stowing it. Jessie was nearly there, walking slowly, clearly trying to work through her bad mood. "Still, the Anal Repository has some clout, and they're allowed to police their own."

"Have been for a while."

"Right. Which is something ye might've mentioned when Jessie was getting ready to battle—and potentially kill—that idiot mage a couple of weeks ago. Kinsella is firmly established in their crap network and she is not. If she'd killed him, she would've had that damn repository breathing down her neck."

"They would've been up her ass, actually, and I figured you knew."

Niamh glared at him, her patience quickly running out. "Ye must be the stupidest smart fella I know. The lot of us have been practically dormant in this small town for…years. Decades! We didn't know when, or *if*, someone would show up to claim the Ivy House magic. We'd all but retired. Then Jessie came to us without any knowledge of magic, so our focus needed to be on training. We don't—or didn't—know bollocks about the current goings-on in the magical world. Hopelessly blind, so we were. How did ye not see that?"

He pulled his lips to the side and squinted one eye as if aiming. "I was scrambling to figure out how to be part of the team and clearly missed the mark."

"Yes, ye certainly did," she said, then picked up her glass and shook it aggressively, the ice cubes making a sound like shrill bells. Donna down the bar put up her finger in a *just a moment* gesture, waiting on a group of younger women with too much booze and too few clothes. "Well, it's a good thing she didn't slit his throat as she oughta've, because the repository would've held an inquiry. Austin Steele wouldn't have let them punish her, and it would've led to war. A war the shifters aren't ready to fight. It would've been a grand ol' mess, sure enough."

"Jessie has enough money to buy the guild."

"Momar basically owns them, from what I've gleaned, and he would never allow it. He hates shifters something fierce. That poor wee lad Sebastian wasn't telling fibs about that. No, it's lucky for us that useless bugger Kinsella took off. The only problem is, he'll resurface eventually, and then we'll have a problem on our hands."

Ulric tensed as a swell of power infiltrated the bar. Through the link, Niamh could feel Jessie nearing the entrance. Ryan, also known as Sasquatch, had gone outside for a smoke. Jessie did not tolerate him on the best of days, and today was far from the best of days.

"She's still pissed that we didn't pull Cyra off her," Ulric muttered, correctly reading the situation.

"That is the general feeling I am getting, yes." Niamh glared down the bar at Paul, helping a crowd of shifters who'd been drinking all day and were ordering shots. Austin Steele was in the backroom and not slinging beers as he ought to be. Niamh had been dry for much too long. People would start to wonder what she was even doing there, sitting at the bar with a computer and nothing to drink. "Don't mind her. She had it in the bag."

"It was kind of a close call, though."

"Nah. Ivy House would've reacted if it had been a close call. Hell, Cyra would've let go. She's been around far too long to get lost to rage. Jessie just needed a moment to push through her fear. Worked out exactly like it should've, with the basajaun pissing himself and everything."

Ulric huffed out a laugh and turned around, elbows pushed back to lean on the back of the pushed-in chair. He'd clearly given up on getting a drink.

Niamh shook her glass again.

"I didn't even know he'd snuck up," Ulric said.

"Only Edgar seemed to notice. That el' vampire is Froot Loops, but he does tend to notice things everyone else has missed."

"She took out a phoenix in one shot, after already having battled everyone for a while." Ulric shook his head, his smile growing. "If we can get her enough training, she'll be a real contender."

"If we can kill Elliot Graves so he'd butt out of her life, we might have a shot."

"Wouldn't we have to deal with the guild?"

"They'd be thanking us. The Anal Repository has a bounty out on Elliot Graves. They're trying to weasel into this thing he's throwing in a couple weeks under the guise of 'discussing the possibility of lifting the bounty,' but Elliot Graves is ignoring them, so he is. The whole situation has social media atwitter. No one can believe he is flat-out refusing them, and they are dying to see what happens. So it seems our Mr. Graves is re-emerging into the magical world on the wrong side of the current pervasive authority."

"Then he plans to pit himself against Momar, I take it."

"If that's what people are thinking, they haven't dared mention it where I can see. Stands to reason, though."

"Still, what the hell does he want with Jessie?"

"To harness her power? I was starting to think someone else might be using Elliot's name, but with his invitation and all the rest of it, that doesn't seem likely. Maybe he's trying a new tactic. Throwing romance and riches at her and promising her the world in the hopes she'll open up that power for him to use, like the heirs before her."

"If that's his game, he's going to get an unwelcome surprise."

Niamh watched Austin emerge from the backroom, making his way behind the bar, ignoring everyone, his eyes on the door. He had clearly come out to greet Jessie.

"I half hope it *is* his game, just so we can see the fireworks," Niamh murmured.

"Fireworks? It'll be a slaughter. Austin Steele isn't rational when it comes to Jessie. He overheard some guy talking about her ass last week and about killed the dude. I saw the whole thing. If that's Elliot Graves's game, he might get his arms ripped off for his troubles."

"Austin Steele is heading toward mating and he's a powerful alpha—he'll get a lot worse before he gets better, trust me. I've seen some things that would curl yer chest hair."

"I don't have chest hair. I'll have to settle for it curling my ass hair." He winked.

Niamh shook her head at the jest, still watching Austin Steele. "Good thing fer his power, too, because if Earl is right, Austin Steele'll have his work cut out fer him, trying to handle her once she finally accepts him as her mate."

Of course, there were so few female gargoyles that few had much personal experience with them. They were going off gargoyle lore, which was hardly reliable, plus a few scraps of knowledge from some book or other Earl had found.

"Mr. Tom said we shouldn't fill her in on how a female gargoyle...goes about mating."

"Are ye daft? Of *course* ye shouldn't fill her in. That's all she needs to know right before walking into a large gathering of experienced and cutthroat mages."

Niamh shook her head. "She's stubborn about some things, and rushing into romance after a divorce is one of those things. Rightfully so. Hopefully she doesn't officially decide about Austin Steele until *after* we're out of the woods."

"Out of the tunnels, you mean, and that's if we make it that far."

"Well, yes, to be sure. But if we don't, we'll be killed, so it really won't matter."

"Comforting."

"What am I, yer mammy? I'm not tryin' ta'be comforting. Ye knew ye'd be in the thick of it if ye signed on to Ivy House. Expect the worst, hope for the best."

"Can I get that on an inspirational poster?"

"I'll tattoo it across yer arse, how's that?"

"It would be hard to see, but I'll take what I can get."

"Based on the women ye go home with, I'd already figured as much, yeah."

Ulric spat out laughter. "Touché. Mr. Tom seems to think she should have played the field more. I get the feeling he'd prefer to see Jessie with a male gargoyle."

"He's a Muppet. There isn't anyone better for her than Austin Steele, wings or no."

The chatter died down as Jessie came through the doorway, her face closed down in annoyance. There was no way of knowing if she'd encountered

Ryan/Sasquatch outside the bar, but she'd taken her time coming inside. Her mood radiated off her in waves of power.

Heads turned her way and eyes widened. People shuffled or stepped out of her way, nodding as she passed by. Many greeted her with "Miss Ironheart," giving her the respect due to an alpha. Others looked down at their feet, acceding to her dominance.

The shifters from the training earlier had already told anyone who would listen that she'd taken out the phoenix. Now they all knew what Niamh had known for some time—Austin Steele wasn't the only power player in this territory.

Niamh sat up a little straighter as Jessie walked toward them, feeling a rush of pride in the Ivy House heir.

Austin Steele leaned forward against the bar, staring at her, ignoring the customers trying to order drinks as he waited for her to meet his gaze. He was proclaiming Jessie the most important person (to him) in the room, a distinction an alpha reserved for his or her mate and children. His intentions were laid bare for all to see.

That she didn't look for him immediately upon entering the bar—his establishment within his territory—sent its own message. She was powerful in her own right, he wasn't her alpha, and she didn't claim him as her mate. Not yet. She held all the power.

Jessie might not realize it, but that was the message she was unconsciously conveying. Austin had told the Ivy House team, in no uncertain terms, that they were not to explain any shifter rules to her. And because fair was fair, he'd asked not to be told how female gargoyles mated. He wanted to experience this as nature intended, apparently. He'd probably live to regret that. Maybe he already did.

"Hey." Jessie nodded at Niamh and Ulric, who immediately moved out of the way. Even though anger still curled through her middle, she'd chosen to acknowledge her team first.

Finally, as Ulric pulled the high-backed bar chair out for her, she looked up and met Austin's eyes.

Her eyes lit up and a big smile spread across her face. Hunger sparked in his gaze, and she blushed and leaned toward him just a little, hands braced on the bar. Thick slabs of muscle popped under Austin's tan, long-sleeved shirt. Power curled through the room, his claim on her manifesting into a surge of magic. She answered with her own burst of power, a feeling like little bubbles slithering across Niamh's skin, potent but pleasant.

"Everyone freeze," Ulric murmured, holding out a hand.

A woman down the bar squealed, another shrieked, and a man's booming laugh shattered the scene.

Austin's focus shifted, his head snapping to the Dicks and Janes down the way.

The pleasant feeling of Jessie's magic changed in an instant, turning pressurized and angry, bearing down. Ulric swore. Pain twisted along Niamh's spine and boiled through her blood. She barely stopped from wilting over the bar.

Grunts erupted all around her, people starting to sink down. Screams and shouts reverberated down the way.

"Silence," Jessie said, her voice a whip crack of power, ominous and full of authority. Niamh's limbs tightened until she couldn't move them if she'd tried. The shouts and screams died off. The entire bar ceased movement until it was dead silent.

"Hi," Jessie said to Austin softly.

His focus came back to her, and passion flash-boiled through the link, Austin's response to Jessie's dominance.

No, his *animal's* response. Her gargoyle was calling the shots right now, and the polar bear in him liked it. She was much deeper into the mating slide, as the shifters called it, than any of them had realized. Earl wouldn't be pleased, the wanker.

For a moment, Austin's brow creased. He looked like he was on the verge of asking her questions, but a rush of wariness flooded the Ivy House link from Ulric. Although no words transferred through the links, just feelings, the message was clear: *Don't question her, just go with it.*

Austin took a deep breath, and his bearing relaxed, his eyes softening. A moment later, a little smile tickled his lips.

"Hey, babe," he replied, easy and confident.

His blistering passion at the dominance she was displaying cut away, as did Jessie's sudden surge of heat. She'd made their link private, keeping her emotions—and his—to an independent line, no longer shared amongst the whole crew.

A soft breeze blew through the stagnant air, carrying the smell of daffodils and crisp mountain mornings. The pain eased from Niamh's spine. A little thrill of adrenaline wormed through her blood, giving her a shock of energy. The bubbles resumed their slide across her skin, pleasant again. A sense of peace filled Niamh as Jessie smiled.

"Good to see you," Jessie said to Austin as she finally lowered into her seat.

Ulric shook himself a little before stepping forward and pushing in Jessie's chair. The pressure from around Niamh ceased, her ability to move restored as the magic ebbed from the room.

Gasps sounded from down the bar, the Dicks and Janes clearly freaked out or at least very confused by what had happened.

"Go sort that out," Niamh told Ulric.

"Yep. Life of the party, coming right up." Ulric peeled away.

Jessie took a deep breath and looked around. The link opened back up, and a thread of confusion leaked through it.

"Want a drink?" Austin asked her, recapturing her attention.

"Oh, uh…yeah." Jessie frowned, tilting her head to the side, and glanced behind her. "I just told everyone to…be silent…right? My head went foggy there for a moment. Is my magic getting away from me again?"

"And why wouldn't ye tell them so?" Niamh said, holding up her glass, the ice nearly melted. "With all that screeching down there, ye couldn't get a word in edgewise, so ye couldn't."

"What do you say we duck out of here early and I make you dinner?" Austin asked her, reaching behind the bar to grab Niamh a cider.

"Get two," Niamh said. "Who knows when the other yuk-ups will make their way down here again."

He pulled out another without looking, his eyes on Jessie as she smiled. "That sounds amazing," she said to

Austin. "Do you mind if I have a glass of wine first? I've had *a day*."

"Of course. I'll come around and join you." He pulled out a bottle of Merlot and poured two glasses then pushed them across the bar and winked. "Be right there."

Jessie frowned again, watching him go. "He winked."

"Did ye fall on a rock and hit yer head? Why are ye so slow all of a sudden?" Niamh stared at her glass for a moment. He hadn't freshened up her ice. What a balls. They needed to get this mating thing out of the way so they could go back to being functioning adults. Watery cider was just ridiculous.

"No, but"—Jessie picked up her glass of wine— "alphas don't show that kind of emotion. It invites challenges."

No one in their right mind would challenge either of them after Jessie's show of power. It was quite prestigious for anyone to land an alpha, but everyone in this bar was quickly realizing that it was just as prestigious to land a female gargoyle.

That would've filled Niamh with pride if the heir's magic hadn't just given her a good rattle, and if she didn't now have watery cider. The joy of her position had gone out of her. She just hoped those Janes at the end of the bar kept their wandering eyes and especially their hands to themselves until Jessie and Austin Steele got out of there. Niamh liked seeing fireworks, but she didn't like being blown up by them.

CHAPTER 4

I SLOUCHED AGAINST the chair and sipped my wine, happy for the background noise of other people chattering. Mr. Tom had been doing my head in, quizzing me on various spells, randomly trying to attack me to see if I could defend myself, going over various clothing options for the trip, and asking if I might want to take Nathanial or a gargoyle in town for a sexual spin for comparison reasons. I think the pressure was getting to the guy. His grip on reality was starting to fray.

After all that, he'd had the gall to ask if I'd "finally" gotten around to deciding how I wanted to reoutfit the house.

I didn't care about home décor! I was about to stumble my way into an impossible situation, and I was starting to lose sleep thinking about the danger I was putting everyone in. It would be better if I went alone, took a magical kill shot at Elliot, and hoped for the best. End of story. If someone went down, it should be me and only me.

"You good?"

Austin's rough voice washed over me in the best of ways. I closed my eyes as his hand touched down on my shoulder and drifted across my back, dropping to rest on the back of the chair. I turned a little, dipping my fingers into his pocket and resting my hand there, pulling him a little closer until his side was pressed flush to my shoulder.

"Yeah. You?" I asked, looking up at his handsome face.

"Very. Should I grab a chair?"

He was asking how long we'd be.

My stomach flipped as I thought of him cooking dinner for me. Of what would absolutely happen once we were finished eating.

"No. Just one drink, I think."

He nodded and reached around me to grab his glass. "So. You took down the phoenix, huh?"

My mood darkened. I scowled at Niamh. "I didn't have much choice. It was that or die."

"Bollocks," Niamh said. "She was fartin' around the whole time until she finally got her head out of her arse and finished things up."

I rolled my eyes but didn't bother to comment. I'd already yelled as much as I cared to. She hadn't backed down then, and I knew she wasn't likely to have a sudden change of heart.

"One shot?" Austin said, swishing my hair across my shoulders. He stroked my cheek, and I closed my eyes and savored the sensation, my heart leaping, his heart beating right beside mine in my chest.

"Mhm," I murmured.

"You did better than I did," he said.

I laughed, my eyes fluttering open again. "Hardly. I didn't get the shot off until after she nearly choked me to death."

"That Cyra is tough, boy," Niamh said. "Jessie raked her across the middle, nearly tore her throat out, and battered her around—she just held on until she couldn't anymore. Everyone knows female phoenixes have more power than the males, but Hollace says she's also one of the oldest and most vicious of the females. Her soul has been around for ages."

The link with Austin sparkled with pride. "And now both of the alphas of this territory have taken her down."

"I'm not so sure I could do it again," I said.

"Ah, would ye *schtawp.*" Niamh gave the ceiling a long-suffering look.

"Was that English?" I asked with a grin.

"Janie Mack, ye're driven me mental, so ye are. Go have dinner. Austin Steele, if ye're goin'ta have all these people in this bar all the time, ye're gonna need more bartenders."

A woman in her early twenties staggered a little as she climbed the steps from the lower area with the pool table and the bathrooms to the main bar area, from which the pool table had been removed a while ago to create space for the crowds. Been there, done that. She was one of the Janes and definitely a tourist.

I sipped my wine, nearly finished, losing sight of her within the throng of people.

"Are you over capacity?" I asked, pulling my fingers from Austin's pocket and tracing them up his hard side.

He glanced around, taking in the crowd. I caught sight of the woman again, all hips and breasts, her miniskirt barely covering her crotch and her tube top covering just a strip of her middle. Her jewelry glittered, layered on her chest. I watched, transfixed like a magpie, an effect of my exhaustion. I could think of at least three outfits I had that would look great with that collection of jewelry. If only it was in vogue to steal so I wouldn't have to go shopping.

It didn't dawn on me that she had drifted a little too close until Austin stiffened, curling his hand around my far shoulder and turning, using body language to advertise that he was with me. I looked at her face; her makeup was a bit smeared from heavy drinking and her lips twisted in a hungry though taunting sort of way.

"Mmm, I like me an older man," she purred, slowing.

I could feel my eyebrows lowering and wondered if she thought that was a flattering thing to say, calling Austin an older man. Didn't men take that as the insult women had been taught to?

But when her gaze roamed his broad shoulders, dipped to his defined chest, evident even through his nondescript cotton top, and settled on his package, the logical part of my brain dimmed. Rage as hot as Cyra's magma bubbled up out of nowhere. My whole being throbbed with it, pulsing with power.

My scope of vision reduced down to the woman, turning a little as she slunk by, her fingertips trailing across her cleavage, tinkling those stylish necklaces. Her predatory gaze darted to me.

She had no idea what a predator really was.

She had no idea who she was challenging.

I pushed Austin away and stood from my seat, power pumping, ballooning out. That distant part of me, the logical part, screamed at me to stop. To control the magic. To reel it back in.

I shouldn't reveal my power to so many innocent bystanders, and I definitely couldn't go after a Jane!

But none of that would register.

My wings itched at my back, my gargoyle threatening to claw its way out, and a pinkish-purple sheen vibrated into being around my body, trailing my movements.

I could have sworn a bell rang in the distance. A death knell. I couldn't tell if it was my imagination, or if Ivy House was fueling the fire, telling me to protect what was mine.

Mine.

A stocky woman with white-blonde hair—Isabelle—stepped forward suddenly and rammed into the younger woman, knocking her sideways into a crowd of male shifters watching the scene with grim faces. She screamed as she tried to correct on four-inch stilettos, but the excessive alcohol hindered her movements. She scrabbled at one of the shifters as she fell, trying to grasp an arm or a hand.

The man, a newer guy I'd seen patrolling the streets in jeans and a white shirt, pulled his hands away and stepped back, getting out of her way. The others followed suit, letting her fall.

"Oh my God, what the *hell*?" the woman demanded, fighting with her long, wavy blonde hair as she tried to look around.

"He's taken," Isabelle said, looking down on her.

"You *bitch*," the woman yelled, pushing to her

knees, but Isabelle was already walking away, her message delivered.

The newer guy looked down at the woman, his face impassive. "If you're smart, you'll never look at him again, not even when he's talking to you. Best to take the warning."

"Oh my God, Brittany, what happened?" Two other women descended, having heard their friend's cries, and pushed through the crowd to get to her. "Who did this to you?"

"Hold my earrings. I'll deal with this," said one of them, a girl with short red hair and big hoop earrings.

"That big bitch that just walked out." The first woman let her friends haul her to her feet, all of them swaying like new sailors on a boat in stormy seas. "Forget her. It's not worth it." Isabelle might have been the one who'd shoved her—and I knew exactly how *that* felt—but the woman had clearly sensed something from me, even if she didn't understand it. She speared me with a glance, hatred burning deep in her red-rimmed eyes. "Whore."

She spun and let her friends help her away, but they weren't agitated enough to leave the bar—they just headed back to their seats. The loud guys I'd heard earlier were probably waiting for them.

"Those Dicks down there are going to take offense

for their friend," Niamh murmured, then took a sip of her drink. "They'll probably start a row."

"Nah." Austin had hardly moved, watching me with hunger plain in his eyes. "They aren't friends; they're just trying to get laid. They're cowards. If they don't convince the girls to leave, I'll have someone escort them out before things…escalate."

I stared after the three women, expecting to feel bad for my outburst. Or embarrassed. Or even fearful. A swell of possessiveness had taken over my better judgment, and I'd almost used magic to strike down a Jane. And although I wasn't even sure what spell would have zipped out at her, I sensed that it would have been a bad one. Maybe bad enough that I wouldn't have been able to heal her.

But I didn't feel either of those things.

I stared after them for a moment longer, that pinkish-purple light still shimmering around me, and Austin's heartbeat felt just a little more powerful in my chest. His presence comforted and soothed me, helping me back down.

"I'm going crazy, that's what this is," I said softly, bracing a hand on the back of my seat. "This magic, or the bond, or my gargoyle is making me go crazy."

"Edgar is crazy," Niamh said. "That fool *Mr. Tom* is crazy, naming weapons based on their 'personality.' The basajaun might just be nuts, as well. The ruling is out on him. Ye aren't crazy, though. Ye're owning yer space, that's all. That trollop pushed into yer space, trying to get a rise out of you, and if Austin's people weren't here to keep the bar in one piece, ye would've pushed her right back out. That's within reason. Sure she started it! How is that yer fault?"

I shook my head and finished my wine.

"Your reaction is expected for a shifter," Austin said, putting his empty glass on the bar. He set his hand on the small of my back. "It was definitely within reason for an alpha sliding toward the mating bond."

"I'm not a shifter."

Austin looked down at me, his cobalt eyes taking on a sheen from the sparkly light still shedding from my skin. "No, you are not. And not a single shifter in the world would hold that against you." He bent down and kissed me softly. "Let's go get some dinner. You'll need sustenance for what I'm going to do to you later."

I smiled at him. "I'm going to hold you to that promise."

CHAPTER 5

AUSTIN COULDN'T HELP but smile back. Jess wasn't his mate yet, so it was slightly unorthodox for an alpha to be so openly affectionate in public, but he felt like a little kid at Christmas. Jess had just given her beast the wheel, and his people had needed to step in to calm things down. They knew the score: Austin would have been powerless to stop her.

Mating bonds were tricky. When a shifter saw that his future mate was defending his claim on her, there wasn't a hope in hell that he'd intervene. Even if his own bar came tumbling down around them.

"I'd never break a promise to you," he said, running the pad of his thumb down the front of her throat.

Her eyes fluttered and she shivered, a shadow crossing her eyes. "I think I understand a little more of what it means to let someone trace down the jugular like that," she said, but didn't pull away.

"Oh yeah?"

"There was a moment today," she said, "when the

shifters got me down, and I had a blast of terror that they'd go for my throat. It felt like death was coming."

He noticed Kace, his beta, threading through the crowd. When he neared, Kace clasped his hands behind his back and turned his eyes downward. He wanted Austin's attention but knew better than to interrupt. Wise. Even a small intrusion wouldn't sit well just now. It was why he needed to get her out of here. Get them both out of here.

This thing with Elliot Graves couldn't have come at a worse time.

"Excuse me," he said to Jess, then looked at Kace. "Yes?"

"Sir, the Janes are getting all riled up. The Dicks they're with clearly don't want to get involved, but it could get…ugly."

"Get the Janes out of here. The Dicks will surely follow."

"Yes, sir."

"I did that," Jess murmured, glancing down the bar. "I made them feel that way."

Austin walked toward the door, sweeping her along with him. They exited the bar into the early evening, the light dwindling.

"Other way around, actually," Austin said. "That Jane got *you* all riled up. On purpose, I believe. I didn't use to know much about women, but I've learned a lot from an insightful and amazing woman I met last fall. A woman who shamed me into realizing I was a selfish jackass—"

"I'm pretty sure that wasn't what I was saying…"

"—but I'm no expert. Still, I doubt she would've been so vocal about her desire for me if you weren't sitting right there."

Jess stiffened and sucked in a breath. She squeezed her eyes closed, and her steps faltered. "Please don't talk about other women desiring you. I am…not well."

"What are you, in a Jane Austen movie? You are 'not well'?"

Her smile was grim. "That's the only way I can describe it without sounding like a jealous teen. Jealousy stems from a lack of trust, but I trust you implicitly. A beautiful woman could crawl into your lap, and I would trust that you—" She stopped, hands balled up in fists, teeth gritted. "I'd lose my ever-loving mind, is what I would do." She breathed deeply. "What's worse, I'd *enjoy* it. I would enjoy ripping her off you and beating her to a senseless, bloody pulp. I wouldn't even feel guilty. I'd feel *vindicated*." She shrugged him off and started walking again, heading to the parking lot out back. "I hate that I feel that way. It's not right. That sort of possessiveness is abusive behavior."

"Everything you've learned in a lifetime as a Jane is warring with your primal knowledge of yourself as a female gargoyle. It'll take time to get used to it."

She shook her head but didn't say anything, clearly at war with her emotions.

"I'm tired," she finally said as they reached his dirty Jeep with mud sprayed up the side. "My guard is slipping."

"Your guard against what?"

"Reality? I don't know. Just let me say things and pretend they make sense."

He laughed and opened the door for her. "Ten-four."

"It would've been disastrous if I'd attacked that Jane," she murmured as he got in and started the Jeep. "She wasn't my equal, and she wouldn't have healed like a magical person. It would have been like a man hitting a woman."

"I would like to see what happened if a man hit you."

"Yeah, right. You'd lose your mind."

"Not if he hit you, no. Only if he pinched your bottom." He grinned at her, feeling a rush of adrenaline. In the past, he would have shut it down forcefully, worrying where it might lead, but this time he didn't.

Austin had always worried he'd lose himself to his

beast. That he'd become like his abusive, no-good father. They had the same animal form, after all, and he'd feared he'd fail in the same ways. But giving in to his feelings for Jess had actually made him stronger. And now, watching her wrestle with her own fear and uncertainty, he felt closer to her than ever. Because he'd been there. And seeing her in the thick of the same struggle actually made him less judgmental of his own floundering.

They were meant for each other; he truly believed that. She made him a better man, and he was uniquely qualified to help her cope with the violence of her creature. He'd lived with that darkness all his life.

"What do you want for dinner?" he asked, driving up the narrow mountain road to his home overlooking the valley.

"Anything. I'm easy."

"That's what she said."

"Who?" She frowned at him, then her expression cleared and she gave him a dopey grin. "Ha-ha." She rolled her eyes, then shook her head. "I'm slow tonight."

"You're too wound up."

"I know. I'm worried about Elliot Graves."

He nodded, resting his elbow on the open window. Two gargoyles flew ahead of them, one pink and blue and one with an enormous wing span—Ulric and

Nathanial—flying low, since this area was so remote. They'd check things out at the house before Jess arrived. "Niamh is working on it. She's turned her barstool into a seat at the library, and she has the whole town looking into things and reporting back. She must've been a political animal back in the day—she makes pretty intricate connections very quickly."

"Really? I haven't heard much of anything. Any time I ask for news, she tells me to stick it up my hole, or some other colorful Irish saying."

"Each of us needs to be an expert in our own right. Trust her to get all the information and deliver it when you need it."

"In other words, mind my business."

"Not mind your business so much as spend your energy focusing on your piece of the pie and don't waste precious resources worrying about what you can't immediately control."

"Right, which is a very eloquent way of saying…mind my business."

He chuckled. "If you say so."

He slowed as he approached the house, giving the gargoyles another moment to look around. A supposedly great mage had put a ward on his house, but Austin's brother had opened his eyes to the fear and hatred most mages felt toward shifters—information Niamh's research had bolstered—and he no longer trusted the protections. With the right training, he knew Jess could fix it, but her magic lessons had been cut short by her tutor's death.

"Hey, I was thinking." He slowly pulled into his driveway. "You're going to have access to a few good mages at Elliot's thing. They won't have as much power as you do—at least, that's what Niamh thinks—but they'll have a lot of experience. Maybe you can ask one of them to train you? You'd have to give them something, and I bet Niamh will have a bunch of suggestions about what to offer, most of them ending in you screwing them over when you get what you want, but it would be worth a try."

"Yeah." She sighed as he shut off the engine but didn't make a move to get out of the Jeep. More gargoyles circled the house and grounds now, scouting.

These gargoyles had answered Jess's original summons and hadn't made the cut for the Ivy House crew—space was limited, and Jess had to be selective—but they'd hung around in the hopes they could be of some use. And they had. Nathanial, the gargoyle who'd answered Jess's last summons, was an alpha in his own right, although not as dominant, and he'd led the host of gargoyles on various missions. They also frequently volunteered for night watch duty when Jess was away from Ivy House.

Five gargoyles landed in the front yard as Austin got out and walked around to open Jess's door. The gargoyles nodded to her and then crouched down and shifted to stone. There they would stay until they were called to action.

"That's the other part of my day that didn't go well," Jess said as she watched them change.

"What's that?" Austin took her hand and entwined his fingers with hers.

"Nathanial tried to teach me how to call the gargoyles that aren't connected to me through Ivy House. He does it with his wings. They make this loud buzzing sound. But my wings are too small. They're runts."

"They're female gargoyle wings. They're the size they should be."

"Not to call my army, they're not."

He started them toward the front door. "I thought you said you didn't want an army? Something about the government, or modern times, or... Help me out; I can't remember the excuse."

"You're going to get the beating of your life if you keep it up."

"Hmm, does that mean you want to be on top?"

Heat kindled through their link, but he could feel her pushing the desire away. She was fighting it with everything she had.

He grinned. It made him want to claim her that much more.

"I'm not actually talking about an army, but I need a way to call the gargoyles without Nathanial. If something happens to him or—"

"They need to ultimately be in your control instead of his," Austin said. He opened the door for her.

"Yes, exactly."

He led her toward the kitchen, passing a small table in the hall with a stack of brochures and binders. Their winemaker had compiled that thick file on the table, full of fliers for various vineyards for sale that might work for the winery they'd purchased together. Although new wines were already in the works, made from grapes purchased from other wineries and locations, Austin and Jess had agreed that they'd prefer to have control over how the grapes were grown.

But all that could wait until Jess wasn't so tightly wound. Basically, until after they sorted out the situation with Elliot Graves.

A rush of adrenaline coursed through Austin, and this one wasn't pleasant. He pushed it away. It wasn't time to deal with his wariness and uncertainty about the Elliot Graves situation.

"Did you decide what was for dinner?" He placed

his hand on the small of her back and guided her toward one of the seats at the kitchen island. If he didn't insist that she sit and stay seated, she'd try to help out of obligation. It was nice of her, but Austin could tell she didn't want to, and it took the joy out of cooking for her.

"Anything, honestly. You know my situation."

He certainly did. She liked to watch. She never tore her eyes away.

As he grabbed the apron hanging on the handle of the oven, her eyes lit with hunger. Her gaze traveled over his shoulders and down his chest.

"Do you ever cook without a shirt on?" she asked, her voice silky.

He paused in slipping the apron strap over his head, his heart beating faster. Her heart beat right beside his, deep in his chest, her presence always there. It grew stronger every day, and he knew it wouldn't be long before he didn't *need* the Ivy House connection. Once their mating bond was solidified, she wouldn't be able to cut off his ability to find her, something he feared she'd do in a life-threatening situation. Jess was absolutely the sort who would prefer to face danger on her own than to have a loved one in the thick of it.

Eyes holding hers, body tightening up and loosening at the same time, he put the apron on the counter and grabbed the bottom of his shirt. He slowly pulled it over his head. "Pants?"

She crinkled her nose. "Keep the pants on. You can't have your ding dong rubbing against things."

He barked out a laugh. "I do have boxers on, but okay. It's your show."

He tossed his shirt to the side, getting it out of the way, before holding up the apron, asking if she wanted him to wear it.

Her eyes increased in intensity. He could feel excitement and anticipation bubbling through the Ivy House link. Lust.

She nodded slowly.

He could barely stand the hunger in her eyes as she watched him secure the apron around his bare waist. Her gaze traveled to his shoulders, met his eyes, and dug deep into his soul.

Her dream had always been to have a man to cook for her. Such a small dream in the grand scheme of things, but the wish had been strong enough that her teenage son had known about it. In her life before Ivy House, cooking had always been a chore—*her* chore. It hadn't been her way of expressing love. Rather, she'd done it out of obligation.

This was the result. Every meal he prepared for her was an erotic experience. He hadn't thought he could like cooking any more than he already did. He'd been wrong.

"Meat or pasta, then? Or both?" He moved to the refrigerator.

"Pasta. I like watching your hands knead the dough."

He pulled out the eggs and closed the fridge before grabbing the flour and placing the ingredients on the island nearest her. "Would you mind choosing some wine?"

"Sure. White?"

"Maybe we can have some sort of seafood in the pasta, then. Shrimp?"

She smiled, getting off her seat and coming around the island. He paused in spreading flour across a large wood cutting board. She reached up and curled her small hand around the back of his neck, pulling his face down to hers. Her lips connected with his, gentle but insistent, tasting of wine, spices, and jam. Their kiss was languid, unhurried, and she released him and trailed an open palm down his chest.

Without another word, she moved away, heading to the wine rack.

He mixed salt into the flour and created a deep well before cracking eggs into it. The cork popped on the wine bottle as he used a fork to whisk the eggs and then unhurriedly pulled the flour from the sides and bottom into the mix.

"I liked…having my episode earlier today," Jess said softly, placing his glass on the counter to his right. She set hers down, too, and ran her palms up the center of his back. "I didn't want to admit that earlier. I still don't want to admit it, but I am so damn turned on that I can't help it. The feeling of…the episode…keeps seeping out."

She slid her lips up the center of his back, and he shivered, trying to focus on mixing but having a hard time.

"I don't want something like that to happen again, don't get me wrong." She kissed one side of his spine, then the other side, on the rise of his muscle. "My God, Austin, you have an incredible back."

"You're killing me."

Her laugh was deep and sultry. Her hands flowed down, over his butt, and then away. When she reached for her wine, purplish-pink magic shivered into the air.

"Is that your magic you're shedding, or power, or…?" He turned his head to catch her as she moved back toward her seat. The same shifting colors drifted behind her, sparkling within the air, keeping his focus. A deep, reverberating need welled up inside him, stopping his heart. He couldn't seem to think, to get enough breath. He'd wanted to experience what it was like for a female gargoyle to mate without learning about it first, and now he was happy for it. Each new surprise was a pleasure. Each new facet had him in rapture. The experience of her was everything.

CHAPTER 6

THE WORLD STOPPED spinning for a moment as I looked at Austin, a cold sweat drenching me, the very center of my being throbbing. He'd just said something, but I didn't know what. I couldn't properly focus. His heart beat a drum in my middle, and my power curled and twisted and danced around us.

His hands had stilled in making the dough.

I glanced down. The room shifted to the side, and I bumped into the island. My glass clinked against the side, and I nearly dropped it. The world shuddered to a start again, but my magic continued to drift around me, playful and joyous.

"You okay?" And I wasn't sure if I was asking Austin or myself.

"I'm good. How about you? Do you want dinner, or do you want me to bend you over the kitchen table and pound into you until neither of us know up from down? I'm good with either."

His words shocked into me, and something deep

down inside of me growled. My eyes widened and I was frozen again, entranced by his cobalt eyes, then distracted by his popping muscles as he finished mixing the eggs and flour and was about to start kneading the dough.

"You're really sexy, Austin," I gushed, unable to help it. "Like really, *really* sexy."

He studied me for a moment. "Dinner, then. Let's work you higher before we get to the pounding, hm?"

Suddenly as meek as a lamb, I nodded mutely and sat down, my lady bits aching in a way that fuzzed out all of my thoughts. I sipped my wine with a shaking hand.

"So you liked guarding your claim, huh?" Austin kneaded the dough, his biceps popping rhythmically, the effect hypnotizing.

"Guarding my claim?"

"You said a moment ago that you liked having *your episode*. From a shifter perspective, you were guarding your claim. A Jane might call it protecting her interests. You were guarding what was yours."

I smoothed my fingers down the stem of my wine glass. "You don't mind being thought of as property?"

"It's not a property thing. You claimed me, and I accepted that claim. I claimed you, and you accepted that claim. It's the same thing Dicks and Janes do in a relationship when they agree to be exclusive. And when a Dick cheats, for example, the scorned Jane might torch his car and burn all his crap."

"That's a pretty extreme example…"

"Magic is even more extreme, which you know."

"Yeah." The word rode a sigh. "It felt good for some reason, but I don't want to be *that* woman."

"I hope you have no choice, because *that* woman turns me on something fierce." He smirked and cut into the dough with a knife, checking for air bubbles before kneading for a bit longer.

"I don't understand any of this."

"I know. It's got to be weird experiencing all of this without any real frame of reference." He pulled out a bowl and dropped the dough into it before covering it with a dinner plate. "What's the verdict? Shrimp?" He looked in the fridge. "Maybe a garlic butter shrimp pasta…" He reached in and moved some things around, the muscles on his back rippling and flexing. "Or maybe a creamy shrimp pasta…" He paused and looked back at me. Before I could answer, he turned back. "Garlic butter. You can't do heavy exercise with a belly full of cream." My stomach fluttered as he took out ingredients. "Or maybe a parmesan white wine sauce… That sounds good."

"I can't believe you do this stuff without recipes." I

watched him pull out a block of parmesan and grab a grater before setting them on the island.

"I can't believe how in awe you are of my cooking. It makes me feel like a shifter god." He chuckled as he gathered the rest of what he'd need, including a pasta machine.

I sipped my wine, continuing to watch him, but my mind wandered to the larger issues at hand. "We haven't gotten any instructions from Elliot Graves yet. Don't you think that's odd?"

"Niamh says it isn't. He won't want anyone to try to sneak in, and the magical world is full of leaks. He's trying to keep the repository out."

"The what?"

He laughed. "Sorry, I meant the guild. Niamh calls it that so much it sticks."

"Yeah, right, that thing. Looks like I caught a lucky break, not finding Kinsella. He ran like a coward and saved my skin."

"For now. For all we know, he might turn up in Elliot Graves's collection of cozy tunnels."

"Too bad we can't bring the basajaun—he'd do okay in the tunnels. He usually hangs out on top of his mountain, but he's equally comfortable inside of one. The roots, he calls it."

"He's been hanging around a lot, that basajaun."

Austin set a skillet onto the stove and flicked on the heat.

"He likes the buffet. We've got plenty for him to eat now that I've figured out how to reverse-engineer that elixir Sebastian made for Edgar's flowers."

"And enhance it to create weaponized sunflowers that try to kill anyone who gets close," he said with a small smile.

"That wasn't my fault! I told Edgar that he had to sing to it in order to teach it friend from foe."

"I thought he did." Austin dropped butter into the pan. It frothed and bubbled. Steam rose into the air and the hood fan clicked on and whisked it away.

"Yes, but his voice sounds like a dying frog. The plant probably thought he was trying to kill it."

Austin laughed as he shook his head and dropped in the shrimp.

"The normal flowers are getting a little out of hand," I said, then took a sip of wine. "The basajaun is keeping them manageable. But the *gas*." I scrunched up my face. "I can't even begin to figure out what part of that elixir is causing him such freaking gas. He sounds like a bullhorn. Mr. Tom is beside himself."

Austin wilted, shaking with laughter. I chuckled a little, because it *was* funny, even if I was put out to be in the middle of it.

"Mr. Tom keeps yelling at the basajaun to have manners, and that the garden is no place for flatulence"—Austin laughed harder—"but the basajaun ignores him, lifts up a cheek, and then *riiip*. It's crazy."

Austin transferred the shrimp to a plate before mincing garlic, his knife descending on the cutting board a mile a minute. He added that to the pan with more butter. "That house is…one of a kind."

"Yeah, it is. But if I had a choice, I'd take the basajaun to Elliot's house, flatulence and all."

"Ask him."

"I mean…" I shrugged, my humor dying. "There's a chance none of us will come back, Austin. He knows we're going. If he wants to come, he'll mention it. I don't want to put him in a position where he feels like he can't say no."

"I think you're projecting onto that creature." Austin added wine, then lemon juice, the liquid sizzling in the heat. He sprinkled in some crushed red pepper. His pecs flared and the muscle along his side rippled. This was, literally, the best show in town, and it came with a happy ending. Two happy endings, if I counted being bent over the table afterward. "If he didn't want to go, he wouldn't sugarcoat it," he continued. "He usually only works with his own kind."

"Yet he moved really far away from most of his family."

"I know what that's like."

Austin turned to the pasta machine, and I got up to help. An extra pair of hands to feed and catch the dough-turned-pasta wasn't necessary, but it made things easier.

I lifted my eyebrows. "I just don't think I can ask that of him. He's a house friend, not a crew member, you know?"

Austin leaned down and kissed me on the temple. "You're a pure soul. Let's hope Elliot doesn't tarnish that when you kill him."

I couldn't help thinking, *Let's hope I don't balk when I get my chance to end it.*

CHAPTER 7

I HELD MY belly as I headed to the deck with my glass of wine, the tangerine sun kissing the horizon. Fuchsia, violet, and deep purple streaked the sky. A shape lingered on the ground below, hunched over the dimming blue and butter yellow meadow flowers that Austin had planted in honor of our first date. The spritz of a spray bottle caught the dying light as the water misted onto the plants.

I laid my free hand on the deck banister, looking down at Edgar. "Hey."

He snapped straight and spun, jamming the spray bottle behind his back. "Miss Jessie, hello. How was dinner? It smells divine."

I grinned down at him as Austin came out behind me, his guitar in one hand and a glass of wine in the other. He didn't seem fazed by seeing Edgar—he just set his things down so he could move the barbecue out of the way and pull the circular gas firepit from the side.

"It was so good." I turned my face skyward. "Fresh

pasta is a treat I'll never get used to, and the sauce just melted in my mouth."

"Oh, fantastic. How about dessert? Did you have that?"

Being a vampire, Edgar's food source was a vein. He had no use or even memory of anything else. He knew I loved Austin's cooking more than anything, though, and never passed up a chance to let me gush about it.

"He had some homemade chocolate chip cookies on hand."

"With walnuts?"

"No walnuts. He made them for me the other night."

"Oh, good, yes. You hate walnuts. It's the fastest way to ruin a chocolate chip cookie, I remember you saying."

Austin put wood into the firepit and lit it before sitting in his chair and lifting the guitar into his lap. He strummed the strings, the notes rising into the peaceful evening.

"What are you doing down there?" I asked Edgar, half wishing the rest of Ivy House had come with him. I loved Austin's house, but the more time I spent here, the more I missed my crew, the strange antics of the house itself. Most importantly, I felt safe on Ivy House property in a way I couldn't feel safe anywhere else in the world.

"Or maybe I just need to remodel and modernize Ivy House and have Austin over more," I murmured to myself, chewing on my lip, wishing I could just transplant Austin's whole house onto Ivy House property. I'd have to install a mountain, though. Because that was something people did every day…

"What's that?" Edgar called up.

"Huh?" Austin paused in playing his guitar.

I shook my head. "Sorry, my mind is wandering. What's in the squirt bottle, Edgar? You're not trying to create attack flowers, are you?"

"Ha-ha-ha…" Edgar's uncomfortable laugh wasn't fooling anyone. "No, Jessie, not to worry. Though, now that you mention it…"

"No, Edgar."

"Yes, Jessie, of course. Of course you're right. The sunflower didn't go well. But then again, it's not like it had legs. It couldn't actually *chase* anyone."

"I love that little patch of meadow flowers, Edgar, I don't want to have to call the basajaun in to eat it."

"Yes, Jessie. Right. Though…the alpha does have a *lovely* singing voice. Better than the artists on my eight-tracks."

"Eight-tracks?"

"Yes. I just never could get into radio. Eight-tracks

have superior quality as far as I'm concerned. But the alpha blows them all out of the water. He could definitely do great things for attack flowers."

"Maybe we'll try again on Ivy House and let him at it, but let's keep those meadow flowers normal, okay?"

"Yes, Jessie. I was just tending them—like normal. Just the normal tending." He paused for a moment, and I wondered why he was hiding the squirt bottle if it contained nothing but the normal elixir... "I must admit, the possibility of militarized flowers has really gotten my ideas flowing. Have you thought about trying to make a potion or elixir that allows plants to speak? Or...maybe not speak but squeal? If someone tricked Ivy House again, and got onto the property without any of us knowing, then the flowers could all squeal and alert us. Wouldn't that be nice?"

"Just this morning I found out the dolls could squeal, Edgar." The music twanged, Austin's fingers scraping across the strings. "I'm not ready for flowers."

"Sure. Yes, it is a little progressive." Edgar nodded. "I've always been a little ahead of my time. Don't worry, Jessie, I'll keep thinking."

"Great," I said dryly.

Spray bottle still behind his back, he started to wander deeper into the woods.

I frowned at him. "Did you plant more flowers in

the woods?"

"Oh no. Who would see them? I don't even think animals come around here—they're afraid of the big bad bear." He sang the last part. "No, I'll just stick around for a while and make sure nothing tries to sneak up on you."

"The gargoyles are here. I think we're covered. I'd hate to keep you away from home all night."

"The thing about the gargoyles is, when they're in their other form...their heads are made of rock." Edgar stared at me. "Their brains are stone."

I stared back at him, not quite sure what to say.

"Can't argue with reason," Austin murmured, and laughter bubbled up inside me.

"I don't mind, Jessie, really." Edgar stepped farther away. "It's refreshing to explore a new area. Maybe some night hikers will wander this way. Or some shifters who plan to attack the alpha and will instead make an unexpected blood donation."

I watched him take incremental steps until he finally stepped behind a tree and disappeared from sight.

"You are the only reason why I allow that sort of madness near my home, I hope you know that," Austin said as I shook my head and took a seat next to him. The flames licked the small logs within the pit and danced into the air. "If you ever wonder how much you mean to me, look no further than Edgar hanging out in my yard with a spray bottle."

"What about Mr. Tom?" I turned my chair with an evil smile, slipped off my shoes, and propped my feet on his thigh. "If you let Mr. Tom hover around in the mornings, getting us stuff, being his weird self, what will that say about your feelings for me?"

The tune he played was soft and sweet, slow and delicious. His fingers moved deftly over the strings, strumming or plucking, sliding and pressing. He didn't speak for a moment, playing that gorgeous melody.

Finally he said, "It would say that I was lost to you, completely, without regret. That I would give you the world if it would make your heart sing." His gaze met mine. "That I would stop at nothing to make you happy and comfortable. It would be my greatest joy as your mate and your lover."

I gulped, feeling something deep move within me. A pinkish-purple halo rose from my skin, shimmering in the air. Pressure filled my chest, and his heart beat a little stronger within me.

"It's my gargoyle magic," I said with a tight throat, blinking back tears. The world stilled again, like it had in the kitchen. "The colors…it's pure magic, oozing out of me. I think it's because I'm opening up to my gargoyle, like when I hide myself near buildings."

"You're giving way to your beast," he whispered, our gazes locked. He kept picking, the melody seeming to swirl within my magic. "It is an incredibly intoxicating sight. You're beautiful, Jacinta. Fierce."

Another question rose, unbidden, as though bobbing to the surface from the very depths of my being. The question tasted sweet on my lips, but my voice turned rough with it. "And what if I were in danger? How would you show you cared for me then?"

His eyes sparked like embers in the growing darkness. Crackling rage pumped through the Ivy House link. Power blasted from his person, so potent and intense, so incredibly dominating, that it made me gasp.

When he finally spoke, his tone made my small hairs stand on end and set my pulse to racing. "I would tear the world apart and shed blood on its ruin. No one will ever harm you, Jacinta, not while I am alive. *No one*," he growled.

I was up and ripping at his belt before I could think. He walked me backward into the house, the twang of his dropped guitar following us through the door neither of us bothered to close. He shoved at my pants and massaged the center of me while I pushed down his jeans and boxers. He tore off my shirt and bra without ceremony before bending and fastening a hot mouth to my budded nipple.

I groaned, dropping my head back, sliding my palm along his hard length. He moved to the other nipple, his teeth scraping against it, sending a little jolt of pain before he sucked, filling my world with pleasure.

He spun me around and, with a palm to the center of my back, pushed me forward. My hands hit the flat surface of the kitchen island. He gripped my hips and thrust forward.

My moan as uninhibited as his, I let my eyes flutter shut with the sensation, so gloriously filled up. He reached around me and continued massaging as he made good on his promise and pounded into me without mercy, pushing me higher with each thrust. Consuming me with each slide of his large, hard length.

I couldn't tell where my world began and ended. I couldn't control my magic or keep it in as the pleasure soared, as my heart—and his—matched it. I hit a peak yet continued climbing. Power pumped through the room, blistering in intensity but delicious in feel, scraping against my skin and cutting into his. He yanked me back by my hair, gripping me against his chest as he thrust like a wild thing, claiming me in body and spirit.

Writhing against him, goading him with magic, crying out from the onslaught, I pushed him on, wanting it all, needing to consume every piece of him, utterly lost to the feel of his body and the incredible sensations filling my world.

He growled with his release, shuddering against me. I cried his name with mine, practically convulsing against him. Magic and pleasure and passion boiled through me before calming, leaving behind a vibrating sort of bliss.

Our rough breathing filled the silent room.

He pulled out of me and turned me around, capturing my chin in his fingers and looking deeply into my eyes. He didn't say a word, but he didn't have to. I could see the intense emotion soaking through his eyes, feel it through the link and the beating of his heart in my chest. My emotions were every bit as strong, but for some reason I couldn't vocalize them. Something was blocking me from moving to the next level with Austin. But it wasn't fear or logic. It wasn't anything trivial like worry about moving on too soon after the divorce.

It was that unnamed darkness within me, I could feel it. It was my gargoyle—or the beast, as Austin called it. It wanted something more. A payment in blood, as was the Ivy House way. But what kind of payment?

I didn't know what would satisfy this strange craving I could feel slicing into my bones.

I didn't know if I could ever rest easy until it was sated.

As if understanding my turmoil, knowing what I felt and wanted to say but couldn't, Austin smirked, unworried.

"You're *mine*, and I mean to prove it. I'll wrestle that beast until it submits." His kiss was bruising. My passion ratcheted up to impossible levels. "In the meantime, I plan to make you scream so hard you go hoarse." He picked me up and threw me over his shoulder, carrying me to bed like a caveman, dragging out my excited laughter. "You will declare your feelings. It's only a matter of time."

CHAPTER 8

THE COOL EVENING worried my hair. Shadows lurked at the bases of the trees at the edge of the grass in my backyard, growing denser, some already seeming solid. The metal of the lounge chair I was sitting on had started to chill.

One week to go.

I had one week before the to-do at Elliot Graves's place.

One week until we were essentially locked in a mountain, our wings no good. I'd have to rely heavily on my magic and the few weapons I could stash on my person. I'd have to rely on the team we put together.

Spells tumbled through my mind, crammed in there from all the intense practice and studying I had been doing. Even so, I was far from ready for someone like Elliot Graves. We all knew that. Nor was I sneaky or cunning like the other mages he'd almost certainly invited. I didn't know how to play false to someone's face with the intent of physically stabbing them in the back. The best I could do was fake politeness, like at a dinner party from my Jane years, and I wouldn't even be able to manage that if someone messed with Austin. Since that night at his house a week ago, when he'd cooked shirtless and then made love to me until the first rays of the sun lightened the horizon, I was not even remotely rational where he was concerned. I completely flew off the handle if anyone threatened or maligned him in any way.

There'd been an episode at the bar the other night. A disgruntled and overly intoxicated regular had caused a scene and taken a stumbling swing at Austin. The threat had been nonexistent, but I'd pounced on the guy and started pummeling him before Austin could throw him out of the bar. Four big pack members had needed to drag me off him.

Strangely, no one had seemed overly upset by the situation. In fact, Austin had been desperately turned on. I, however, had been mortified.

The only thing I could say for myself was that I hadn't gone for my magic this time. I had no idea why I hadn't, since I hadn't even remotely been in control, but it had saved the man's life. Still, I couldn't be trusted. The situation made me incredibly nervous. I hadn't been out in public with Austin since.

I wouldn't be able to section myself off from other

people at Elliot Graves's place, though. And if Kinsella was any indication, some of the guests would be vocal about their dislike of shifters. To put it mildly, we were headed for a dicey situation.

The basajaun entered my woods from the other side, moving fast, heading for the house. No one was with or in front of him.

Good. I didn't need more drama. In a few moments, I'd be heading inside to officially welcome the three new people to the Ivy House team. Hollace, the newly reincarnated Cyra, and Nathanial had all agreed to join my circle. They'd get the magic, we'd get a link between us, and our team would be stronger than ever.

I ached with guilt for putting them in danger.

Austin's footsteps touched down on the front walkway. His heart beat comfortingly in my chest. We'd slept in the same bed—whether his or mine—every night this past week, but I always missed him the second we parted. Even now, knowing he was coming around the house to me, I felt a pull toward him.

The basajaun kept coming as Austin started around the side of the house. Austin came into view first, wearing a dress shirt that molded to his perfect torso and a pair of fashionably faded jeans that showed off his powerful thighs. His hair was styled, short on the sides and messy on top, and his expensive watch flashed within the motion-sensor light that clicked on as he passed.

I glanced down at my stained and mud-splotched purple sweats, mostly shapeless on my body. I hadn't changed since the practice session had ended a couple hours ago. I hadn't even moved from this seat, choosing instead to sit here in partial misery, going over all the spells in my mind again and again.

"Hey." Austin took the chair next to me, leaning back as I was doing and putting his feet up. "Just taking in the night?"

He knew I wasn't. He'd be able to feel the worry dripping through me like acid, churning my stomach. I wasn't hiding it from him as I was from the rest of the crew. I didn't hide anything from him anymore. I never deadened the Ivy House link between us. There was no need. He never judged me or held my feelings against me. That wasn't in his nature.

"The basajaun is nearly here," I said, watching the tree line. "You look handsome, by the way."

He reached over and squeezed my thigh. "Any idea what the basajaun wants?"

I shook my head as the basajaun slowed near the tree line, utterly invisible in the dwindling light even though he should've been in plain view. His ability to blend into his natural surroundings was incredible.

No, it was magic. Sometimes I forgot that magical creatures each had their own special blend of it.

"He wasn't at training today. Maybe he wants to see what he missed." I watched the spot, finally seeing him as he pushed out through the tree limbs. My eyebrows pinched together. "What in the heck?"

The hair all over his body lay flat and tamed, almost like it had been lightly spritzed with gel and then combed. His long, usually bushy beard had been re-braided, no part of it out of place. The hair on his head had been parted on the right and slicked over, and a bow tie adorned his hairy neck.

"That's my cue." Austin swung his feet off the chair and stood.

"What cue? What do you mean?"

"He wants to talk to you privately."

"How do you know? Is it the bow tie?"

"Body language. I'll be right over there, okay?" He pointed toward the back door. "In case you need anything."

I frowned but nodded, and he bent down to kiss my forehead. The look he shot the basajaun as he walked toward the door was long and poignant, not so subtly making a statement that if the basajaun acted out of turn, there'd be hell to pay.

My stomach fluttered and a strange fizzy sensation

bubbled through my blood, like I was being aerated or something. Odd.

The basajaun stopped in front of me. "Miss Jessie Ironheart."

Bewildered or not, it felt like I should be standing for this, whatever *this* was.

"Hi." I grimaced as I stretched, stiff from sitting still for so long. "What's up?"

"Basajaunak, as a whole, are family-oriented creatures. We typically stick with our own. If something happens to one of us, vengeance can be claimed by all of us, and often is."

I hoped I was keeping my frown of uncertainty off my face. The basajaun had strange rules I usually only half understood, and when you slighted him, he went crazy. I sincerely hoped this wasn't his way of telling me that I'd unintentionally wronged him and his entire family was about to hunt me down. That would not be a good time.

"I love my family, of course," he continued. I nodded. "But they can be stifling. I am what's known as the black cow of the family."

"Black sheep, I think you mean—"

"I wanted my independence and to see more of the world. I wanted to choose my own mountain and enforce my own rules. That is not usually done by one so young as me."

I had gotten the impression that he was quite old. I wondered how old his family was.

"I think it was the stars that led me to my mountain," he went on. "Every so often, the stars choose a basajaun and lead him, or more likely her—our females are usually more courageous—to a great future. A future the family can be proud of. I think the stars have chosen my path."

"Hmm," I said, having no idea where this was going.

"It is not for me to decipher the journey of others," he said, "but it is an interesting thing that we should meet under the mountain, forge our friendship in battle, and that you should then find yourself facing down another battle under a mountain."

I'd been really working on controlling my reactions, but I was pretty sure a brow furrow seeped through. "Mhm."

"It is a clear sign if ever there was one," he went on. "So…" His voice drifted away, as though he was waiting for something.

"It probably is a sign, yes," I said vaguely.

"Yes." He nodded as though that answered that. I still didn't understand what I'd agreed to, which was probably a mistake. "The stars, as I thought. This is the right way."

He took a step toward the back door of Ivy House, and I stepped with him.

"I thought we were supposed to dress up a little?" the basajaun asked, taking another step.

I ran a little to keep pace. "For what now?"

"For the ceremony. I thought we were supposed to dress up?"

"The ceremony…" I stopped and faced him again, my eyebrows climbing and my shock too great to be hidden. "Wai—"

"Yes, the ceremony. I thought you agreed? It is not easy to decipher the stars, but they didn't even attempt subtlety this time. My job, when we first met, was to guard you under the mountain."

"Your job wasn't so much to guard me as it was to keep me from escaping—"

"We helped each other that day—you generously promised me flowers, and I allowed you to escape."

Well, sort of. He'd feigned an injury so the mages who'd enlisted his help wouldn't accuse him of dereliction of duty. The prison I'd been held in was in his mountain, which apparently meant it was his role to guard it.

"We have battled together often since then," the basajaun continued. "You have assembled a fearsome collection of magical people, from an alpha who gives me pause to a mythical creature I could not fight." He was talking about the phoenix. The night Cyra had showed up, he'd tried to help take her down, but the burns had incapacitated him. "My ancestors will not be disappointed to see me join such a crew, especially since I was led by the stars. I have debated the decision for months, of course. I do not like to be tied down, which is why I left my family in the beginning. I do love those redwoods, but I do not like being governed. So I have been watching you. The alpha is strict with his people, yes. The gargoyle is strict with his gargoyles in town, yes. But you are not so strict. You merely ask that we all respect one another. That we help fight and protect one another. That is how a family should work. The grievances of one can be claimed by all."

"Right. Except…" This was blindsiding me. I would never in a million years have guessed he'd want to join the Ivy House crew. It had never even occurred to me, mostly because of all the things he'd said about moving away from his family and living alone on his mountain. "It's just that you live really far away—"

"And then I heard your next battle is to be under a mountain."

"It's a different mountain, though—"

"My first introduction to you was guarding you under a mountain. The job that cements me to you will be guarding you under a mountain. That fits. The stars led me here—me and the alpha and the rest of your crew—and here we will bind together. A strange sort of magical family. I will be laughed at, yes. But I have always been laughed at, and when they see a female gargoyle and the phoenix and the thunderbird... The basajaunak will come around. It is as the stars will it."

I stared at him blankly, my mouth gaping open. This was all coming out of left field. I didn't know if I was comfortable with having him on my team. Sure, he was an amazing asset in a battle, and he'd hung around often enough that I was comfortable with him personally, but he was picky about his rules. He traded for the simplest of things.

Which reminded me...

"Would I have to trade for your involvement on the team?" I asked.

"It would not be a trade, but a basajaunak partnership. Like family. If I am slighted, this small magical family will be entitled to claim vengeance, and vice versa. If your family is in trouble, like young Master Jimmy, it will be within my power to go to his aid. The same would be true if my family were in danger."

"We doing okay?" Austin approached us from the house, glancing back and forth between us. He rested his hand lightly on the small of my back.

"The basajaun thinks the stars led us all here," I said, "and it's a sign that Elliot Graves's stronghold is embedded in mountain tunnels. He wants to join the Ivy House crew."

Austin's expression didn't change, and no surprise trickled through the link. He'd clearly been in hearing range, because otherwise I didn't know how all that hadn't blown his hair back.

"He says that if he joins the crew," I went on, "then it basically joins our families. So if something were to happen to Jimmy, he'd...probably pop heads off and spike them like footballs, as he likes to do, and if something happens to his family...I guess we need to return the favor?"

"Yes. As is standard," the basajaun said.

"As is apparently standard, sure..." I said.

"Can I speak to you for a moment, Jess?" Austin asked, oddly formal.

"Yes, sure."

We took a few steps away, and I covered us in a soundproof spell.

"Is this not throwing you for a loop?" I asked Austin the second we were cut off from the basajaun's hearing. "Everyone has always been surprised that the basajaun even fights with us. I got the impression basajaunak families are very tight-knit and don't care for outsiders. I don't want to piss them off. And…what if the basajaun wants to live in Ivy House? I don't have a bed that big. Does he shed? Mr. Tom would pitch a fit if there are rolling balls of hair all the time." I ran my hand over my face. "I know that I should be jumping for joy, since he is a very good creature to have in my corner, but this has really taken me by surprise. I wasn't ready for it."

"It's ultimately your decision," Austin said, bending a little to catch my gaze. "But you should know that this is an incredible honor. This basajaun is essentially offering to add you—all of us—to his family. He is connecting us with the rest of the basajaunak the world over. You're right about their usual attitude toward outsiders. They rarely bother with anyone but their own kind unless it is to get something they need or to claim vengeance for a perceived wrong. Usually their council of elders would need to approve of this decision, and maybe he got it to them somehow. Or he might just assume they're on board. The thing he said about being led by the stars…he's talking about fate. He thinks fate is guiding his feet—all of our feet—and their kind do not turn their backs on fate." Austin glanced back at the basajaun, in his bow tie with his freshly braided beard. "If you take him on, you'd have the whole of the basajaunak at your disposal. You'd be their family, and they would protect you with their lives."

My stomach dropped out of me. I didn't know what to say. I didn't know what I *could* say.

Austin nodded slowly. "Yes, this is a big deal. A huge honor, like I said. It has happened occasionally in the past, but it is incredibly rare. You are on the precipice of securing a powerful ally."

"But what if they refuse to honor the connection?"

"I'm sure they could cut him out of the family if it came down to it, but special allowances are made for situations like this one. The basajaunak really do believe in following the stars. From what I understand, anyway. I'm certainly no expert."

"You think I'd be crazy to pass this up?"

"I think you need to be comfortable with your team. That's the most important consideration."

I glanced over at the basajaun, who was now eyeing the nearest flowers. "I mean…the hair…"

"I doubt he will want to sleep inside. That's not really what they do."

"Right, true. He was really good with Jimmy when he was here. And he's always been nice to me, in his way… I mean, if I had thought he'd ever want the position, I totally would've offered, but it was just such a surprise that it threw me for a loop."

"What will you do?"

CHAPTER 9

I TORE THE privacy spell away and took a deep breath. "I usually do dress a little nicer for these things," I said, offering the basajaun a nervous smile. "I'll head up now and change. I've just had a lot on my mind—"

"Yes, with the trials ahead." The basajaun nodded gravely. "I can help. I am as proficient under a mountain as I am atop one."

"So…you know that Graves's lair seems to be a collection of tunnels within the mountain, not necessarily below it, right?"

"Yes." The basajaun frowned at me.

"Right. Just…making sure. Yeah, okay, sure, come inside. I'll go get changed for the ceremony."

For the first time in a couple weeks, the stress in my shoulders and the coiling in my stomach relaxed a little. Having the basajaun with us would be an incredible help, especially if he felt at home in the underground lair that would have the rest of us itching to escape. An *incredible* help. The fact that he'd actually sought out an invitation eased my mind too. He knew exactly what he was getting into, and he had chosen to add his name to the roster. That was good news.

"Miss—"

"Hah!" I jumped and karate-chopped the air, three feet from Mr. Tom waiting near the table in my room. I could feel him both through the link and through my awareness of everyone on the house's grounds, but given he was basically white noise to me, I never bothered to check his location.

Mr. Tom pursed his lips. "I do hope you will refrain from that method of attack once you are among the other mages. I can't imagine it'll be a good look."

I let out my breath and clutched my chest. "You know I try not to use my magic in the house. The last thing I need is to accidentally kill one of you after a jump scare. Why are you standing in the shadows like a creep?"

"It is not creepy to wait patiently while conserving electricity."

"Yes it is. Take a note."

"You're running late. The others are nervous that you're having second thoughts."

"No. The basajaun showed up." I told him about our conversation.

"I wondered why he was showing such an interest,"

Mr. Tom said as I took out some slacks and a blouse. "I must admit, I didn't expect that."

"Yeah, me neither. Austin said it isn't for me to ask about how that decision will go down with his family, but...it's definitely on my mind."

"Basajaunak are certainly touchy about dealings with their families. They are very private, even within their own species. Definitely better not to mention it."

"So does that mean soon he'll be touchy about all of us?"

"Likely. Now, hop into the shower and wash away some of that stink. I'll refresh the champagne and tell them you'll be down in a minute."

I paused in turning around. "They're nervous I had second thoughts? They're eager to join, then? Even though it'll be really dangerous?"

"Nathanial knows there is no higher honor than to protect you from danger. The more intense the danger, the higher the status he'll gain within the gargoyle community. All of us will. The others answered your summons when they could have resisted, and they were immediately confronted by Austin Steele's incredible power and your ever-growing strength. They aren't fools; they see the vast potential in this outfit and want to be on the winning team. Of course they are eager to join, miss. You are not seeing your worth clearly, which is why your decision not to *play the field*, as it were, concerns me. Have you even considered anyone with wings?"

"Oh my God, what is your malfunction?" I said on a release of breath, and turned toward the shower. He'd always been weird about my sex life, trying to get me to bang everyone in town, it seemed like. I had a man. I wasn't like the gargoyle guys—I didn't need more than one, especially not at the same time. I'd tried that in college once. More than one dong just got tedious after a while.

Clean and dressed, I hurried down and found everyone in the front sitting room, the basajaun among them, sipping their champagne and talking quietly. They fell silent as I appeared in the doorway, Mr. Tom approaching with a glass immediately.

"Welcome everyone," I said, because I didn't really know what else to say. Other than the basajaun and Austin, they all lived here, so why was I welcoming them to their own sitting room? "Do you want to follow me back?"

"Me first." Cyra shoved Hollace, who rolled his eyes at her toddler antics. To be fair, she was only a week old in her current iteration. The dolls, scattered around the room, ran forward with their glasses or cups of water, liquid sloshing down their fronts. Cyra wasn't even shedding fire at the moment.

"It's not first come, first served," Hollace drawled as he followed her. A doll ran across his path, and he kicked in its direction. It swerved just before his foot could connect. They were getting smart to his antics. Too bad.

They followed me down the hall, the others behind them. At the door to the council room, I stopped for a second and took a deep breath.

"Here we go," I said quietly.

I'd already explained what kind of magic they'd get: a sort of fountain of youth in every way but one. They'd feel younger, with more energy, stamina, and ease of movement, but they'd retain their current appearance. They'd become immortal unless killed, if they weren't already. I'd also explained the link that would develop between us, and between them and Ivy House. I'd laid all this out before asking if they'd like to join the team.

They hadn't hesitated then, and they didn't hesitate now, filing into the room behind me and spreading out, sipping their champagne. Their sparkling eyes and smiles indicated that Mr. Tom hadn't been feeding me a line. They were definitely eager to become part of the Ivy House crew, as weird as we were.

I walked around the large, ornate chairs, positioned in a circle, and entered near the little flag marking the first chair. Once in the middle, I felt the pull of Ivy House magic, directing those in the room to their rightful seats, one at a time. I chose my crew; she chose where they sat in the circle based on their importance to the group as a whole.

Austin walked forward, taking his seat in the first chair, my most important asset. No one needed an explanation as to why. Niamh would usually step forward next, Ivy House having placed her in the number three spot before I was even chosen as heir. But she didn't move. I frowned as Ulric walked toward the little flag, his face screwed up in confusion. He nodded to me as he passed, then took a seat in the number six spot. Jasper came next, in the number seven chair, and Mr. Tom claimed the number nine spot, which only proved that the order was based on fighting prowess and not the council members' relative importance to my life and wellbeing.

Edgar came last, offering me a smile before sitting on the chair on the other side of the flag, number twelve.

"*There has been a change,*" Ivy House said to me in our magical language.

Cyra stepped forward with a big smile and her lensless glasses. Fire dripped from her fingers, and I was starting to wonder if she leaked when she couldn't totally control her emotions. The dolls thudded after her, water sloshing out, little streams of smoke rising from the snuffed-out flames. I'd need to constantly replace the rugs in this place until I had a handle on the elemental magic.

She passed by Austin, smiling down at him as she did so. She stopped in front of me and offered me a bow.

"I pledge to you my allegiance, and in so doing, place with you the honor of the phoenix. You are a friend to my kind. When in great need, call to us and we will answer."

I widened my eyes as she about-faced. She hadn't mentioned that part of it.

"*She is strong for her species, power incarnate,*" Ivy House said. "*She does your circle proud.*"

"The house is controlling me, Hollace. This is neat." Cyra laughed as she started forward, aiming for the number two spot. She lowered next to Austin and then beamed at him.

The basajaun's hair puffed out and he tensed.

"*Don't try to force him,*" I told Ivy House quickly. "*This is not the time for a battle of wills. Remember when Austin pushed back? You'll probably get the same thing from the basajaun, only a lot more violent.*"

She was quiet for a long moment. The basajaun

tensed further, proving she hadn't backed down.

"*Fine...*" she finally said, but I could sense her annoyance. She was playing along, for now, but she'd probably try to mess with the basajaun in the future like she had with Austin. I wondered how that would go. Austin wasn't the epitome of patience when someone was messing with him, but he was ten times more civil than that hairy beast.

"*What's the story with Niamh?*" I asked as the basajaun finally started forward.

"*Niamh is very valuable, but when I appointed her all those years ago, I could've never imagined the power you would amass. You have already collected more power than any of my other heirs did, with a larger variety. You were a good choice, and your circle shows your merit. I must change the positions as befit the players. None of these places are ever set in stone.*"

That was news to me. I wondered if she changed the rules as the game continued. I wouldn't put it past her.

Not like it really mattered. I didn't treat anyone differently based on where they sat.

The basajaun stopped in front of me, towering over me. "May the stars guide our feet," he said, his beard starting to come loose from its braid. The hair on his neck nearly covered the bow tie.

"Thank you for joining," I said lamely. "Welcome."

It would've been cooler if I'd had some snappy answer. I needed to work on that.

He turned and took the third seat, his size making Cyra look like a child.

Hollace stepped forward next, grinning as he reached the flag. "What a trip."

"Right?" Cyra said.

At least they'd fit in. No one seemed to regard this as the solemn occasion Ivy House probably wanted it to be. Which was kind of nice, but I should've lit some incense or something to pacify her.

"Thank you for asking me," Hollace said as he stopped in front of me, also bowing. "It's an honor. I look forward to serving on the most powerful magical team in the world." His smile was infectious as he took the fourth seat.

Finally Niamh stepped forward, nonchalant as she took the fifth chair next to Ulric. Nathanial was next, and I had to wonder why Ivy House hadn't replaced Ulric or even pushed Niamh farther back. He was an alpha in his own right and had the ability to lead the gargoyles. His call could rouse them from stone or summon them from town.

"This is an incredible honor that will bring much status and attention to my family," Nathanial said, offering me the deepest bow of all. Given I was one of the near-mythical females of his species, it surely meant more to him.

"Welcome," I said, still feeling lame. I hadn't had a chance to think of something better yet.

He skipped the chair after Mr. Tom, taking the eleventh spot, next to Edgar.

"*He is your anchor,*" Ivy House said. "*He is a solid choice and an excellent specimen of the species. He will lead your gargoyles well.*"

"*Then why put him so far back?*"

"*I just said—because he's the anchor.*"

"*Right, but...Edgar is the twelfth spot. Isn't he the anchor in this setup?*"

"*Edgar fits nowhere and everywhere at the same time. He's necessary but forgettable. He adds incredible value, but it's hard to pinpoint exactly how until it's happening. Honestly...I didn't really know where to stick him, so I just tacked him onto the end.*"

I stifled a laugh. Poor Edgar. He did, absolutely, add incredible value to the team. He took random jobs no one else really wanted, and he did it without needing to be told. He always just...filled in the holes, preventing the enemy from getting through in ways that defied planning. But yeah, I got what she meant. It was hard to actually assign value because, well, he was just so weird and you never knew what would happen next with him.

I looked at the two empty spots, seats eight and ten. I wondered which of those Sebastian would have taken—or would he have earned a seat closer to Austin?

"Oh no, she's sad. Do you feel that, Hollace?" Cyra pushed halfway to standing. "How do we handle this? Human women hug in these situations, don't they?"

"We quietly allow her privacy unless she expresses a need." Mr. Tom sniffed, and I wondered who he was trying to fool.

I quickly muted my links to everyone except Austin. I'd need to get used to feeling the new people, and I didn't have the mindset right at the moment.

"Okay, well…" I held out my hands. "This is what we have so far. All of us will be going to Elliot Graves's…meeting next week, along with an additional three shifters, hand-selected by Austin. That's all we're allowed, fourteen in all. In case you haven't heard, we'll have our own room in a wing within the mountain. We'll have facilities with which to cook and store food, all of which will be provided for us. We can use the cook and cleaners provided to us or not, but we cannot bring a cook and cleaners."

"Well, that's Earl uninvited, hey, Earl?" Niamh said. "Back to useless again."

"I'm not the one who lost her seat," Earl responded.

"Might have lost my seat, but I'm still ahead of ye.

How's that feel, then?" she retorted.

"Okay, okay." I rubbed my temples. "We have a week to go, and then things get serious. So let's make the most of the time we have. Once we set foot inside that mountain, it'll be a game of hide-and-seek, except the loser dies."

CHAPTER 10

"**Y**OU SENT IN our list of attendees?" I pointed at Niamh as she kept pace, walking down the line of limos waiting on the street next to the house. We didn't need six limos to carry fourteen people to the jet that would fly us to Elliot's collection of mountain tunnels, but we apparently did need plenty of room for all the luggage.

"Yes. But I was vague about what each one of us is, magically speaking. Elliot Graves doesn't need a detailed rundown, are ye jokin'?" Niamh frowned. "He gets to know head count, and that's about it. He can be surprised like everyone else."

Given we hadn't been told to stay home, he was apparently fine with that.

The crew waited outside the limos, dressed in pristine suits or flowing dresses, looking the part of a prestigious magical unit.

"Jet is standing by?" I asked, approaching Austin at the back of the group, standing beside his people with an air of patient confidence. Nothing but tranquil waters drifted through the link. He clearly wasn't worried about the unfamiliar conditions we'd be facing or the danger from Elliot Graves and the other mages we'd be meeting.

"Yes. Waiting for us on the private magical airstrip."

"How is that even possible, to have a private airstrip for magical people? That doesn't make sense," I mumbled, stopping in front of the shifters.

"It's a private piece of land owned by magical people." Niamh stopped with me. "We pay a fee to use it. Honestly, girl, where is yer head at?"

Kace stood beside Austin, his face hard and his onyx eyes tracking me.

I nodded at him, then nodded at Isabelle beside him. Good additions to the team.

I hadn't met the guy next to Isabelle, though, and his whole vibe sent shivers racing across my skin. I backed up a step, unable to help it.

A wicked scar ran down his cheek and pooled under his severe jaw. Sharp cheekbones set off a narrow nose, ending in a little uptick that would've been cute on anyone else. His eyebrows rose over heavy-lidded eyes with long black lashes. He topped Austin's height and then some, probably six-five, but his huge shoulders nearly made him look shorter. But it was his eyes that tripped me up. They weren't just hard—they were off-kilter. When this guy looked at me, I felt like shrinking into myself and waiting for death. Pain lurked in those eyes. Imbalance. As though he'd been broken ten times over and had barely stitched himself back together.

"You remember Kace and Isabelle," Austin said. I nodded. He motioned at the man on the end. "This is Brochan." His name sounded like the word "broken" with a lilting accent. It fit perfectly, and I half wondered if he'd named himself. "He's something of a unique situation. I hadn't thought to include him originally because of his newness to the area, but after learning a bit more about his history, I figured he'd be a strong asset for our team."

"Well, I didn't send his name in," Niamh said, bracing her hands on her hips. "What sort of unique situation? Because this isn't the time for Jessie to be meetin' someone new, and it definitely isn't the time for some unhinged shifter to lose his marbles and act the bollocks."

Brochan's stare rose from the ground, where it had been resting after I had—quickly—broken eye contact, and narrowed in on her. Darkness moved within that gaze, raw and ruthless, setting me on edge.

Niamh's eyebrows lowered. "Goin'ta give me that

look, are ye? Don't think I know yer type, do ye? I know what kinda guy sits in the corner, back to the wall, and drinks by himself until he staggers from the bar. And he's not the sort we should trust in close quarters, especially since he hasn't trained with Jessie these last few weeks."

"I trust Austin's judgment," I said, feeling the urgency to get moving. We had to get on the road if we were going to make our time window at Elliot's, between two o'clock and two eighteen. We needed to be punctual. "If Austin thinks Brochan is a good fit, I'm okay with that."

"Well, don't come crying to me if they don't let him in because his name isn't on the list," Niamh murmured.

"Austin only brought three, so he's clearly replacing someone. We'll just give him that person's name," I replied.

"Shauna? He doesn't look like a Shauna."

"I don't mind being a Shauna," Brochan said. "Maybe Sue for short?"

"Yeah, fine, whatever. Let's get going." I made a circle in the air with my finger and turned for the lead limo.

Mr. Tom struggled to drag a large suitcase without wheels toward the open trunk of the middle limo.

"What do you have in there?" I asked, hurrying to help.

"My disguises," he said as we labored to fit the suitcase into the space.

"Why do you need... What kind of..." I just shook my head and stepped back. "Fine, are you ready? We need to go."

"Yes."

Austin met me at the front limo. I stopped beside the open door, the driver waiting to close it behind us. Ivy House sat in the morning sun, large and hulking, a magical shadow hanging from it like a curtain.

"I hope this isn't the last time I see this house," I murmured. "You never even got to decorate it properly."

"Oh, *I'm* decorating it?"

"Yeah. You're good at that stuff. Surprise!"

He slid his arm around my shoulders and pulled me close. "You'll see it again, I promise."

With a last look at my crew and the shifters waiting for my cue, I ducked into the limo.

"Since Brochan will be going with us, I figure I might tell you about his history," Austin said once we were both inside, the door closed behind us. It would just be the two of us in this limo. Mr. Tom had decided that was more prudent, his reasoning made clear when he tried to force condoms into my handbag and muttered about wings and just making do with what I had.

"It's not like you to make a hasty decision," I said as the limo got underway. A time check said we were only five minutes behind schedule.

"It isn't. And if it weren't for something the basajaun said, I wouldn't have."

"What did he say?"

Austin hit a button above him, and the divider between us and the driver rose.

"He said that it is wise to harness the power of revenge, as long as it is used for good."

I slipped my hand into Austin's, frowning. "I always thought revenge was problematic. That it ends up eating a person from the inside out so that when they finally get it, they're basically just a shell of a person."

"Brochan's case is different. He never planned to seek revenge. He was a man defeated. He had a well-established pack with a healthy dose of power, and a mage completely steamrolled them."

"But if he is a man defeated…"

"He came to the area a month ago, shortly after we sent Kinsella running. A few of my people tipped me off that another alpha had arrived, and I could sense his status as soon as I saw him. It was obvious from the way he held himself. I looked into it, and he used to be alpha of a good-sized pack in Ohio. The pack was prosperous and established, on the land for generations. He took it over from his father, who had taken it over from his mother, and so on.

"They ran into trouble when a fairly powerful mage moved his operation close by, liking the somewhat rural area. As you might guess, the mage didn't at all respect the territory boundaries or the prior claim on the area. He used Brochan's land for hunting, gathering supplies, felling trees for wood, and after Brochan started defending his territory, the mage resorted to burning land and trying to push the shifters back.

"A man like Brochan—like me—isn't the type to be pushed anywhere. He continued to defend his territory, growing increasingly violent. Shifters started disappearing, and some were attacked and left for dead. Any of the mage's people caught on Brochan's land were killed. It came to a head, and finally the mage led a full-scale attack.

"He came through at dawn with all his people and a group of mercenaries in tow, not unlike the forces we met with Kinsella. They had magic and they had numbers. The mage killed nearly all of Brochan's pack, including older people, pregnant women, and children." A nerve pulsed in Austin's cheek. Anger roiled through the link. "Brochan's pregnant mate and two young children were also slain. He almost joined them, and I think he wishes he had. He certainly blames himself for what happened."

"Oh my God," I whispered.

"After he healed, he had no choice but to move on—to find a new place for his people. And he did. He shouldered his duty to the last, even though I imagine all he wanted to do was wither away and die. Once he had a new situation established for them, he relinquished his alpha position to someone capable and moved on. He wandered as a nomad for a while, doing his own mercenary work."

"So he kinda drifted here?"

"He came here after hearing about Kinsella. He told me, just recently, that he'd wanted to see what kind of alpha could withstand an attack from a mage and a host of mercenaries."

"Kinsella wasn't the one who killed his family…"

"No. Not Kinsella. Someone else who's rumored to be going to this meeting."

I bit my lip, suddenly unsure about all this.

Austin nodded, feeling it through the link, or maybe just reading my face. "I wouldn't bring him if I thought he was bent on getting revenge. He's trying to find purpose again. Protecting you—his alpha's future mate—is giving him that. Being a part of a greater cause is giving him that."

"Or maybe he sees that you can give him an element of safety. You weren't defeated by an attacking mage."

"That shifter doesn't crave safety for himself; he craves providing it for others. He doesn't fear death, especially now."

"So he came here to see about an alpha who didn't lose everything to an attacking mage, and then just hung around in the bar for a while, or... Because you didn't have him training with us, and even though Niamh has clearly noticed him, I haven't seen him around the streets or anything..."

"He did hang around for a while, but he did it by the book. Given that he isn't an alpha with a territory, he didn't need to introduce himself or ask for passage. Many people who have been alphas for a while can't help dominating those around them or comparing status." Kingsley had been like that on his visit. *He* certainly couldn't help it. "Brochan didn't do any of that. He kept his head down. Then, a couple of weeks ago, when he decided to join my pack, he approached me directly and explained his history. He wanted me to know he'd been an alpha, and also that he'd hung up his desire to reestablish a pack. He would never be an alpha again. He was content to follow someone else's rule; he just needed to make sure that someone was strong enough to lead him."

"Which you are."

"Yes. I think the first two weeks was him assessing the situation. Me, basically. When he challenged into the pack…" Austin shook his head. "I had to stop three fights and take over. No one could handle him. He's better than anyone in my pack now, even Kace. He's on a level nearly as high as Kingsley. He'd be my beta, no problem, if not for his emotional issues. First we need to see if he can get beyond them. If he gets a handle on himself, and learns to live again, he might still be my beta."

"If you can trust him."

"Yes. For the last couple weeks he's been training with the pack and doing very well. He's a strong addition. He could be to me what Nathanial is to you."

"If you can trust him."

"Right."

"And how did you decide you trusted him enough to bring him?"

"Because even though he'd heard by that point which mages were going, he never once asked to come."

The limos pulled off the highway, the land flat and covered in dried golden grass. Smaller planes were parked to our right, and a few jets were stationed a little closer.

"Oh," I said, taking in what Austin was saying. "But won't it mess with his head if he sees this mage?"

"Maybe. But then the basajaun said that, and…" Austin shook his head. "Something clicked. I can't describe it. I feel it in my gut that he should come. That he needs to be in the tiptop of my hierarchy. He will help me protect my mate better than anyone else in the world, because he knows what it's like to lose one. He won't wish that on anyone."

The limo slowed as we passed a mostly empty parking lot. A small building accompanied by a tower rising into the sky hunkered in front of us. An open hangar sat to our right, a large jet waiting for us to board.

Butterflies swam in my stomach. I'd never so much as flown first class. This was a sort of luxury I'd never experienced, and it was somewhat alarming that my excitement level was competing with my churning worry about meeting a bunch of conniving mages and a guy I was going to try to kill in not-at-all-cold blood.

"My life has taken a very strange turn," I muttered to myself, nearly plastering my face to the window so I could stare at the jet. "Ever since my divorce, my life has been just plain weird." After a moment, I asked, "Did you ask him how he might react if he sees that mage?"

"Of course. I also asked him if he thought he could handle standing idly in a room where that mage might be sneering at him. He said it wouldn't be a problem."

"I find that hard to believe. Oh my God, Austin, there's even a red carpet." I beamed at him, patting his arm. I felt like a little kid in a candy shop with unlimited funds and zero restrictions. "There's a red carpet. *Look!* The door thing is coming down. The steps. This is awesome. I mean, the whole nature of this trip is the pits, but this one shining moment is awesome."

"I found it hard to believe as well, until I realized that Brochan is emotionally dead where his family is concerned. He cauterized the wound, shoved it into a cold, dark box, and shut the lid. He won't have a problem handling it because he won't be able to feel at all. In theory."

"That's not healthy, Austin," I said, shifting away from the display of luxury to look at him. "One day he'll snap."

"Yes, he will," he said, his eyes full of fire. "And so help me God, I will arrange it. I will get him into a room with that mage, flip the lock, and let Brochan have his vengeance. No one should be allowed to get away with what that mage did. He created an altercation where there wasn't one, he wouldn't back down when he should've—when he was in the wrong—and he mass-murdered innocents. Children! If the Mages' Guild allowed something like that to happen—if this is what it looks like when they 'police' their own—then I'll take matters into my own hands and police them myself. Sebastian was right. No one comes together like shifters do."

The limo stopped in front of the red carpet, my door perfectly aligned with it.

"Oh my God," I muttered, "this is my best life and worst nightmare, all wrapped up in the same day. Why can't I just have normal good things going on without the crap that always seems to go with it?" I pushed out a breath, trying to still my excitement. Trying to force down the swell of anxiety. But neither emotion cooperated.

The limo driver opened my door, and I tried to remain calm. I took his hand and stepped out in my long, swishy black dress and my neck full of jewels. I'd nearly forgotten I was wearing all of that.

"So what you're saying is…" I stepped to the side, waiting for Austin to get out on his side and come around. Apparently, the old slide across wasn't in vogue.

The rest of the limos were stopping behind us, lining up for their turn on the red carpet.

"Oh my God," I said again, butterflies fluttering through my stomach. "I hope there are, like, little baskets of goodies and chocolates and stuff on the plane. That would really make this amazing."

Austin dropped his hand to the small of my back and guided me toward the steps.

"What you're saying," I started again, "is that you will build a castle around my keep, manage the very powerful creatures I have called in, and *also* create some sort of massive shifter organization that sticks it to the Mages' Guild and Momar?"

Austin paused as I grabbed the railing and started climbing the stairs in black three-inch stilettos. I should've worn flats.

"Yeah," he said, following me up. "Might as well, right? Beyond the initial meet-and-greets, your people don't seem to need much muscling around. I might as well look for a bigger challenge."

I laughed and stopped on the stairs, stepping down one so my back connected with his front. He placed a hand on my hip, and I paused for a moment.

"You're a good person, Austin Steele. I'll help you claim vengeance for him, and for every other shifter they've wronged. If I live, obviously."

"Of course you're going to live," he said softly, waiting for me to keep going. "You'll be the heir that lives forever."

Shivers covered my body and lead filled my stomach. I hoped those weren't his famous last words.

CHAPTER 11

A FLEET OF limos awaited the Ivy House crew at a
nondescript landing strip at the base of a mountain range in Colorado. White peaks rose with jagged
edges into the sapphire blue above, the air scrubbed
clean by the dense trees surrounding them. A single
tower rose into the sky behind the woods.

A prickling of warning moved across Austin's skin,
prompting his animal to grow restless, urging him to
shed his skin and slip into those trees, to scout the area.
Brochan stepped up next to him, his body tense, his
eyes distant.

"Do you feel that, sir?" he asked, in a submissive
way to alert Austin to the danger. If Austin had needed
it, here was further proof the shifter had no problem
relinquishing his alpha mantle, even in pressurized
situations.

"Yes." Austin watched the basajaun descend the
stairs and then strut off into the trees, disappearing
immediately. "The basajaun can speak to trees. He'll

assess the danger."

"I wondered how that other one up north knew I was in its territory," Brochan said softly, scanning the area. "I was roaming when I caught its scent. I didn't feel like circling around, so I changed my direction to downwind and hightailed it. It got around and in front of me. That thing was not fun to deal with. I hoped never to see one again."

"Please tell me you didn't kill it."

"Are you kidding, sir? I'm not that stupid. No, I fought it until I could prove I was a risky challenge, and then I bartered with it. I didn't know they could talk to the woods. I've always heard they're prickly to deal with and they don't often bother with anyone but the basajaunak."

"Usually that's true, yes. Until Jess charmed this one, I'd given him a large berth. He's downright placid when it comes to her. It seems he thinks their fates are intertwined."

"Ah yeah. Fate. Tricky bitch."

"Yes. Very. But this basajaun has been incredibly helpful to have around."

"It's magic." Jess stopped next to the open limo door, the driver waiting beside it in a tux similar to Mr. Tom's. "What you're all sensing is magic. It's every-where around here—on the runway, draped between the trees, on the ground… It's basically an elaborate tripwire system, but I don't sense anything terribly dangerous. Roam at will."

"In other words, they think anyone sneaking into the area will be using an airplane," Hollace said, following her.

"Yes." Jess checked her watch. "We need to get going. Basajaun!" she called. "Come on. You can check things out when we get closer."

The basajaun emerged from the trees, his hair sticking up from his shoulders and his bow tie absolutely ridiculous. He was taking a page out of Mr. Tom's book, apparently.

"There is nothing around this area. No watchers," he said.

"Magic is doing the watching. They don't need people." Jess gave the jet a final, forlorn look before ducking into the last limo. Her team would arrive right before her and spread out around her for cover so as to give her a grander entrance.

"Yes, miss, I know you are severely disappointed." Mr. Tom walked closer, frazzled, his arms braced on his hips and his wings rustling behind him. Niamh and Edgar walked behind him. "But how was I supposed to know they wouldn't stock the jets with snacks and drinks? Really, all that expense and they only provide water and ice? I think they cut corners for magical people, that's what I think."

"I think they expected magical people to read the fine print when *that is their job*," Niamh berated as Jasper descended from the jet. He immediately turned to monitor the service staff carrying down the luggage.

"I looked over the fine print, I thought," Mr. Tom murmured, turning and walking back toward Jasper, scanning the luggage as it was brought down and put in a neat pile to be divided up between the limos.

"Beautiful." Cyra sauntered in front of Austin and spread her arms, gazing at the mountains around them. Fire ballooned up around her like wings. "I would love to take a moment for flight."

"No time," Austin responded. "We'll make sure to take advantage of the area before we leave."

"If we aren't being chased out." Edgar scratched his head, and little white flakes drifted to the ground.

Nathanial stopped with Austin and Brochan. "Barring any unforeseen challenges, the gargoyles from town should arrive tonight," Nathanial said. "I haven't heard of any problems, so I assume they are on track. They have been instructed to touch down a ways from the entrance. Hopefully there'll be a place to land that is hard for non-fliers to reach. They'll turn to stone until needed. I don't know if we'll be able to use them, but if we can, they'll be on hand."

Austin nodded as Cyra neared the trees, fire swirling out around her.

"Why didn't we fly them in, sir?" Kace asked, joining their gathering. Brochan stepped back and out of the way, deferring to Kace's higher standing in the pack. Isabelle stood just beyond him.

"Here, miss." Mr. Tom jogged back to Jess's limo with a paper bag in one hand and a white plastic medicine bottle in the other. "Look at this! I completely forgot about this! A few chocolates for the car ride."

"Ye should've given them to her when she was looking for snacks on the plane." Niamh started forward. "Ye ruined her whole experience."

"Ah, but look!" Mr. Tom jiggled the bag, more flustered and panicked than Austin had ever seen him. The way he was carrying on, one might assume he'd made a critical error that would cost lives. "Chocolates, miss! They are only slightly melted. Well, not melted *now*, per se, but melted at one time and reformed into…rather lovely…artistic shapes. You won't even taste the difference. A little whitened, but that's okay. It's still chocolate. I know how chocolate calms you. It's like catnip for Jane women, right?"

"No thanks," Jess said. "Let's just get on the road. I'm sure they'll have food for us when we get there."

"Or, look…" Mr. Tom held out the white medicinal bottle. "Chocolate-flavored stool softener. It will taste good and maybe loosen up the bowels. I know you've been nervous. Stress can cause lots of problems for the body. This will keep you regular *and* fulfill that chocolate craving you were clearly having on the plane."

All the shifters turned to stare, their expressions flat but their poise and body language screaming their utter bewilderment. Austin thought about reassuring them that they would eventually get used to Mr. Tom's antics, but he didn't want to lie. Apparently, when he got flustered, Mr. Tom not only got weirder, but he started making very questionable decisions.

Austin turned away from Mr. Tom, shifting his focus back to Kace's question. "The jet needed to have a manifest of passengers, which we suspected Elliot Graves would be able to access. We don't want him knowing we have backup." The basajaun bounded back from the woods, shaking his head. "Basajaun, take the second-to-last limo." He'd be a spectacle. Better for him to get out toward the end so he wouldn't take much focus away from Jessie.

"Mages don't think about the wild lands other than to hunt and collect supplies for their craft," Brochan said, his tone flat, emotionless. "Even to do that, they distance themselves from nature. They use vehicles whenever they can, guns, metal traps—they are more similar to Dicks and Janes than shifters when it comes to nature. It won't occur to them that anyone might sneak in through the trees. They might not even realize there's a threat of fliers showing up. The roads leading in and out are probably closely monitored, along with this landing strip and the entrances and exits for the lair. But mages are shortsighted. Extremely powerful but narrow-minded in their thinking. Hard to combat them unless you have a magic wielder, though."

"Which we do," Edgar said, still standing off to the side. Austin had nearly forgotten he was there. "We have the most powerful magic wielder in the world, actually. She can fight face-to-face combat, and we can rush in from the sides and behind."

Austin nodded, because that was exactly right. They could handle mages—the battle with Kinsella had made that entirely clear.

"Load up." Austin made a circle with his finger. "Let's get to it before Mr. Tom convinces Jess she needs some Ex-Lax."

"Hopefully the miss isn't so nervous that she allows that to happen," Edgar murmured, watching Mr. Tom straighten up and glance back. "Maybe he's the one who should be asking for retirement."

Niamh laughed, getting into a limo near the front.

"Brochan, check in with Jasper and make sure everything is coming along." Austin broke away from the others and found Jess in the interior of the limo staring down at her hands. "Mr. Tom failed you again, huh?"

Her smile didn't reach her eyes. "He found those chocolates in the bottom of his toiletry bag, did you hear that part? Who puts chocolates in a toiletry bag and how long have they been in there? He's been at Ivy House for...*years*. When was the last time he traveled? Because looking at them, there was no way he recently packed those things."

"I thought you always said never to question Mr. Tom?"

Her eyebrows flared and she looked out the window. "This is true. Did the basajaun feel anything? I couldn't hear over the growling of my stomach."

He slipped his fingers between hers and bumped her leg with his knee, knowing she was trying not to focus on her extreme discomfort with what they were doing. He played into it, knowing it wouldn't do any good to try to convince her that they would pull through this. That he would make sure she made it out one way or another, with or without him.

"No, all is quiet. Listen, I think I have some caramels in my sock. Want me to dig around for them?"

This time a real smile peeked through. After a moment she said, "I did get my hopes up that there would be a big spread in the jet. I thought that was kind of a standard thing. You got, like, an air hostess and some...awesome little nibbles, or...I don't know... *Something.*"

He laughed as the limo got underway. "My brother always has those things when he flies in a private jet, yes, but he has an experienced staff to handle stocking it."

"Hmm."

The narrow two-lane road led away from the landing strip. It didn't take long for them to start climbing into the mountain range, the limos slowing down to take turns that would have been better suited to different cars.

"We didn't hire these limos," she whispered, now chewing on her nail. "We're already in *his* power."

Austin stroked her thumb with his, holding her hand tightly. "We are never in someone else's power. When you were in a cage hanging above spikes without access to your wings, you still weren't in anyone else's power. You were just...put out for a moment."

"We could be ambushed."

"What a horrible surprise for them, trying to ambush a basajaun."

"We might get out of the limo and be killed immediately."

"That's why Cyra will be getting out first, because she comes back to life."

"He might finally succeed in capturing me, his sole goal all this time."

"That has hardly been his sole goal. I'm sure he has much more sinister plans, like trying to make you fall in love with him so he can steal your magic, like what happened with the past heirs. Good thing you don't want to fall in love, huh? He's got his work cut out for him."

"That's not true. I lo—" She gritted her teeth, her whole body tightening up.

She'd been just about to say that she loved him, Austin knew. He could see it in her body language. He could feel it in his gut.

He breathed out slowly, everything in him pounding, wanting to take her right then, right there, feeling how close they were to completing the mating bond. Something was stopping her, and he would bet anything it was her beast. The female gargoyle was not sated. It wanted something more.

Austin just wished he knew what it was. He wished Jess did.

After this was all over, he was going to cheat and ask Ulric to tell him what it would take to impress her beast.

Whatever it was, he'd do it. He'd claim his mate.

He just had to wait until they had a week or so to explore their new bond. That wasn't something he wanted to happen in enemy territory.

"It's the unknown that is giving me hell," she said after a while, the limo winding higher into the mountains. "I hate the unknown. Whenever I went on vacation in the past, I had the itinerary all laid out. I knew where we would be staying, how we'd get there, places in the area where we could eat, places to avoid…"

"I think we're headed into a place to avoid."

"Yes, we are. And it isn't just a bad neighborhood— it's a bunch of caves closed into a mountain and filled with cutthroat, homicidal magical people." She met his gaze and then looked away. "This isn't your average work trip. We might not survive, Austin. I could be responsible for all these people dying."

He touched his palm to her jaw, guiding her face back to him. When she was looking at him, he kissed her lips gently, and said, "I know this is playing hell on your nerves, and nothing any of us say will ease this burden for you. It feels different when you're walking into danger instead of defending your home against it. But Elliot Graves left you no choice. He's caused a lot of problems and a lot of bloodshed, and someone needs to end it. You are the only one who can. The people who joined you today *want* to be here. They want to fight. Please remember that when the guilt pulls you down."

She blinked her glassy eyes, looking up at him with a wide-open gaze. A tear slipped out and rolled down her cheek.

"What would I do without you?" she asked quietly.

"Probably go on more internet dates that would end badly."

She huffed out a laugh and pulled him in for a kiss, lingering for a moment. When she pulled back, he wrapped her in his arms and held her close.

"We both know that as soon as you get there," he said into her ear, "you'll go into overdrive, and you'll handle whatever comes at you. You will dazzle them with your weird team—"

"Eccentric."

"—and you will show them that you are not some-one to trifle with."

"Or I will hear someone make a snide comment about you, go absolutely crazy, and start a war."

"An enemy's lair isn't the most romantic place to spend the week with a new mate, but we can make it work if we must."

"Especially if Mr. Tom is in charge of the snacks, am I right?" She released a breath. "I almost wish I'd taken some of that chocolate. That's how unsettled I am. I'm so off-kilter that I would eat some old chocolate Mr. Tom randomly found in his toiletry bag."

"As long as you don't reach for the chocolate stool softener. What could he possibly have been thinking?"

She shook with laughter in his arms. "Yeah, well… Honestly, there are no words. There just aren't."

"Let's hope this week doesn't frazzle him more, if this is the way he reacts to nerves."

She paused for a moment, serious again. "It won't last a week. It will only last as long as it takes for me to get a clear shot off at Elliot Graves."

CHAPTER 12

THE LIMO ROLLED up to a large tunnel in the center of the mountain. A cement arch curved over the narrow, two-lane road. Past the entrance, there was only darkness.

"This is fine," I said into the deathly quiet limo, my heart nearly choking me. "This is okay. Ivy House is shadowy too, and it's lovely."

But it wasn't lovely, Ivy House. It was a nightmare for anyone who wasn't welcome, which was nearly everyone.

"Does it have animated dolls? That's the question," I said.

Austin still held my hand. He gave it a squeeze but didn't comment. He'd put his game face on. Normally that would make me less nervous, because he would surely have my back, but in this situation there was probably very little in the world that would have eased my anxiety.

The car entered the tunnel, and that thick, choking

darkness washed over us. The driver must have turned on his lights, but I couldn't see my hand in front of my face. How could he see the road?

"Oh crap, oh crap, oh crap, it's happening. We're going to be attacked." My magic ballooned around us, and my power ripped outward, seeking out danger. It found some sort of spell promoting blindness. I tried to blast through it and took out the window instead. Glass shattered, but the limo shuddered and kept moving. I belatedly thought to try the door. Locked. "We are not in his power," I reminded myself in a whisper as panic ate at me. "No one has power over me!"

I fired off spells as quickly as I could, no idea how to counter whatever was making me blind but figuring I could create havoc in the meantime.

"Get clear," I yelled at Austin.

His hand ripped free of mine, and I felt him practically dive forward in the limo. I could've just shielded him from what I was about to do, but I was acting faster than I was thinking, and that thought was belated as well.

I slammed a spell into the door. The back tire bounced into the air, the sound and sensation jarring as it came back down. Metal squealed and twisted. More glass shattered. Finally, the door ripped off and cool air gushed in, smelling of exhaust.

Darkness still cocooned me. The limo slammed to a stop.

"Do not go out that door," Austin growled, clearly realizing I'd blasted it off. He didn't need to tell me twice. I was no fool.

I tried a ball of light, but the magic creating the darkness swallowed it almost immediately. I tried again, and this time I pumped all my power into it. I didn't care if it morphed the spell into something unexpected. I needed to see!

Before I fired it out of the limo, I felt out my people through the link and put a protective spell around them, making it a little larger to encompass the shifters I knew were near them. That done, I let loose.

White cracks formed within the blackness, spiderwebbing out. They grew and spread, almost like pressure fractures in a wall or cement. My spell was battling that of Elliot Graves, power against power. We'd see if I was any match for him.

While I waited for the verdict, not able to pump more power into the spell after shooting it off, I threw magical bombs, blasting the other door off and blowing out the rest of the limo's side windows.

"Am I magically covered?"

"Hah!" I slapped out my hand in a stupid karate chop, uselessly striking Austin's shoulder. I hadn't heard him crawl back toward me. "Yes, yes, yes, though some of my more adventurous spells might physically jolt you."

He squeezed my knee and brushed past me as he exited the limo from the hole on the other side, where the door used to be. Or so I thought. I obviously couldn't see my handiwork.

Light forced its way through the inky blackness like the roots of a great oak, undaunted by the resistance, undeterred in its goal. I blasted the area directly in front of us, behind the next limo up, and heard metal pop, followed by a heavy thud, like bouncing.

I felt my people scramble toward the right, hurrying. Austin was around the back of the limo, already heading back toward me, moving faster than a non-shifter could, relying on his other senses to show him the way.

My magic blossomed through the sky, peeling back the blackness. It showered the curved sides of the great tunnel and shone against the mangled metal around me. Glass spread across the cement outside my door, Austin stepping on it in his fine suit, his hands at his jacket edges, ready to strip if he needed to change. A moment later, my stomach dropped.

My people were all standing on a cobblestone sidewalk in front of a large entryway, their eyes wide, hands hanging at their sides as they gaped at me. Behind them, glass littered the floor. What had once been a large glass double door was now a hole. Men and women in red suits, like hotel staff, cowered in the corners of the large room beyond with their arms over their heads.

Austin let go of his jacket and smoothly stepped toward me. I could feel his utter delight through the link but had no clue why.

My spell drifted away, taking the lingering blackness with it, and I noticed the lovely ornate gas lanterns suspended by chains above the road, the magical flames purple, blue, and pink. It almost reminded me of the crystals at the core of Ivy House. More lights glowed from the sides of the tunnel, highlighting the narrow road, the yellow line down the middle easy to see.

Given a couple of the limos had made their way to the curb and the rest were in the process of doing so, I suspected only the passengers had been magically blinded. Though, given the fact that everyone had made their way to the little sidewalk in front of the destroyed doors, maybe the others hadn't been blinded for long. They'd all known exactly where to head when they (clearly) thought I was about to blow them up.

Smoke rose from one of the limos in front. I could just see another with the trunk all twisted. Someone's luggage had probably suffered from that one.

Absolutely no one moved in the ensuing silence.

"So…" The glass crunched under my stiletto as I stepped forward, my voice echoing around the cavernous space. The late-afternoon sunlight shone through the large tunnel entrance behind me. "That was some sort of welcome, was it? Some sort of magical…howdy-do?"

"Maybe you should've taken some of that chocolate Ex-Lax," Ulric said, and the pressure released. The people in red coats slowly pulled their arms away from their heads, peering over their shoulders. Limo drivers poked their heads out from around the ruined entrance, seeing if the coast was clear. Cyra's fire swirled around her, and everyone else gave her a lot more room than she actually needed.

"Seems to me," Mr. Tom said to Niamh, "that you failed to tell her that mages typically give a show of their power when their guests first arrive."

"That might've slipped me mind, yes," Niamh said, dusting the glass from her shoulder. "But now we know that our Jessie has more power."

"*Shh*." Mr. Tom batted at her, then looked upward and into the corners of the door. "They might have surveillance out here."

"She's not telling them anything they didn't just realize." Hollace stepped forward and looked away from us, down the long tunnel and out the small hole on the other side. "What should we do about the basajaun?"

"Did he run?" I asked in disbelief, slipping my hand through Austin's held-out arm. I could feel the basajaun now, walking back toward us.

Mr. Tom sniffed. "Your limo driver took off running like a coward. The basajaun went after him. Apparently he didn't like the idea of anyone getting away. Cyra, you are making black spots on the cobblestone. For a centuries-old soul, you are horribly bad at containing your magic."

"It's harder to control after rebirth," Cyra said. "Doubly hard after many rebirths in a short period of time. It usually takes me a few months to level out."

"I never thought I'd miss the dolls," Hollace said. "Let's hope there's a lot of rock in this place, which won't catch fire, or I'm going to be sprinting out of here like the basajaun. Only I won't be trying to catch anyone."

"Niamh didn't tell you about the show Elliot Graves would put on either, huh?" I asked Austin quietly as everyone set to work wrestling the luggage out of the trunks with twisted metal. Thankfully, they all (loudly) blamed it on Niamh.

"She did—" Austin cut off as he walked me through the ruined glass doors and then stopped, surprise blistering through the link.

He'd clearly expected some dark series of tunnels, small spaces carved into the rock with low ceilings, rough rock walls, and uneven ground. And if not that, something other than the luxurious setup before us.

Cream walls rose to the curved ceiling, sporting a rectangular square of muted light surrounded by thick white paneling. A large gold chandelier hung from the middle of the ceiling, dripping with crystals. The metal frame curled up and supported a candle with a flickering magical flame. A design of large blue flowers with darkened violet middles was painted on the walls, their deep brown stems painted close to the ceiling so the blooms hung downward, with pops of yellow birds flying or sitting within them.

"That reminds me of the flowers you got me on our first date," I mumbled, tracing their path along the walls. "Different flowers but similar color scheme."

In contrast to the white paneling around the glowing patch of light, dark baseboards lined the floor and the large open doorways leading away from the front room. A couple of blue velvet chairs, the same shade as the flowers on the walls, waited in front of us, pushed up against a small table as though inviting us to sit until our accommodations were ready. There were more small seating areas beyond that, situated in front of large ornate mirrors to make the room look bigger.

"Niamh did tell me he'd put on a show," Austin said, picking our conversation back up as he guided me to the chair setup. I sat down happily enough. There was plenty of luggage outside, but I wasn't supposed to help my people get it. This week, I would act like some sort of duchess, expecting everyone to do everything for me. I wasn't all that put out by that.

He sat down in the other chair. "Given your reaction, however," he continued, "I assumed we were being magically attacked."

"I mean…we were. With blindness. I feel like that's an attack."

"It can certainly be construed as such." Austin crossed an ankle over a knee and extended his arm until it was resting across the back of my chair. "Not all mages give a show of their power. If the host knew the mages he'd invited were more powerful, for example, he wouldn't take the risk. A more powerful mage would tear the spell down and send a message, not only for the hosting mage, but for everyone else at the…meetup. Or party. Elliot Graves put on a show to declare that he is the most powerful mage here. He holds all the cards."

"And by tearing it down…"

"You've just sent your message."

"Except I didn't know I was doing it," I whispered.

"You knew exactly what you were doing. You just didn't know it was a statement. You also wrecked his transportation and blew a hole in the side of his—certainly warded—front door. If there was ever a question of who had more power, you just answered it. We just have to be more careful now, is all."

"Why is that?"

"Because he'll know that, head to head, your brawn will win. If he comes at you, it'll be from behind. When you least expect it."

CHAPTER 13

S EBASTIAN SAT AT his desk and watched the cameras in utter delight. The heir of Ivy House had made an entrance that would be gossiped about for years to come. Her team apparently hadn't alerted her to the protocol at one of these things, and wow, he marveled at her sense of survival and her reactions in a tight situation. Blowing out the limo doors and the entrance? Scaring the staff?

That display would create fear-soaked rumors that would travel to the other mages, no problem. She was wild and unpredictable. Incredibly powerful. She'd broken Sebastian's spell from the inside out. Cracked it open like an egg. No finesse, no meticulous approach, just brute strength.

No one else would be able to counteract that spell. Not in the time allotted. The drivers had been given precise instructions on how fast to drive from the start of the tunnel until they pulled up to the curb. Not even Sebastian could work a counter-spell—or counter-curse, if you wanted to be dramatic—in that amount of time. Not with the precision it required.

Still, every single mage he'd invited would try to do the impossible. They'd experience the power of the spell for themselves, which would make it even more difficult for them to believe *she* had torn it down. They'd probably tell themselves the staff had gotten it wrong. Or maybe they'd convince themselves the shifters—the *animals*—had wrecked the place.

But that would scare them, too. This was a no-lose situation. Ivy House would be proud of her heir's debut in the magical world; Sebastian would make sure of it. He might die for his troubles, but magic was risky.

The huge and hairy basajaun entered the screen on the main camera, angled to pick up the loading zone. The basajaun held his prize, a scared-senseless driver who would almost assuredly quit and take whatever punishment he was given. Sebastian wasn't sure he blamed the guy.

The driver hung upside down, his palms over his face and his ankles captured in one of the basajaun's giant hands. It was the worst game of peekaboo the world had ever known. For that driver, anyway.

"Sir, the living quarters are ready for—What in the…"

"Yeah, yeah." Sebastian motioned to Nessa, his

right-hand woman, organizer of all things, and the only person he could really call a friend in the magical world. "Get a load of this." He pointed at the screen, then gestured to all the other screens showing the entrance-way and tunnel.

"Oh wow." Nessa leaned closer, pointing at the basajaun. "You weren't kidding. Holy hell, that thing is huge."

"And ferocious. Seriously, you will pee your pants, I am telling you. I hope they sign up for the trials. I half wish they didn't have to be a secret until the last minute so I could have gotten a general feel for if she'd go for it."

"She wants to kill you. She'll sign up."

"Let's not dwell on the details."

"She did all that? Or did the shifters help?"

"No, no. She did all that. Amazing, right? She liter-ally blew through my magic. Like…blew it up, I mean."

She gave him a look that was half amused and half perturbed. "Normal mages wouldn't be tickled by that fact."

"And they also wouldn't get the opportunity to train an ancient, fabled magic that will dwarf all other magics."

"If she doesn't kill you first," Nessa said dryly. "Your sister didn't finish her *Sight*."

A heart attack had knocked Sebastian's sister out of her trance right before she made it to the outcome of the final battle. She'd died five minutes later, before they could get help.

Sebastian had been preparing for years, counting down to this meeting, with the blind hope that the heir wouldn't kill him in the final moment. He very well might have been planning his death all this time. It was a helluva leap of faith, but he'd clung to his sister's dying words, which she'd struggled to say right before giving in to eternal night. "*You must…walk this journey. You* must *follow the stars.*"

Follow the stars. It sounded lofty and full of purpose. Or so he hoped. It was what he'd clung to this last decade.

The waiting was almost over. The pivotal scene was upon them.

He was doing everything he could not to think about it. His elaborate game of cat and mouse with the other mages showing up would hopefully distract him from the possibility that he might be about to follow Jala into death.

"Oh…hel-*lo*." Nessa looked at the screen showing the waiting area. An attendant had stopped next to the couple, no doubt relaying the information that their rooms were ready. The alpha stood, helping Jessie up after him, both of them dressed to the nines. "He is *all* man."

"Don't even think it." Sebastian put his hand in front of the screen. "Don't even look. Ever. Eyes and especially hands off him, unless you want a world of hurt."

"Don't worry, I'm not going to try to steal the heir's man. But I don't mind looking, not one bit. You said he was in shape; you didn't say he was a god. The guy is H-O-T, *hot*." She fanned her face, nearly salivating.

"Seriously, Nessa, I'm not joking. That female gargoyle is entering the mating phase—or maybe she's in it by now—and she will literally tear your face off and wear it like a party favor if you encroach on her territory. That man is her territory. Do not pass go; do not collect two hundred dollars. He likes violence, too. He'll like watching what she does to you."

"All right, all right," she said softly, her gaze still lingering on Austin. "He's incredibly handsome, though. And just...so...*masculine*. They don't make mages like that."

"They don't make shifters like that either, I think. From what I've seen, he's unusual for his kind. More powerful and more intense. It has something to do with his father and mother—I couldn't get a straight answer out of anyone. They only trusted me when Jessie was around, and I didn't want to make her suspicious by asking too many questions. Just wait until you meet him in person, though. He is terrifying. More so than the basajaun. Or the phoenix. Or the thunderbird. Or even the vampire. That one is wily, the vampire. Half the time, he didn't make sense—he'd just pop up next to me randomly, offering some strange sort of floral anecdote. He kept giving me doilies, too. Oddly shaped doilies. I couldn't tell if it was a threat or a joke or… He really unnerved me—I got the feeling he was intentionally trying to disorientate me. He definitely didn't trust me, that was clear. I think he knew I was hiding something. I kept waiting to turn around and find him sinking his fangs into my neck. It was a crazy couple of weeks."

"So you've said. Who is…" She leaned closer to one of the lower screens—the whole office was covered in them, every inch of Sebastian's compound affixed with cameras, recording to the cloud. He wanted to know every important detail of the meeting and hopefully glean secrets from the visiting mages that he could use against them. He also wanted to watch over Jessie and make sure she didn't get tangled up with one of his other visitors. "Who's that? I don't recognize him. He's a looker, too. The scar on his face makes him seem…dangerous."

"He's a shifter—he *is* dangerous," Sebastian murmured, squinting at the screen. "I haven't seen him before. He must be new. What's it say on the roster?"

Nessa pointed at each member of Jessie's party in turn before landing back on the incredibly large shifter who looked like he was draped in a black cloud. "That doesn't look like a Shauna to me."

"A guy like that can go by whatever name he wants. I'm not judging."

Nessa took a step forward and grabbed the office phone off the cradle. She hit three buttons and waited for a moment.

"Yeah, Rick, hey…who's the stand-in for Shauna? He hasn't been approved." She waited a moment. "Yeah, patch me through."

Sebastian watched one of the screens as a red-coated woman holding a clipboard glanced at the phone resting on a nearby end table.

There was no cell service in this mountain. The only way to call for help was via landline, wired in a few of the tunnels and in select rooms. The chances of finding one of those landlines and getting help in time was next to nil.

Sebastian hit a few keys and turned up the volume near the woman.

"Hello?" the woman said.

"This is the captain," Nessa replied, a title she'd chosen for herself. She hadn't revealed her name to the staff, just like Sebastian hadn't informed them of his real name. They were Elliot Graves and the captain, never close enough to strangers to be vulnerable, feared the world over. It was necessary, the anonymity, and it made life much easier. If people feared you, you got results. The shifters knew something about that. "Who is that man standing in for Shauna?"

The woman had the presence of mind not to turn and look.

"They introduced him as Shauna, ma'am. Sue for short. Well, actually, it seems like they call him 'broken Sue' or something… It's hard to tell. The driver that the Bigfoot chased down—"

"Don't call him Bigfoot!" Sebastian practically yelled, unable to help himself. He calmed himself down. "Don't call him that. He gets riled up. Call him basajaun—or whatever he asks to be called."

Nessa relayed the information.

"Thank you, ma'am. I'll make sure to pass that on. As I was saying, the driver that the…basajaun chased down has been crying uncontrollably and screeching about being eaten, so it's made things a little…chaotic. You'd said not to clean up, though, so we've left him in a ball in the corner."

"Yes, fine." Nessa covered the mouthpiece with her

hand. "That rodent talks back far too much. I'd planned to discipline him anyway. This will do nicely." She took her hand off the mouthpiece. "Did they give any reasoning for…Broken Sue not looking like her—his picture?"

"Yes, ma'am. The…puca said he'd been in a traffic accident and came out uglier. We didn't really know what to do with that."

Sebastian huffed out a laugh. "Let them through."

"Thank you, corporal." Nessa hung up the phone. There weren't ranks within the staff—there was one captain, and the rest were corporals. It was a little absurd, but it enhanced the eccentricity of Elliot Graves, so Sebastian had never commented on it. "They made a swap right before go time and clearly didn't care if we noticed."

"Seems that way."

"He's fit, too." Nessa was looking harder at the screen. "I'll take a boy named Sue. How do *you* do?"

"Okay, that's enough. Don't chase the shifters until after you've met them face to face. You might change your tune."

"I'm not trying to marry one of them, Sabby. I just want to take one of them home and play with him for a little while."

Sebastian rolled his eyes with a grin. Nessa had been

friends with Jala, Sebastian's sister, which was why she sometimes called him Sabby when she was being silly. It grounded him. "Explosive action with a heavy side of danger? Yes, *please*."

Sebastian watched Jessie follow the attendant down the largest tunnel to the plushest collection of rooms Sebastian had, save his own quarters and Nessa's rooms. The alpha was just a little behind, his hand on the small of her back, his eyes straight ahead but his senses probably on overdrive, sussing out danger. The rest of the crew followed them.

"They are lining up according to power level, then," Nessa asked, studying them, no longer ogling Broken Sue. It was time to do her job.

Sebastian rifled through his memory. "Looks about right. Except the shifters aren't in the rear because they're weak. When a shifter expects danger from behind, one of the strongest will take up the last place. An alpha or the next best thing, I think."

"Broken Sue is clearly the next best thing." Nessa bit her lip. "It's impossible to gauge how the heir's people will fare against the magical might you have coming in here. I've read up on the various creatures, but…" She shook her head. "How they will do here is a blind spot for me."

"They'll be a blind spot for everyone. So will Jessie.

Honestly, wait and see. I wasn't telling tall tales."

"Yeah, yeah, sure, sure." She checked her watch. "We have our first mouse landing at the airstrip in thirty minutes. Have you decided how many of these mages you'll leave alive?"

"No. It depends on how the week unravels."

"Well." Nessa straightened up and headed for the door. "Don't get soft. You have a reputation to uphold. That reputation is your safety net. Keep it taut."

"Yes, captain." He was supposed to be some evil overlord, but he constantly got pushed around and told what to do by his underling. He was pretty sure he was doing it wrong.

He noticed the tension in Jessie's eyes as she passed from camera to camera. She didn't understand why any of this was necessary. But it was. Sebastian was only setting her up because he hoped to save her life.

He just hoped, when the time came, she'd return the favor.

The attendant stopped in front of her door, explaining some details about the quarters she'd been given. When she was finished, she left them to it.

Jessie opened the door, but the alpha stopped her, wrapping her in his body and his protection. Sebastian doubted any of the other heirs had found a man like him. A man who wouldn't hesitate to put her safety over his own. That was why the Ivy House magic was designed to be shared between the heir and her chosen protector: he could fight for her safety if need be.

It was said that Tamara had built that little "safe-guard" into her magic at her lover's insistence, and the loophole had accidentally been passed to the house along with the magic. At that point, it was impossible to remove.

Sebastian wondered about that, however. From his readings, Tamara had seemed like a whip-smart woman who'd made a youth's mistake in love. At the end of her life, she could have struck out at her attacker, her lover, and died in the process, but instead she'd chosen to protect the magic. Stripping herself—and him—of magic and transferring it to the house had taken time. She'd had enough of it to consider abolishing the protector's role. But she hadn't. She'd chosen to keep the magic sharable. And in so doing, she'd ensured a long line of heirs followed her fate: going for the wrong guy and paying the ultimate price.

Maybe Sebastian was just a hopeless romantic at heart, but he didn't think Tamara had done it out of bitterness. He believed with all his soul that she had transferred the magic that way—sharable—out of hope. He believed she had wished for a future heir to find the kind of partner she'd always wanted—and to give him the magic with an open heart and solid trust so that he might use it to protect her in a way no one else could. In a way she couldn't protect herself.

The other heirs had all been young, however, and young people were more liable to make mistakes when it came to love.

Miss Jessie Ironheart was in a different phase of her life. She'd learned from her mistakes and had the wisdom to show for it. In her new life, she was more discerning, which was why she'd found what the other heirs had not—a partner who was worthy of her.

Austin Steele was everything Tamara would've wanted. He was designed for the protector's magic, and he'd know exactly how to use it, Sebastian was positive. Austin probably wouldn't even want it, or think he needed it. Which, of course, meant he was exactly the right person to wield it.

What a treat it would be to see it all unfold.

If Jessie didn't kill Sebastian first.

He watched as the other shifters pushed to the front and entered the room first, moving as a collective unit.

Sebastian put his elbow on the desk and leaned his chin against his fist, watching in fascination.

They cleared one room at a time, like a police force in the movies, but without all the halting and hand gestures. They worked seamlessly, somehow communi-

cating without speaking, utterly fluid in their movements. Having checked all the adjoining rooms, they
returned to the large community room, which Niamh
and the phoenix had since entered. The shifters nodded
to them before retreating back against the walls.

Mages and shifters. What an amazing pair they
would make.

"Uh-oh, Earl, the bad guy has shown you up,"
Niamh called out with a grin.

Sebastian grinned, watching Jessie's face as she finally entered the room behind a couple of others.
Surprise and wonder lit up her expression.

"I knew it," Sebastian whispered, his smile spreading. She'd always liked to nibble, he remembered. She
liked cheese plates and chocolates. He'd figured this
setup would be her speed.

A moment later, her expression shut down, but he'd
gotten the payoff he was looking for. He turned off the
cameras in her area to give her some privacy, something
he wasn't allowing anyone else.

She'd taken care of him in O'Briens, treating him
like one of the team and trusting him with her life.
She'd taken him at face value and judged him only by
his actions and his integrity. He wanted to thank her by
making her feel welcome too, even if she didn't know it
was in good faith. Not yet, anyway.

He was glad she'd come. He'd missed her—he'd missed them all. He'd missed training with an equal who didn't judge him. Learning about shifters and other magical creatures. Feeling the thrill of fear—of being *alive*—and working as a team. He missed Ivy House.

He hoped to go back there someday.

He hoped Jessie didn't kill him before he could explain.

CHAPTER 14

I TRIED NOT to be impressed by the grand tunnel, lined with that lovely paneling that created a border around the rectangles of light, giving the impression of skylights in the middle of a mountain. I tried not to admire the cozy seating areas cut into the walls—an armchair on either side of a table holding a vase with blood-red roses, mulberry tulips, or butter-yellow daffodils. I desperately tried not to appreciate the murals painted on the walls, like looking through a window at the valley far below, the scenes rendered in a way that gave the tunnel more depth and an illusion of size. I tried, and I failed. Whatever else Elliot Graves may be, he had an eye for comfortable décor. He knew how to make his guests feel welcome, even in a collection of tunnels with no immediate escape.

It was dangerous, feeling that way in this place.

The tunnel ended at a red-brick wall with a white double door in the middle. Our guide reached into the pocket of her coat and fished out a large, rustic bronze key like one might see in a castle. She held it out for me.

"This is your collection of rooms," she said. "You may assign the rooms as you wish. I was instructed to tell you that the lock and key can't be relied on for security. Any decent mage, of which there will be plenty, can open a locked door. Inside, on the table, you will find a few spells for warding your space, generously created and offered by Elliot Graves himself. You would do well to pick the spell outlined in red, as that is the most powerful, and besides him, you're the only one who should be able to do it. He'll look forward to testing your work."

I narrowed my eyes but said nothing. I wasn't in the habit of shooting the messenger.

"We have a commercial kitchen on site," she went on. "If you would like to order meals to be brought to you, that is no problem. Otherwise, the kitchen in your quarters is fully stocked, and if you need anything, or have any dietary restrictions, please let us know so that we may accommodate you. You will find only one item on the schedule so far, and that is dinner tomorrow night. Details are enclosed in the packet. At dinner you will get a new schedule, based on your choices."

Based on my choices? I didn't like the sound of that.

"Your luggage will arrive shortly. Please let us know if you need anything." The woman bowed, slipped around our group of people, and hastened down the hall.

"There's no magic on this door," I said, trying the round bronze handle above the old-fashioned keyhole. Both matched the look and feel of the key.

The handle turned easily, but Austin stepped forward as soon as I pushed the door open, his front against my side and his hand taking over the handle. His other arm curved around me, pulling me in close, creating a protective layer around my body.

The shifters walked up the sides of the group, having stayed in the back to watch our six. Now they filed to the front and went through the door.

"Let them have a quick look," Austin murmured, his voice low and rough. "They'll be able to smell it if people have been tampering with things."

"What about magic? They can't see if any magical traps are laid."

"Elliot Graves wouldn't have gone through all this trouble to kill you so quickly. We'll be safe until the dinner tomorrow night."

Cyra walked through the door, followed shortly afterward by Niamh.

A few moments passed by, and I could feel Cyra and Niamh having a look around the room just beyond the door.

A moment later, Niamh called out, "Uh-oh, Earl, the bad guy has shown you up."

"What is she talking about?" Mr. Tom pushed his way to the front of our group and walked into the room.

Cyra's disembodied voice floated out. "I volunteer to sample everything first, as the official poison control."

"Oh, heavens," Mr. Tom said, and I could tell he was deflated.

I couldn't wait any longer. I wiggled out of Austin's grip.

A large room opened up before me, with a couple of conversation areas formed by cream couches and chairs clustered around coffee tables, a pool table, and darts in the back, next to the open-concept kitchen. There were little side tables throughout the room, accompanied by more stools for sitting. Every available surface, it seemed, was laden with goodies, from the chocolate-covered strawberries I'd craved on the plane, to cantaloupe wrapped in prosciutto, a selection of breads and cheeses, a platter of sandwiches, nuts, other fruits, and a bowl of what looked like truffles that Cyra was currently sampling.

"Mmm." She tilted her head back and looked at the arched ceiling. "This is delicious."

A long table was pushed against the brick wall that

held the doors. The spells were there, ready to lure me into some sort of trap, probably. An engraved invitation informed me of the details of tomorrow's dinner, including where and when, the number of people I could bring (one guest and a food taster), and the dress code. The last item on the table was a manila folder with the label "maps and accessible areas." It held details about our quarters, directions to a garden, exits (with a note about how heavily warded they were), a bar, and other amenities, like something you'd see in a huge hotel at a vacation destination.

"Here, Jessie," Niamh called out, opening the fridge, "maybe ye better have Elliot Graves stock the plane on the way back."

"I make one simple mistake…" Mr. Tom murmured, looking over the selections with an expression of abject horror.

"This all seems safe," Cyra said, munching as she crouched down to a low table holding a selection of cheeses. "Can you imagine if we had a dog? It would roam through here and make short work of all this."

Hollace frowned at her then shook his head, strolling to a fondue stand on a large table in the corner. "This is swank. They really went all out."

"He plays a great host." I ignored the food as I looked over the sheet describing the layout of this collection of rooms. Austin stepped beside me, poring over it with me.

Each person would have their own quarters, the rooms mostly small, with a bed, a small table, and a chair with what looked like a reading light perched over it. I doubted the drawing was totally accurate, but it served its purpose. All of those were connected by a hallway, and they formed a sort of rough circle around a large room in the middle. Mine, apparently.

"Does it matter where we put people?" I asked Austin.

"I'll check it out. There might be a rear exit that isn't mentioned. If not, then the strongest go in the front as our first line of defense. Are you going to do one of those spells?"

I handed the paper off to him and grabbed up the spells. "I want to look at them first. Who knows what they actually do?"

The top popped on a can, and I knew Niamh had found a beer.

"Well, miss, it seems I must go the way of Edgar and ask that you retire me," Mr. Tom said, standing in front of me with his head held high. "As your butler, I must own that I have failed you, and now I've been shown up by our biggest enemy. It is a bleak day, I can assure—"

"No." I held up my hand. "Not now, Mr. Tom. I

have enough to handle as it is."

I took a deep breath and made my way to the largest room, although I grabbed a bacon-wrapped shrimp on the way. Some things were worth being poisoned over, and bacon was one of those things.

Once there, I sighed in utter defeat. Mr. Tom-level defeat.

A bed with a dark gray frame took up the middle of the space, pushed against a slate-gray wall. The bed faced a fireplace, which had to be either decorative or magical, with a TV mounted above it on a sort of column with rock facing, similar to the style of Austin's house. A plush cream rug with cloud-gray squares etched through it covered the floor, and there was a seating area off to the side of the bed. An enormous gift basket wrapped in a red bow sat on the cloth-covered bench at the end of the bed.

Heart sinking, knowing this was going to be amazing, I gingerly sat beside the basket and pulled it closer. The first thing I spied was a blue box with Tiffany & Co. written across the front. Another with Gucci. A third with a name I didn't recognize, all stacked on a bunch of other goodies.

"Damn him," I murmured, my stomach fluttering despite my best efforts not to react.

I wouldn't accept any of this. I couldn't. He'd invaded my house, attacked my people, hired people to kidnap me, and killed my trainer. My friend.

He could not buy me things so I would forget. I would not forget.

That didn't mean I couldn't at least *look*, though. I was only human.

I pulled the cream-white ribbon from the blue Tiffany box and gently lifted the cover. Inside was a rose-gold cuff with a ring of diamonds on each end. In the middle sparkled an infinity sign, rendered in diamonds. A tiny square of paper lay within the hollow of the cuff, and on it read, *You'll be the only heir to live forever.*

The breath left me, and I nearly threw the box and contents across the room. Instead, I lowered it to my lap and looked at it for a moment longer. It wasn't just a costly gift—it was thoughtful, too. He'd seen one of my fears, somehow, and thought to settle it.

He was good.

I replaced the cover and set it aside, lifting the long Gucci box. This one proved to be a black clutch with a diamond insignia. The note read, *In case you don't have any high fashion for dinner. This will go with everything.*

I had high fashion. Mr. Tom had insisted on it and also called me ridiculous for worrying about the price tags when I didn't ever have to worry about money again. Old habits died hard.

An Apple box was next. I expected some sort of high-end electronic, but a glittering gold and diamond iPhone case stared up at me.

"I'd break this in a heartbeat," I muttered, picking up the note inside and turning it over to read it: *A ridiculous display of wealth. I'm guessing you'll re-gift it to someone you have to impress. Like I did.*

I stared at the note for a second and thought about laughing. And then thought about crying. Why did he have to seem so human? To do what I needed to do, I had to think of him as a monster.

I opened a small black velvet box, and a note fell out and fluttered onto my lap. The white-gold ring boasted a translucent, emerald-cut ruby bracketed by two diamonds. I bent to grab the note.

Red diamonds are the rarest in the world. They are absolutely priceless. Just like your magic. Full disclosure: I stole this one. The owner was a real dickhead. Don't worry, someone else has killed him since. You're free and clear.

I looked closer. I hadn't even known red diamonds existed.

The box with the name I didn't recognize, Piaget, yielded a gorgeous watch with a deep blue face marked with what looked like white-gold numbers, surrounded by white-gold casing inlaid with baguette diamonds.

The deep blue leather band matched the face. It was probably ungodly expensive, but it looked simple and elegant.

The note: *Just a pretty, everyday watch I thought you might like.*

There were notes with each and every thing, explaining why the gift was in the basket. They were all thoughtful. They all implied he knew me.

Bose earphones. *To drown out the others while you are confined in this tiny cave.*

A box of Swiss truffles: *This is the best chocolate I've ever had. I am submitting it to you for your assessment. Everyone knows women are the chief experts in these things.*

The last thing I pulled out was a fountain pen shaped as a quill, its stand designed to look like a bottle of ink. The note: *I confess, I got carried away. I thought it was cool until I got it. Online ordering, what can you do?*

"Hey…" Austin poked his head in. "You okay?"

"Yeah." I placed the—actually quite cool—fountain pen back into the basket and started loading everything else up. "What's up?"

"Did you get any good stuff?" He walked in, cool and confident, the swagger of a king. "You should see the watch I got. It's a Patek Philippe Grandmaster

173

Chime out of his personal collection." He searched my blank face. "No? Well, trust me, it is a helluva watch. He somehow knew I was a watch guy."

"You're not freaked out about that fact?"

"No. He just wants us to know he's done his homework. He has the home-court advantage, and he's showing it. I'll wear it to dinner tomorrow night."

"You can't wear it to dinner tomorrow! It'll look like he has the upper hand. Or like he's buying us. We can't accept this stuff."

"Wearing it will show that I am taking all of this in stride. Which I am. I don't care about these little things. The food, the accommodations, the note in the room next to yours, where the watch was waiting for me, suggesting I place the *second* most powerful person in our crew there, since I'll be sleeping with you…" Austin looked around the room and then shrugged out of his jacket. "This is much nicer than I was expecting. More spacious and defensible, too. We're trapped in here— there are no exits save the door we came through—but there is a limit as to how many people they can send after us. The bodies will pile high before they can get through the door. They'll create their own barricade."

"Gross."

He laid his jacket across the back of one of the chairs and undid the cuff link on his right sleeve. "We're going to be okay. We're going to get a good night's sleep tonight, we'll explore a little in the morning, looking for exits and places we can sneak the gargoyles in, and tomorrow night we'll assess the danger with the other mages. You might actually be able to make a few connections while you're here."

I blew out a breath. I felt too jumpy to network. Like I'd try to karate-chop anyone who came up to me.

"Remember," he continued, shutting the door and throwing the lock. He undid his other cuff link before starting to unbutton his shirt, walking toward me. "Everyone here is in the same boat." He pulled his shirt from his muscular shoulders, exposing his perfectly cut torso. He worked at the button and then zipper on his pants, pushing the fabric down and stepping out, toeing off his shoes and then his socks as he did so. He stood nude before me, his hard length at attention. "Elliot Graves has been missing from the magical world for a long while." He stepped around me, and I felt his lips on the curve of my neck, his fingertips like butterflies across my back before they took hold of my zipper. "Before that, he was the most cunning, ruthless mage the world had ever known. The crime boss of all crime bosses." My zipper whirred as it lowered, the fabric of the dress loosening and falling open across my back. "He killed, maimed, and stole his way to an empire. He never took on a partner." My dress slid across my skin, silky smooth, until it pooled at my feet. "For the first time it seems like he's inviting people to work with him, and everyone here will be as eager as they are cautious."

His lips trailed a line of heat down the center of my back. His fingers curled around the sides of my panties before he pushed them down my legs.

"Everyone here is doubtless also wondering if he plans to kill them to make a little more room for his reemergence into the magical world." He stepped in front of me before sinking to his knees, looking up at me. "No one here has the team we have. No one here is as safe as you are." His gaze held mine. "You are being professionally wooed by this man. This place, its setup, the expensive gifts... He wants an audience with you, and he is not going through all of this trouble just to kill you. Not right away. Not before you have an opening to kill him first." He leaned forward, his cobalt eyes still connected with mine, and licked up my center.

I sucked in a breath, tingles spreading across my body.

He pulled back just a bit. "I need you to go out there tomorrow like you're headed into battle. I need you to own who and what you are, and take no prisoners. These mages can smell weakness. You can't show any. I know you're anxious and stressed, so I will spend a great deal of time and effort helping you relax to-night..." He sucked on the little bundle of nerves at the top of my sex, gently scraping it with his teeth and flash-boiling my blood. "I will serve you dinner in bed after I pleasure you, before pleasuring you again, until you are boneless and unable to keep your eyes open. We'll sleep in late, and then you will strap on your armor, knowing that you have the absolute best team in the world at your back. And then you will lead us into danger."

I ran my hand through his dark brown hair...and opened my legs a little wider.

"That's my girl." He took to me like he was starving, sucking and licking and making my eyes roll into the back of my head. His fingers dove and retreated as his mouth worked in tandem, winding me ever tighter.

I let the sensations move through me, focused on his ministrations and his proximity, allowing myself to let go. My hips swung toward him and away as his plunging fingers sped up and his suction increased. The orgasm swelled out of nowhere, sweeping me away. I shuddered above him, crying out his name and yanking on his hair.

He gave me a hearty growl before standing and picking me up, carrying me to the bed.

"I don't want you to hold on to anything tonight,"

he told me, ripping back the covers and settling me in. His body pushed me into the soft mattress. "I want you to release it all onto me. Any lingering doubts or worries—release them to me." He ran his teeth up my throat, and I shivered. He kissed my lips firmly before sweeping his tongue through my mouth. His thrust drove the air from my lungs. "I will hold all of that for you." He started to move, his eyes on mine, so intense. "I will hold your concerns and your fears so that you can focus on kicking ass. Trust me, Jacinta."

I sighed, arching back, wrapping my legs around him.

"Mmm," he said, his thrusts a little harder, a little fiercer, pounding his need into me, giving me a promise of protection.

His heart within my chest thudded a steady rhythm. Something deep inside of me moved, yearned to break free. To explode outward. I swung my hips toward him, feeling my control ebb. Feeling the pleasure build.

"That's right, baby," he growled into my ear, striving harder, driving the exquisite bliss through me.

"Harder," I groaned, out of breath, clutching onto him tightly. He was the only thing in the world at that moment. I lost myself in him, giving myself to him so totally that I didn't have to think. That I *couldn't* think.

My body wound tighter. The sensations rose higher until passion flooded me with a sweet release. I shuddered against him as he quaked above, panting.

He took only a moment to gather himself.

"This is the first time I'm not on call," he said. "Nothing will interrupt us tonight. I can completely give in to this never-ending craving for you." He lifted up between my thighs, his delicious body glistening. "Which position would you like next? Pick any one you want. We'll get through them all before I pound that stress out of you, I think." But he didn't wait for an answer. He just sat on the bed and pulled me up on top of him. I wasn't surprised to feel he was already hard again, already ready for me. "How about this one?" He kissed me deeply as he guided his hardness into me. Against my lips he murmured, "Are you ready to tell me how you feel yet?"

Just the mention of it made me constrict my arms around him. I jerked my hips, grinding against him. I yanked his head back by his hair and harshly dragged my teeth up his throat.

He shuddered. "Hmm, that's how it's going to be, is it?" I could hear the excitement in his words. "So be it."

He trapped me to him, lifted me a bit, and then hammered into me, over and over, driving the pleasure deep. Inwardly smiling, outwardly grunting with the onslaught, I slipped into the feeling and said goodbye to reality. I'd deal with our situation tomorrow. Tonight I'd think of nothing else but Austin.

CHAPTER 15

"WHAT'S OUR STATUS?" I stood in the center of the common area and popped the best truffle in the world into my mouth.

Austin had urged me to keep all the stuff in the gift basket. According to him, I could chalk it up to collecting my dues for all of the mage's badgering, treat the gifts as participation trophies for bothering to show, or assign no emotion to them at all and immediately forget where I'd gotten them. Thanks for the goods, what was your name again?

Given that literally no one else had any reservations about keeping their gifts, each having been given one or two things perfectly suited to their interests and taste, I'd decided to compromise. I would pick and choose a few things to keep. The truffles were the first things out of the basket.

Cyra jogged out of the hallway that led to the rooms, dressed in a black pantsuit with a ruby pin on her lapel. Designed to look like a phoenix shedding flames, it was her gift from Elliot Graves: a magical memento that would help her control her fire shedding after rebirths.

His thoughtfulness was starting to get on my nerves.

Brochan emerged from the hallway in a black suit with a red pocket square. As he came closer, he gave me a once-over before minutely nodding—and then immediately tensed.

"I apologize, Miss Ironheart," he murmured, veering to the side and turning, clasping his hands in front of him and looking straight ahead.

"For what?" I asked.

"Force of habit."

"What's a force of habit?"

Edgar lingered in the far corner, ready and waiting. Niamh was back by the fridge, hunting for food or beer. Everyone else was still getting ready for the day, their slow speed indicative of the danger they thought we'd run into.

I belatedly noticed that every single surface contained at least one cream-colored doily, all a little misshapen, none of them symmetrical. Edgar had apparently decorated, and it was clear he still couldn't create the perfect doily. There was no way I was asking why he'd trucked all these here. Even though I'd taken Austin's (many, many) ministrations to heart, and decided not to give in to my fear and worry, I was still on shaky ground with anxiety. I needed to stick with what I was good at—magic—and leave the political maneuverings for the rest of my team. The last thing I needed right now was to fall down the Edgar-weirdness rabbit hole. If anything could derail a person, that surely would.

"I haven't been to a formal meetup since I was an alpha," Brochan replied. "We lived in a rural place and didn't dress up very often, so when we needed to, I had to check everyone to make sure they fit the requirements. I didn't mean to do it with you."

I waved his apology away. "I don't care. Mr. Tom basically dresses me. He has oddly great taste. Hence this very fashionable pantsuit thing that is both striking and functional if we have to fight."

"Yes, he does. You fit your part perfectly. If you'd allow me…" He paused, and I checked the time on my new watch, something else I'd plundered from the basket.

"Yes?" I answered when he didn't continue.

"When you go to dinner tonight, wear expensive jewels. Based on the gift I received, these cats have a bunch of money."

"What gifts did you receive?"

"A cashmere scarf and a lady's Rolex. Very lovely."

"And you're not wearing them?"

"I might actually wear the scarf. It's cream, so it'll go with a formal jacket in the winter. The Rolex looks ridiculous on me. It's much too small. I tried it."

"I'll trade you a man's Rolex for the one you got, how's that?"

His brows pinched together and he checked my wrist. "That's not a Rolex, and it would also be too small for my wrist." He held up his wrist and pulled back his sleeve. That thing was easily two of mine or more, his forearm lined with muscle and scars.

"I meant I'd buy you one and we'd switch," I said.

"Oh. Right." He shook his head. "I'm slow."

Mr. Tom bustled out, checking all the sparkling surfaces and clucking his tongue at the doilies. A sour expression crossed his face. He'd cleaned last night with gusto, clearly determined to take back his role as provider of food and clean surfaces. Hopefully he didn't also reprise his role as off-kilter life coach.

"Edgar, why must you clutter the space with these odd things?" Mr. Tom asked, whisking two doilies up.

"I figured we could all use a little taste of home," Edgar answered. "A little comfort."

"This is from *your* home, not ours, and the only thing comfortable about these misshapen things is the thought of throwing them in the fire." Mr. Tom stacked up two more. Brochan looked on with a furrowed brow. He was new to the weird. It would probably be a bumpy ride as he got accustomed to it.

"An artist must not bend within the weight of misguided critique," Edgar replied. "I must strive on, unfettered. The perfect doily is out there for me."

Brochan's brow scrunched further.

"Just ignore it," I murmured to him, trying to follow my own advice. "Don't try to understand it. It'll give you brain bubbles."

"Miss, do you need anything before you go?" Mr. Tom asked, paused halfway between me and the kitchen before pursing his lips at Niamh, her head still stuck in the large refrigerator. "A to-go cup of coffee, perhaps? You didn't sleep much last night, and the tunnels in this lair are probably extensive. You don't want to run out of steam halfway through exploring."

"No, I'm good."

Ulric and Jasper came out right before Nathanial, their black suits similar to Brochan's, but with white pocket squares.

The other shifters weren't long after, their pocket squares red. The basajaun had on a black bow tie and a bunch of hair, like yesterday, and Hollace wore a purple pocket square.

Niamh finally straightened up, wearing a pantsuit

like Cyra's but with a holster for a flask. She had a pink pocket square.

"Well, wait," Mr. Tom said, looking around, his gaze finally landing on Edgar. "Even you, Edgar? Everyone has a pocket square but me?"

"Well, if ye weren't so busy hemming and hawing, about messing up the plane ride," Niamh said, walking over to stand beside Brochan, "ye would've heard us plan it out, ye gobshite."

"Each species gets a color," Brochan said. "Yours is white."

Mr. Tom straightened himself a little higher. "I'm no ordinary gargoyle. I am also the butler and personal assistant to the heir of Ivy House."

"Well now, personal assistant, is it?" Niamh asked, a twinkle in her eyes. "What, then, do ye personally assist? Her travel arrangements?"

"Okay, okay, enough." I rubbed my temples. "Mr. Tom, wear whatever color you want. Or none. It doesn't matter. You have wings; they'll get the idea."

He lifted his nose. "I will wear white in solidarity."

"Then why were ye on about yer extra failed tasks that ye do?" Niamh hollered at his retreating backside. "Jaysus, Mary, 'n' Joseph, that gargoyle would drive ye to drink."

"That's your gift, then?" I pointed at her holster and

flask.

"Aye." She patted it. "The *finescht* whiskey that ever graced the land, kept nice and handy."

"Which whiskey is that?" Brochan asked.

"No idea. I didn't recognize the name and can't taste the difference. But the note said it was the best, and so I'll believe it. It sounds better than saying I got some eld slop he threw my way and don't care regardless."

Austin emerged last, his suit molding to his perfect body, his swagger on point, and his face hard. The alpha was ready for a gentlemanly battle of wits.

He looked around the room, checking out everyone's clothes, before his gaze landed on me. His once-over lingered in a way Brochan's hadn't. He didn't nod at the end, just took his place by my side and quietly waited for Mr. Tom to finish fiddling with his pocket square and join us.

"What took you?" I asked him.

"You won't heal me. I'm still sore. I was stretching."

I could feel his humor filter through the link even though it didn't show on his face. I hadn't healed myself either, and I was still a little sore today despite my fast healing abilities. I liked it. I liked the reminder of what Austin had done to me last night, how often he'd done it, and how hard. We'd kept at it into the small hours of the morning, only stopping to eat and lay a tripwire spell. I'd decided it was too risky to use one of the warding spells.

Even after all we'd done last night, I still craved Austin, the need for him unquenched, my desire still pulsing hot.

"Okay. My apologies." Mr. Tom filed in, holding a tray of shot glasses filled with the revealing potion I'd made at home and packed. It would hopefully help us see any mages using an invisibility spell.

If we got out of this, I would set to work trying to figure out a potion that allowed me to see invisible people while being invisible myself. It didn't make sense that that wasn't a common thing. It had to be doable.

Sebastian would have been able to help me with that, I suspected, a thought that steeled my resolve.

"We all know our tasks?" I asked after everyone had drunk it, touching Austin's pants pocket and feeling the crinkle of the map. Hollace had asked the service staff for more copies, and they'd complied without complaint, giving us a stack. We'd break off into teams of three or four, each of which would scout a specific section of the tunnels before reporting back and sharing notes.

Everyone murmured their assent as Edgar drifted in closer.

"I'm still unclear as to what to do about trouble,"

Edgar said.

"Try to avoid it, and if you can't, fight back," I said. "The Mages' Guild can't get in here, and Elliot Graves is on their list of top offenders—it doesn't sound like he'll report anyone. Don't start anything, but go ahead and finish it."

I waited for nods from everyone before I turned and pulled down the tripwire spell. We marched down the hall to the main entrance, utterly silent but for the swish of our clothes and my footfalls. I still wasn't very good at being quiet.

A man sat in one of the blue velvet chairs, an open newspaper in front of him and his ankle over his knee. A steaming white mug sat on the table by his elbow. Service staff bustled around outside, sweeping up debris left over from my episode, or maybe someone else's. The glass double door hadn't been fixed.

"Hello," I said demurely as we crossed the entranceway to the other opening that would lead way back into the mountain, or so we figured based on the twisting length of the tunnels. I was in a wing of my own, it seemed. I wasn't sure if that was good or bad.

The man pulled down a corner of his paper, and I realized belatedly that I probably shouldn't have said anything at all. A lifetime of politeness with strangers had gotten the better of me.

His cold blue eyes assessed me for a moment before flicking to those around me, lingering the longest on Austin. I continued my progress undaunted. Mostly. Staring like that was incredibly rude.

"You're the Jane, are you not?" he said as I entered the doorway.

I paused and turned back. "Sure." It was easier than explaining why he was an idiot or coming up with a scathing put-down.

He folded his paper and placed it in his lap. His gaze went back to Austin. To his credit, he didn't give any of his thoughts away. "And that's your shifter?"

Again, many possible answers came to mind, but I settled on: "Sure."

"And your crew."

"No. They just followed me in off the street."

Everyone had a breaking point.

His lips tightened, his gaze mostly steady on me, but flicking to Austin every so often. The silence stretched. Was he waiting for something?

As if reading my thoughts, Niamh said, "He's waiting for ye to recognize him."

"Oh." I squinted one eye and half smiled. "Right. Uhm…" Only Niamh hadn't told me anything about the other guests. I belatedly realized I was flying blind.

"Don't bother," Niamh said. "He's nobody. Walk

189

on."

I couldn't stop my eyes from widening. Sarcasm was one thing, but blatant rudeness entirely another. It wasn't something I was comfortable with.

Austin applied pressure to the small of my back. Mr. Tom's steady gaze on my face said to comply.

I held my breath and turned away, burning with shame. This was not like my "training" at country clubs and work functions. Politeness had always been key in those situations. There were certain protocols to be followed whether you liked the person or not. Maybe especially when you didn't like the person. This was worse than high school, and I hadn't exactly been a mover and shaker.

I followed the wishes of my team, though, and started walking. Many—some?—of them were experienced, if rusty. Besides, eccentricity! That had to count for something.

"Your shifters tore up the front area," the man called.

I kept walking, separating from Austin's touch, and alarm rang through the links I shared with the team. Hadn't they wanted me to keep going? I stopped in confusion and turned around. These were very mixed signals.

The man was leaning forward to see me around the

doorframe.

"Your shifters tore up the front area yesterday," he said again, having dropped the paper between his spread knees so he could lean without looking too eager.

"I mean…" I raised my hand in exasperation. "Sure, why not."

"How'd they beat Elliot Graves's spell, though?"

I squinted at him, then shot a confused look at Niamh. Why was he going through mental aerobics to assure himself that I had played no part in the destruction? What could I even say to him without it devolving into insults?

"Yes, Miss Ironheart," Mr. Tom said. "Sometimes dealing with mages of a lower thinking capacity can be a lesson in patience."

Hollace's lips quivered as he tried to suppress a smile, and he half turned away to hide it. He wasn't as good as the shifters at keeping a straight face.

Edgar raised his hand. "If I may?"

I lifted an eyebrow, not quite sure what Edgar was asking, but totally willing to let someone else take the lead.

"Sir." Edgar clasped his hands in front of him, bowed, and gave the man a comforting smile. With all that fang, though, I doubted he was comforting anyone.

"Shifters are good at a great many things, like stalking you without your knowledge and snapping your neck when you least expect it. Or working together to close in on you, fighting through the pain of your spells so they can snap your neck. Or even—Well, you get the point. They are very good at killing people." I was pretty sure I was watching a train wreck, one that would give us the reputation as the weirdest magical crew. Not that we had any competition. "But shifters are very cool and collected creatures, prone to rage but not panic. Miss Ironheart, on the other hand, is the only being in this underground complex capable of laying ruin to a powerful mage's headquarters out of panic. Because she didn't like being in the dark. You may not want to admit that a past Jane is more powerful than you, but...well, you'll just look stupid if you don't. Best board this train rather than *rail* against it—get it?" He paused to see if his joke had landed. The mage stared, and no one on earth was good enough to keep confusion from their expression after a talking-to from Edgar. The vampire continued, "Because when she's not panicking, well..." He held up a shaky finger at Brochan.

"I'm Brochan Sue," he growled. "How do you do?"

"Jaysus," Niamh muttered.

Without comment, I turned and started walking.

Really, what else was there to say? That last bit had made zero sense. I'd be a laughing stock, if I wasn't already.

Austin lowered his hand on the small of my back in no time, and I could feel the mixed emotions through the link. Through my link to Hollace, all I could feel was his urge to laugh hysterically.

"I'm not sure if I just created an enemy, or found someone who will take pity on me," I murmured, walking stiffly.

"He's one of the highest-powered mages here besides Elliot," Austin whispered. "Let's hope it's pity."

CHAPTER 16

A COUPLE OF hours later, Austin, Brochan, and I walked down a small tunnel with low ceilings, dim lighting, and rough, slightly damp walls. It was a far cry from the tunnel leading to our rooms. Light fixtures hung from the ceiling on chains, weak magical flames flickering within them. There was supposedly an exit at the end, but the tunnel was much longer than the map suggested.

"Look at this," Brochan whispered, always behind us but now slowing until he lagged.

I looked up from the map and glanced back. Brochan was pointing to a strip of lettering above a row of men's portraits, surprisingly clean in this dank place.

"'Wall of Death,'" he read.

Austin looked both ways down the tunnel and then back at me before stepping closer to Brochan. I waited for a moment, not really wanting to look, but curiosity got the better of me.

Shadows flickered across a dozen or so faces, all

rendered in black-and-white photographs enclosed in cheap plastic frames. Each had a date below it, and I pushed in closer when I saw the last face.

"Kinsella," I breathed out, pointing. There wasn't a date associated with this one.

Austin pointed at others. "Frauchini. Cross. Stokes. All mages Elliot Graves killed in cold blood, or so I've heard."

"But Kinsella?" I pushed in even closer to make absolutely sure.

"Yup—"

"Hah!" I spun and flung out my hands, but instead of a karate chop, I slung a blistering spell that crackled the air and burned through a man's middle.

He flinched and looked down, but the spell had gone right through him—and kept right on going until it crashed against the tunnel's soft turn and sent sparks into the air.

The man shimmered, like a hologram, turning around to see the damage the spell had wrought.

"I don't smell or sense his presence," Austin murmured, pushing away from me somewhat, eyes on the man and ready for action. He obviously didn't want me to get hurt in the crossfire.

The man, about mid-thirties, with slicked-back black hair and pale blue eyes, surveyed me with a little smile, his hands lodged in his pockets.

"You don't smell or sense me because"—he lowered to a whisper—"I'm not really here…" He smiled, smug and self-assured. His image flickered a little more, then wavered before mostly solidifying again. "I think I might like shifters best of all. I know, I know, it's out of character for a mage." He shrugged. "But you are correct, Sir Alpha. Nice watch, by the way."

"Yours as well," Austin replied. "A vintage guy, I see. That is one of the rarest finds on the planet."

I glanced down at it, finding a vintage watch with a black leather band.

"How kind of you to notice. I stole it, of course. From…" The man pointed at the row of faces. "The man in the middle, there. Jacobson. He didn't deserve it, and the crows in his employ wouldn't have appreciated it."

"You're Elliot Graves," I said, my anger bubbling up, hot and heady. Magic pulsed around me, eager to be used.

His focus was acute and his smile disarming. "Hello, Jacinta. Lovely to finally make your acquaintance."

The slicked-back hair—I recognized it from the first time I'd seen him, the night I'd claimed Ivy House's magic. He'd blown me a kiss that had turned into words. He'd had facial hair that night, but today he was clean-shaven. And the pale blue eyes—those belonged to a delivery guy about half this guy's age. He'd delivered a note from Elliot Graves and then disappeared in his truck on the street. Clearly Elliot Graves could change his appearance at will.

He'd also attacked me, tried to have me kidnapped, had his people spy on me, killed my—

"No, no, no!" He bent and pushed out his hands, but my spell had already been let loose. It passed straight through him again, cracking into the wall on the other side of the tunnel. A deep rumble rolled beneath my feet. Elliot looked at the ceiling. "Keep doing that and you'll bring this mountain down on top of us."

"Why does it go right through you?" I asked, taking a step forward. Could an illusion be this lifelike?

Austin stepped with me, staying even.

Elliot laughed softly, shaking his head. "You are something. You've grown in might since I last..." His speech hitched, but then he spread his hands wide. "Let's just get it out there, shall we? Since I last spied on you."

A boot scraped the ground. Austin spread his fingers in a stop motion, keeping Brochan from doing whatever a moving boot indicated.

"Ah yes, the new shifter. Broken Sue, wasn't it? How

do you like your Rolex?"

"It'll fit perfectly around my dick," Brochan growled.

I widened my eyes. That was unexpected. And strangely hilarious.

Elliot took a step back and then shivered. "I'm not even there in the flesh and that freaked me out. You're quite the power player. Austin Steele has found a protégé."

"Why aren't you in the... *How* aren't you in the flesh?" I asked.

He winked at me. "It's a pretty common practice for those of us *in the know*. And with enough power, of course. One of the mages at this party is too weak to manage it. I invited him to attend so as to make a fool of him. It's a personal grudge. Petty, some might say, but..." He shrugged. "And then there's you—you have plenty of power but not enough experience."

"You aim to make a fool out of me, then?"

"Hardly." He chuckled. "I would like to inform you, however, that you will be the only female head mage at this gathering. That was an intentional decision. I fully intend to demean many of the mages here, one way or another. To taunt or condescend to them. Since female mages are routinely treated that way in the magical world, I didn't want to add to their...misfortunes.

They're also better at ignoring such behavior, which makes them more dangerous. It's also simply more fun to taunt those who are not used to being taunted. They get angry and flustered. It's comical."

"Then why am I here?"

"Not because I thought I could get one over on you, that's for sure." He paused, and I just blinked at him, waiting for the answer. His smile told me he knew what I wanted and didn't intend to offer it up. "All the other mages have only been granted one seat at the table. You get two, one for you and one for your shifter. This is because you treat him as your equal, do you not?"

"Yes, I do."

"It'll raise contention with the others. Make you look weaker. Are you sure that's what you want?"

"Yes. He's my date."

"I thought as much. You don't care how people perceive you…"

I shifted from side to side, frustrated. After all these months, I'd actually gotten an audience with the guy who'd been plaguing me, and he wasn't physically in front of me. Worse, he was one hundred percent leading this conversation. He held all the cards.

I pointed at the wall. "Kinsella."

"Ah, yes." He took a step closer. "He gave you some trouble, I believe."

"What is this wall?"

"That wall represents my illustrious status as the Mage Most Wanted. I am claiming my kills to serve as proof that I have done what the Anal Repository Guild, as some call it, says I did. One of the mages that walks these halls is on the cusp of financial ruin. Given the repository has a *huge* price on my head, I suspect our greedy little mage will try to cash in."

"You're intentionally painting a target on your back?"

"I always have a target on my back, Miss Ironheart. All powerful mages do. You will have a larger target than I do, just you wait. Your power level, your power type, and your dirty little fetish for laying animals…"

His eyes glinted, and a deep, dark rage washed over me, followed by a powerful undertow, sucking me under. My magic stuffed the tunnel, churning and spitting and electric, a hairsbreadth from being un-leashed.

"Not here," Austin said softly, and I felt his calming touch on my back and through the link. "Don't unleash whatever that is, babe. I hate to say it, but he's right. It could jeopardize the structure of the tunnel."

With incredible effort, I forced down the blackness seeping into my blood. The rage. The disgust. I blinked, trying to clear the red haze from my vision.

"I apologize," Elliot said, his smile dripping off his face, his eyes laser-focused on me. "I was just testing your…closeness to your alpha. I didn't mean the last. Don't get me wrong, that will be a common thought, but it isn't shared by me. As I said, I think shifters are my favorite magical type. I would've liked being a shifter. Anyway, yes, Kinsella was one of the mages that I took out. Quite recently, in fact, as I'm sure you know. You just met him, didn't you?" He touched his pointer finger to the edge of his nose. "I'm well informed." He surveyed the wall again and slipped his hands back into his pockets. "There are many, many more faces that could go on that wall, but the repository doesn't care about lesser mages, or those without money. It's a pay-per-play system, you see. Bribe them, and get protection and what passes for justice. Ignore them, and if you're small potatoes, you are also ignored. But if a wealthy, powerful mage like me ignores them, they won't stand down so easily. You might want to establish that professional relationship soon. It's easy for bodies to pile up in this business."

"Why did you kill him, though? Where did you even find him? He ran away from me."

"Maybe someday I will explain. Maybe I won't. We shall see."

Frustration still ate at me. "And Sebastian? Why

isn't he on that wall?"

Elliot's grin faded. "He was just a kid who liked doing magic. The Mages' Guild crunches up people like that. They don't respect them, and they certainly don't waste time looking into their murders. They are the small potatoes I spoke of."

"You also crunch up kids like that. Since, you know, you *killed* him."

"He chose his path. He accepted what came. As we all will. It's been really lovely talking with you, Miss Ironheart. Don't bother looking for those exits—if you break through the wards, I will know, and you'll be in a world of hurt."

Out of the corner of my eye, I saw Brochan tense. His fists clenched.

"My goodness," Elliot said, his gaze slipping to Brochan. "Broken Sue is a good name. His leash will prove faulty. I don't envy the person who gets on the business end of that wrath."

"When do I get to see you in person?" I asked him, anger brimming.

He took a step back. "You'll find out this evening. Goodbye."

His image vanished.

"He looked like a hologram," I said, staring at the empty place he'd been standing.

"I wonder if they can use an invisibility potion when they're like that." Austin turned, facing me, able to watch both directions of the tunnel out of his peripheral vision. "I couldn't smell, hear, or sense him."

"Even if they can't... They can all do that," I murmured, starting to walk again. I wanted to see the exit for myself, warded or not. "The high-powered ones can all do it. They can spy without putting themselves in actual danger. Unless there is some sort of risk..." I shook my head. "I'll need to add that to my list of spells to research, which doesn't help at the moment because there's no internet in this godforsaken place."

"Alpha," Brochan said, his voice gruff. "I think I was mistaken. When that mage was threatening your mate... I don't think I have as much control as I thought I did. I might be a danger to your efforts."

"Understood," Austin said. I suspected his need to suss that out was the reason he'd brought Brochan with us instead of sending him off with another group.

"Don't worry about being a danger to our efforts," I said. "I don't recall you trying to blast a hologram twice in as many minutes. You're the least of our problems. I nearly brought the mountain down on us."

A roar echoed through the tunnel, thick and ferocious. The basajaun ran into view at the other end, his hair puffed out, making him look even larger. He stopped in the center, facing us, and let out another roar. The mountain trembled beneath our feet, as if quaking from the force of his anger.

"Where is the threat?" the basajaun said, looking around wildly. "I felt your blast through the mountain. It quails under your might."

Niamh and Ulric caught up with him, eyes wide, faces long.

"It's over," I said, putting out my hands and glancing behind us down the hall. "Shh. It was a magical trick, basically. I'll tell you about it later."

"He crushed someone who barred his way," Ulric said, breathing hard. "I don't know if it was friend or foe, but one of the mages has one less person on the payroll."

"He wasn't barring the way," Niamh said. "He was frozen in fear."

"Well…it comes down to the same thing," Ulric replied. "He wouldn't move, and the basajaun doesn't say please."

"Jessie, ye might have a problem dealing with that wee hiccup come dinner," Niamh said. "We weren't exactly defending ourselves on that one. That was all our fault, so it was. That death is on us. Without internet, I can't figure out whose camp he might be in, either."

I sighed, hands limp at my sides.

"Definitely don't worry about being a danger to our efforts, Brochan," Austin said. Dark humor and bewilderment trickled through our link. I fell in step with him toward the supposed exit. "You'd be hard-pressed to even stand out amongst this crew."

"I'm heading into dinner after insulting one mage and killing the staff member of another," I murmured as Austin and I took the lead. The dim lighting was somewhat welcome. It felt like I was hiding from my problems in a strange way. "Dinner might just be a grudge match."

"Let's just hope that's all it is."

CHAPTER 17

MY BRIGHT RED dress covered my shoulders but plunged deep down my neckline. The hem reached the floor, but a large slit worked up my leg to my upper thigh, with the loose fabric flowing around it. The material was somewhat stretchy, and the dress could be shed in a hurry. It had almost certainly been dreamed up by a straight male designer envisioning his perfect date.

I hadn't wanted to wear any jewelry, because I didn't know if I'd have to assume my gargoyle form, but Austin had strongly encouraged me to rethink that stance. In this crowd, wealth and prestige went hand in hand, and he thought I should look the part, as did Mr. Tom and the rest of them, so I gave in.

Austin had chosen a black tux that fit even better than his expensive suit earlier, if that were possible, with a red tie and pocket square that matched my dress and fit with the shifter color code. A watch encircled his wrist, different than the one he'd been given, and his shoes had been polished to a mirror shine.

We walked down the tunnel, my dress swishing around my legs, a sparkly clutch in my hand (courtesy of Mr. Tom, not Elliot Graves's gift basket) and flat-soled ballerina slippers on my feet. I didn't care who said what; I could not run in heels, and I was not wearing something I couldn't fight in. Case closed.

"Have I told you how beautiful you look?" Austin asked as we sauntered down the hall, a little late but not hurrying.

Cyra followed behind us, without an invisibility potion, and the basajaun, Niamh, and the shifters were behind her, all under the protection of my invisibility spell. Sebastian and I had found this particular blend in one of Ivy House's training books. Technically speaking, I was only allowed to bring Austin and my "poison-control specialist," but the rest of them would stand invisibly by in case something went down.

"Only twice since you saw me in this," I said, then bumped his side. "Have I told you how incredibly handsome you look?"

Humor leaked through the link. "You told me you wanted to rip into my clothes and suck on anything that popped out."

I smiled, having decided to continue to let Austin handle my worry. It might kill me in the long run, but right now it felt like it was worth the risk. "Did I?"

"Maybe that's just what I heard."

I laughed as we passed through the entranceway. The woman who stepped out was the one who'd led us to our rooms yesterday.

"Miss Ironheart." She bowed as we came to a stop. "I will lead you to dinner."

"Wonderful." I gave a graceful nod like royalty in the movies.

Once we were underway again, she glanced back to get my attention. "Miss, Mr. Graves would like to know why you didn't use the ward spell provided. He thinks the tripwire spell beneath you."

My perfectly penciled eyebrows climbed up my forehead. "I didn't trust his spell."

"Yes, miss. He thought you might say that. He'd like you to know that he only offered the spells to you—a concession because you are so new to the world of mages. He suggested that your tripwire spell would be too easy for most of the higher-powered mages to pull down. If you use his spell and put all your power behind it, Mr. Graves himself won't be able to get in."

"Why is he telling me this?"

She hesitated. "Honestly, ma'am—miss, he didn't specify. I'd recommend asking him when there are no other mages in the room. But I know he was worried about the integrity of the mountain and your...inability to properly control your reactions, begging your pardon."

"It's a fair point," Austin said. His alpha mask was on, but I felt his compulsion to laugh.

"You can also change the spell he gave you," the woman said, "to fit your needs. He said it was...robust, I believe. Easily adaptable."

"Thank you. I'll think about it."

"Yes, miss."

She took a right at a fork, heading down the tunnel that Nathanial, Isabelle, and Edgar had explored earlier. They'd made it to the end, only to discover a big, fat wooden door—similar to what we'd found at the end of our exploration—that could not be moved by magic or physical force. There would be no fast exit, and given the magic I'd seen around the exit we'd investigated, there'd be no sneaking in. We couldn't even ask the town gargoyles what lay on the other side, since they were in rock form, and even if they weren't, there wasn't cell service and the cave phones in our rooms didn't call out.

There was one glimmer of hope: the basajaun thought there was another grouping of tunnels elsewhere in the mountain. Above us, he thought, or maybe in a sister mountain. Possibly both. All mountains were different, it turned out, and this one was hard for him to read.

The question was, could we access those other tunnels through this grouping?

He didn't know the answer yet, but he hoped to keep exploring and figure it out.

Like the tunnel I'd explored with Austin and Broken Sue earlier—that name was too good not to use, especially since Brochan didn't seem to care—the space and light diminished the deeper we went, the tunnel a little cramped. The basajaun would have to stoop back here, which meant we were probably getting close to one of the exits.

The woman stopped beside a double door painted green, covered in a mural designed to make it look like the grand entrance to a dining hall. Magic crisscrossed over it. She wiggled her fingers and the spells bled away.

"They'll have to stay outside." She gestured around us, and I didn't hide my confusion. My people had already lagged back so I could assess the situation. They weren't crowded in around us like she clearly thought. Which meant she couldn't see them but still knew they were there.

"What?" I asked, squinting at her.

"I am equipped with a revealing spell, and your people will need to stay outside. Except for the phoenix."

I huffed out a laugh. "Good guess, obvious lie."

She paused. "Beg your pardon, miss?"

"You can't see my people. Yes, I have some, but no, they aren't where you're guessing. Did Elliot tell you his revealing spell probably wouldn't be powerful enough to break my invisibility potion?"

She stared at me for a long beat. "Yes, he did. Your honesty is…odd."

"Yeah. I probably shouldn't've tried to smuggle them in," I mumbled.

"We have spells that should still work to point them out. I should've run interference to make up for my lack of sight, but I am not used to being in this situation. I've never met anyone that has more power than Elliot Graves. Please, after you." She gestured me in.

The room on the other side had a high ceiling, brightly painted walls, and a stage for a small band. Currently a string quartet was stationed there, quietly playing soothing music into the dim light provided by several hanging chandeliers.

A large table spanned the space to my right, and the eight filled spaces save one flickered with holograms of varying strengths. The other was a gaunt man with graying hair, loose skin, and spindly hands resting on the table.

"No, no, Burke..." Elliot sat at the head of the table, his hologram the strongest of the group, barely flickering. "No hands on the table for those here in the flesh. You know the rules."

"What are you going to do about it?" the man sneered. "You're too chicken to show your face. All of you are."

"What is there to fear? No one sitting at this table in the flesh is worth half a thought," said a young man with a snooty voice, blonde hair parted pristinely to the right, wearing a perfectly knotted bow tie the basajaun really should study.

The woman in red closed the door after Cyra before leading Austin and me to the two empty chairs next to each other, in between two holograms. Cyra would apparently need to stand behind us.

"Is it Jane culture to be late?" asked a man opposite Austin's place, his face pulled tight like a rubber band. Clearly he lacked the ability to pull off a convincing magical illusion and had chosen to pay a plastic surgeon. White hair crawled out of his ears and nose.

"Yes," I said as Austin pulled out the chair for me and waited for me to sit. "It's called fashionably late. Do you not have TVs in the magical world? That's not a new term."

Elliot rested his elbows on the table and steepled his

fingers, watching me as Austin sat down.

The man across from me didn't take his hands off the table, and the corner of his upper lip pulled back from his teeth as he watched Austin.

"Since when do we allow animals at the table?" asked a mage with reddish hair and thin lips, seated next to Elliot. It looked like someone had been about to blow freckles onto his face like pixie dust and then accidentally sneezed. I pegged him for late twenties. At least, he *looked* that age. I had no idea what age any of these people actually were, since they could probably all mess with their appearance, with magic or money.

I breathed through my mouth and closed my eyes, forcing down my instinctive reaction to hearing any insults to Austin.

"One day soon, I don't think anyone will say that to their faces, Noah." Elliot smiled behind his steepled fingers. "Burke, I will only ask you once more: please follow the rules and remove your hands."

Burke huffed, staring at Austin, and then slowly removed his hands from the table.

I turned to Austin. "I really wasn't worried about it, were you?"

Austin placed his napkin in his lap before meeting Burke's stare with a pulse of primal aggression and power. It slammed into Burke so hard that he jolted.

His eyes widened and he sat back in his chair like he was in a very fast car and the driver had just slammed the gas pedal.

"No," Austin said with an extra hint of gravel in his voice.

"And why would you be?" Elliot said as a side door opened and two service people in red coats walked in carrying bottles of wine. "Those of you who are joining us from the comfort of your…quarters, or wherever you had to hunker down in order to cast your soul's shadow into this room—please, synchronize your dinners with us. It doesn't work when some of us are eating and some are not."

The people in the red coats split up, one walking toward Austin and me while the other went around the table to serve Burke. I leaned back in my chair to make it easier for her to pour.

Cyra stepped forward immediately, pushing between me and the person next to me, a chubby man in a light gray suit, sticking her butt into his hologram as she reached for the wine. "I got it."

"Meet the phoenix, everyone," Elliot said. "Cyra."

Cyra straightened up, her nose in my glass, inhaling deeply. She swirled it, nodded, and held up her finger for the service person pouring Austin's glass. "I'll have one of these too, please."

"Yes, of course," Elliot said. "I would never pass up an opportunity to serve a legendary creature such as yourself. After we discuss business, we'll happily make room for another animal at the table. Or do you count as something different? I can never tell how this stuff goes."

Cyra shrugged as she tasted, lowering the glass slowly. "Hmm, that is very good." She set it down in front of me. "Wait a moment. If I don't die, you may drink."

"I would never destroy such a great power as yours, Miss Ironheart. You have no need to worry," Elliot said.

Noah snorted.

"Did you have a comment, Noah?" Elliot asked, hands still steepled.

"Forgive me. I thought you were telling a joke. Since…" Noah gestured at me.

"No, Noah, please. Enlighten us. I'm sure Miss Ironheart would dearly like to hear your thoughts on her…setup."

Noah frowned and looked at the other hologram mages down the table, each of them smirking, snickering, or, in the case of the man who'd been reading the paper in the lobby earlier in the day, blankly staring. Noah shook his head. "Isn't it obvious? When she's not being a Jane, she's one of them stinky gargoyles, and she has filthy animals around all the time. She doesn't even have the power to cast a soul shadow. She's a hot piece of ass, but—"

Rage blistered through the link, and it wasn't mine this time. Every muscle on Austin's large frame went taut. His jaw clenched. He slowly clasped his hands in his lap, his stare of death beating a promise into Noah's head.

The situation would have been very precarious for Noah if he'd been present in the flesh. And he knew it. His mouth clicked shut and his eyes widened, just like Burke's had.

Actually, just like Burke's were doing again. Still leaning back in his chair, he lost what little color he'd had left.

I sipped my wine, basking in the glow of Austin's rage, something within me purring at the feel of it.

"Yes, they are something, aren't they, these shifters?" Elliot said.

The appetizers were brought in, and the server put one plate each in front of Austin and me.

"Here we have, mini cornbread crab cakes with a lemon-caper sauce," she said softly.

"Thank you," I said, setting down my glass. Cyra drifted up, on Austin's side this time, sticking her butt in the fairly weak hologram of a man who looked old enough to be Father Time's brother.

"Now. The subject that has been on everyone's mind and all over social media for the past month…" Elliot pulled his hands away and leaned back, being served wherever he was. The others did the same. Once settled, he picked up utensils that didn't show in his hologram and cut into something off screen. "Why are you here?" He smiled and popped a bit of nothing into his mouth, like a mime. The others followed suit, and suddenly I was mighty uncomfortable. Mimes had never been my favorite, although I guessed it wasn't as big of a deal, since these guys could still talk.

Cyra finished her bite of Austin's crab cake and tried one of mine. "Hmm." She nodded as she chewed. "Very good. I have the best job there is."

"Okay, but…" I picked up my fork and knife. "The wine I get, but if they poisoned the crab cakes, they could've poisoned only one of them, hoping it wasn't the one you actually tried. You'd only have a one in five shot of tasting the poisoned one."

Across the table, Burke stopped chewing mid-bite, his poison person having already been sent back to the wall behind him.

"Well spotted, Jessie—" Elliot's voice hitched, as though he'd caught himself making a mistake. He cleared his throat into his fist. "I assume it is okay if I call you Jessie? We're friends now, aren't we?" He didn't wait for a response. "Usually the first course is soup, since a person on poison duty would catch that, even with a slow-release poison. But individual morsels are more likely to make it through. Rest assured, I do not poison people that I mean to kill. It is much too simple and, quite frankly, boring. I prefer to play with my food, so to speak."

Movement slowed and all eyes drifted to Elliot.

He wiped his mouth with an invisible napkin. "So, back to it. Why are you here? You must be incredibly curious. It's simple: I mean to return to the magical world, and when I do, it will be with an ally. My intention is to pit myself against Momar and reclaim my title as the most powerful mage in the world."

"You've been gone a long time," the man next to Austin said. "Some might say you are out of the loop."

"All would say that, I think," Elliot responded.

"Which means you'll have to build yourself back up. You'll be vulnerable to attack in that time. I've seen your staff. You're a little light on mages. There's even a rumor going around that your head mage left."

"Heard that, did you?" Elliot's eyes flicked to me and then away. "He left for greener pastures, yes. I had to track him down and kill him for his disobedience. Quite the shame. Luckily, I am more than capable of taking over my lab."

These mages clearly didn't know I was the greener pastures. I wondered how they'd heard the rumor so stripped of detail.

"Maybe," the man pushed, "but the fact remains that you will be vulnerable. Momar is more ruthless than you ever were. He's not as cautious—"

"It was never caution, Rufus. It was strategy. In order to achieve a complete victory, one must crush the opposition in its entirety. Pull out the root. That takes time and planning. Otherwise your enemies will come back to haunt you. Isn't that right, Chambers?"

The man with the bow tie's eyebrows lowered, and I suddenly wondered which one of these guys had been responsible for ruining Broken Sue's life. Could that be what Elliot meant?

"Momar doesn't seem to have any trouble with his swifter approach," Noah said with a full mouth.

"He has left severed roots all over the world," Elliot replied. "They are under the ground, slowly growing toward the surface. They merely need to be tended before they will sprout once more."

"Yes, well…" Rubber Band Face shook his head. "Momar took down the power players. He might have left some of the crumbs, sure, but no matter how much you tend those, they'll never grow into…flowers or trees or whatever it is you're talking about. They're useless."

Elliot grinned slyly. "That's the difference between you and me. Between me and Momar. Big-picture thinking. Trees and flowers and ferns and critters—they have more power than you would think when you group them together and give them purpose."

Chambers leaned his elbows on the table. "Is that the power you are hoping to amass? The failed leftovers of Momar's battles?"

"That is the power I will collect, yes. That I will prime and prepare for use. But I won't tell you how. Only my ally will be privy to my plans. Otherwise I will gather a network and a staff, like I have in the past. I doubt the world has changed that much."

"It's changed more than you think," the paper reader said.

My empty plate was cleared away and a steaming plate was set down in its place, no time to rest between courses. Cyra stepped forward immediately, and Rufus paused, probably wondering if he was about to get a butt in his hologram again.

"Roast beef tenderloin with red wine sauce," the server murmured softly. "Haricot verts and a buttery garlic mashed potato."

I nodded as Cyra barged in and took more than the couple of needed bites. "This is good," she said around her food. "Hire these cooks instead of Mr. Tom."

Rufus waited until she was done. "Even if you are correct, Elliot…" He cleared his throat. Gesturing to Paper Reader, he said, "And I'll mention that Maverick is—"

"Maverick?" I blurted out with a laugh.

Everyone paused and looked at me.

I covered my mouth with my napkin. "Sorry. I didn't know his name. Just…surprised me, is all. Does he have an assistant named Goose?"

Elliot laughed heartily. Maverick's eyebrows settled low.

"As I was saying," Rufus continued, "I would agree that the world has certainly changed more than one might think. You won't be able to hide away in your mountain and expect to be left alone while you plot."

"Yes," Maverick said, undaunted by my reaction to his *Top Gun* name. "When you rose the first time, you were unknown. You claimed your mantle almost out of the blue. You are watched now. The Mages' Guild has their eye on you. Momar is aware of this meeting and eager to know what comes of it. You won't get a chance for a mistake, and you might not even get a chance to emerge as you plan."

"Yes, you're right," Elliot said, wiping his mouth. "And I'd be quite the simpleton if I hadn't thought of all of that. Coming up out of the blue the first time wasn't a stroke of luck, however. It wasn't a surprise to me like it was for others. You'd best remember that."

"Do you expect your ally to cover your back while you make your…return?" Noah asked.

Elliot pushed an invisible plate away and went back to resting his elbows on the table. He squinted at Noah. "Cover my back? No. Keep my whereabouts secret? Possibly."

Burke huffed. "How would that even be possible?"

"For you?" Elliot tapped his pointer fingers together. "It wouldn't. You're here to make everyone else feel good about their status. Including the Jane."

Anger crossed Burke's face, but it was insanely hard to feel bad for him. It was a bummer that he was the only mage physically present. He was the kind of blowhard you'd decline an invite to a really great-sounding party just to avoid.

"So you expect us to sign on to be your ally," Maverick said, pushing his own invisible plate away, "without telling us any more about it?"

"Yes. You have it exactly right." Elliot dropped his hands.

"What sort of assurances do we get?" Maverick asked.

Elliot pursed his lips. "I'll discuss all of that with the

person I choose to partner with."

"And…" Maverick crossed his arms over his chest. "How do you plan to choose?"

A grin spread across Elliot's face. "Easy. A good old-fashioned gladiator arena where you will compete against each other to sit in a room with me and hash out the plans. It is the only way you will get to see me in person. I did not hide all this time to stick my neck out the first time I have visitors. If you want your chance with me, you will have to prove your worth first."

My stomach sank into my shoes as I looked around at the other, *much* more experienced mages sitting at the table. I might have more power, but that didn't mean squat in a face-off-type battle, not without Ivy House at my back. My team was newly formed, and I was a novice. Our chances of winning were next to nothing.

"I'll play your little game," Rufus said slowly, leaning back and crossing his arms over his chest like Maverick had. "It does not mean I consent to work with you, but I will hear you out."

"You will attempt to claim his audience, you mean," Maverick said. "I, too, will play this game. I see the value in a partnership and have some ideas about how we can work around Momar to achieve our goals. With some…restrictions, of course."

"I'll play." Noah threw an invisible napkin onto his plate. Maverick and Rufus gave him condescending looks. "There is more to winning than the head mage's power. My team is infinitely superior to yours. I've spent years building it. I'll clean up, no problem."

"That's the spirit," Elliot said.

"I'm out." Burke sucked down the rest of his wine. "To hell with this." He stood from the table. "Been nice knowin' ya, Elliot. Momar is going to make an example of you, and that's if the Mages' Guild doesn't get you first."

"Hmm," Elliot said as Burke stormed out of the room, his poison-control person hustling behind him. "Anyone else want to acknowledge their lesser magical stature?"

"I'll acknowledge my sanity, how's that?" Rubber Band Face rose. "I'm not going to stand against Momar. I don't want that kind of heat."

"And that is why you have never risen above your paltry station." Elliot was taunting him, no doubt trying to get him to change his mind, or apply pressure to the mages who hadn't spoken up yet.

It worked on Chambers. "I'm in. Screw it."

"Mhm." Elliot nodded. "You would certainly work."

The table was quiet, just the chubby man and me left.

Cyra, who'd eaten about half my roast beef, dropped my plate back and pouted when she saw that Austin's had been cleaned. She nudged me to get me to answer.

"Nah," the chubby man said, standing, and I wondered why these people went through the action of walking out when they could surely just blink away like Elliot had earlier. "No disrespect, Mr. Graves. I would love to work with you. I think you are heads and tails smarter than Momar, and twice as cunning. But I can't compete with these guys at the table. There wouldn't be a point in trying."

"I completely understand." Elliot nodded as the man left. His gaze settled on me.

"Did you bring her here for lion food or something?" Noah asked.

Elliot barked out a laugh. "How could I, when it is she who brought the lions? Or whatever animals her shifters turn into."

"Yes, but way back when they brought lions into the—"

"We knew what you meant, Noah," Elliot said. "It is our patience that is lacking, not our intelligence."

"Speaking of patience, this is no place for a Jane," Chambers said, "and even less of a place for her circus animals."

I stared into Elliot's hologram eyes. I felt Austin's steady encouragement and the confident impatience of Cyra. The only way we were going to get in front of Elliot was by winning these games. If I didn't take Elliot out, he could capture me at will, and when I refused to work with him, if that was what he wanted, he'd probably kill me and my people. Even if he let me leave, he'd continue to mess with me until I finally gave him whatever he wanted.

I didn't have much of a choice.

"Yeah," I said. "I'm in."

CHAPTER 18

"**O**KAY, THEN." ELLIOT gave me a little smile. "We have our contestants. A schedule will be delivered to your rooms tomorrow. We'll waste no time. I suggest you get your beauty sleep."

He waved his hands, and the holograms of the others blinked out, leaving only the Elliot hologram, Austin, and me at the table.

"You can make them disappear?" I blurted.

"My ward can keep them out, or toss them out. The power is mine. Speaking of which, I suggest you erect one outside of your door. A tripwire won't stop these mages from having a look around."

The server took my plate, and I lifted my napkin, getting ready to go.

"No dessert?" Cyra asked, disappointed.

"Of course dessert. What do you take me for?" Elliot flicked his hand, and the server bustled away with the dirty plates. "Now, down to business. Let me see this watch of yours, Mr. Steele. You are clearly showing off."

Austin pushed his chair back gracefully and walked toward the hologram, sticking out his wrist.

"Yes, I knew it." Elliot laughed and shook his head. "Who did you steal that from? Because that is not a collector's item anyone would willingly sell."

"I took it from my father, a long time ago."

"He didn't ask for it back?"

"He didn't know I'd stolen it until it was too late. By then, he had too many of his own problems to get it back. Problems that took him to an early grave."

"Hmm." Elliot looked me over. "It seems Miss Ironheart didn't like the gifts she received."

"How do you know that name?" I asked.

"I know many things about you, Jessie. I do my homework. Rest assured, you'll do well in the games. I wouldn't have made them a requirement if I'd thought you'd suffer."

"Wouldn't you? Hmm." I leaned back as the server came back with three dessert glasses filled with chocolate mousse and topped off with puffs of whipped cream sprinkled with chocolate shavings. Apparently, Cyra was now free to join us.

"We've had our differences, Jessie," Elliot said as Cyra sampled our dishes and then started in on hers. "But we don't have to be enemies. There is room in the magical world for the demon and the angel to coexist."

"Not happily," I replied.

"Well. That remains to be seen." Elliot stood, and I noted that he didn't have to push his chair back to do it. "Please, bring in your people and use the room for as long as you would like. No one will bother you here." He stepped away from his place. "You'll be going first, by the way. I'll pair you with that fool Noah. Like ripping off a Band-Aid."

And then he was gone, disappearing on the spot.

The breath went out of me and I sagged over my dessert. "So this is really happening."

"That man is confident about regaining his status in the magical world," Austin said, still standing after playing show and tell with his watch.

"He called in some power, too," Cyra said through a mouthful. Her dessert was nearly done. "A couple of those mages seem like heavy hitters. Elliot Graves would do well to team up with either of them. Too bad he'll be dead."

"*Shh!*" I wrapped a protective soundproof bubble around us. "He might be gone, but that doesn't mean he's not listening somehow."

Cyra shrugged. "He's not stupid. He knows why you're here. Do you think he's afraid of the others? Not a chance. They want to use him, not kill him. He knows you're different. He knows you'll hit him with a kill strike the second he's in view."

"She's right." Austin put out his hand for me. "Would you care to dance?"

I felt my eyebrows climb. The string quartet was still playing, and the room was empty but for the two of us and Cyra. Still…it was enemy territory.

"Ahhmm…" I took his hand gingerly.

Austin helped me out of the chair and led me around the table to the dance floor in front of the string quartet. A balding man with a round nose and thick glasses smiled at me as he played his violin.

"You went through all this effort to get ready." Austin rested his hand around my side and pulled me in close, his other hand holding mine. His smell permeated my world, clean and spicy and masculine. "At least you can show off how beautiful you look."

He bent to kiss me softly before he started moving, his steps graceful and sure, his prowess on the dance floor unsurprising. My dress swished around my legs as he swung me and then twirled me, one hand always holding mine, the other directing me.

My stress unraveled within minutes, and I smiled up at him as he spun me. I was rusty, but it didn't matter, not with his firm and commanding leadership, never letting me stumble, making me look good with each move, even if it was just Cyra and the musicians watching us.

"We've battled mages in hairy conditions," he said softly as we danced. "We've always been the underdog. We've always been inexperienced or way outnumbered. And yet we've come out on top time after time. With or without Ivy House. Keep the faith, love."

Warmth filtered through me at the term of endearment. He'd said he loved me once, but not since. I knew he was waiting for me to go first before he said it again. He clearly wasn't planning on hiding his regard, though.

My heart squished and I leaned in a little closer.

"The other heirs went for bad men," I said as he turned me. "Men who ultimately killed them. Why did the gargoyle magic let that happen if it won't let us finish the mating slide?

"You have no idea how those men started. Power corrupts." Cyra had a refreshed dessert, clearly having asked for more. "Regardless, I suspect your gargoyle is feeding off your own hesitation. You are a woman of strong character, Jacinta Ironheart. You know what happened to the other heirs, and to your own first marriage. You know what's riding on this—your future. Your safety. *You* are feeding that gargoyle, I think, and that's why it's holding back. It's looking for more validation that he is worthy of you. That's a guess, of course, but it stands to reason. You will be the greatest heir of all. Or…if not the greatest, then at least the one that lasts the longest."

"Well." I resisted Austin's leading enough to get it across that I wanted to slow down. He wrapped his arms around my waist and the music slowed. I looped my arms around his shoulders. "Why haven't you proved it, then?"

His eyes flashed. His kiss stole my breath. He didn't respond, but I knew he felt the challenge. I knew he would rise to the occasion and answer it. Somehow.

✧　✧　✧

THE NEXT AFTERNOON, I led my team down the halls and to one of the exits in the smaller tunnels. We'd gotten the schedule earlier that morning. As Elliot had promised, we were going first. I was glad for it. I'd never been good at hanging around, waiting for something to happen.

The large wooden door over the exit was thrown wide, but there wasn't a hole in the mountain face on the other side, as I'd expected. Another tunnel, darker than the one we'd been traveling, curved away and out of sight.

"Good thing we didn't try to break out this way," Niamh murmured as I stepped into the rougher-hewn tunnel and followed it away left.

Austin stayed by my side, in sweats and a T-shirt, face hard and power brimming.

"I wonder if they're all like this," Ulric said from the middle of the pack.

"Quite the fire hazard," Edgar said.

"When you're trapped in a mountain with a bunch of mages," Mr. Tom said, "fire is the least of your worries."

"You say that now," Edgar replied. "Just wait until you're *also* trapped with fire."

The tunnel sloped up and bent around left, the space closing down.

"I forgot to mention—I'm not the best in small, confined spaces," Hollace said, his voice strangely muted.

"Just think about if you were trapped with a fire in a small, confined space," Edgar replied.

"What is wrong with ye?" came Niamh's voice.

"Oh. Quite a lot, I think," he replied. "I just keep trucking on and hoping for the best."

"Jaysus," Niamh muttered, and Cyra started laughing.

"Basajaun," I called back as air fanned across my face. We were getting somewhere.

"Yes, Miss Jessie."

"You good? The ceiling is a bit low. Are you hanging in there?"

"I do not have a problem with caves or tunnels. It will be a while before my back starts to ache from bending over."

"Just don't fart," Ulric said. "My face is much too close to your butt. My view is not great."

"You weren't thinking when you let me go first," the basajaun replied.

"This isn't how normal people walk into battle." I smoothed my hair back.

"Yes, it is," Nathanial replied. "It is exactly how people walk into battle. Confident people. People who know that victory is at hand, and losing is not an option."

"Hear, hear," Jasper intoned.

But I knew they were just trying to bolster me.

Light filtered through the dimness as the tunnel bent right, still sloping upward. We were reaching the end of the tunnel.

"Good news," Hollace whispered.

No door barred the way this time. Little green shoots led to the tunnel opening and patches of lush grass grew beside the entrance. The intensity of the sun blinded me at first, and I screwed up my face and blocked the rays. An electric blue sky looked down on us, not one cloud to mar its beauty.

"Wow." Ulric stepped up beside me, hands braced on hips, and I had to agree. Gorgeous.

Stone steps led down to another tunnel, disappearing into a grassy berm. On the other side, the land flattened out into a huge meadow high off the ground between the peaks. All around us the land dropped away steeply, giving way to the mountain face. The horizon stretched out before us, peeking around distant snow-capped peaks. The view was breathtaking, the air impossibly clear and fresh.

"We'll be able to fly," Hollace said as I started down.

"No." I pointed at the shallow magical dome straddling the path we currently walked, keeping people put, and then the larger dome encompassing the meadow. "Well, not you, at any rate. Ulric probably could. Maybe Jasper. Cyra. The rest of you would be hindered. It would be like the basajaun in that tunnel."

"I was fine in the tunnel," the basajaun said gruffly.

"I mean, the way you had to bend over—"

"I could have fought easily. Called on the mountain to help. It senses the violence within it. It will have its share of blood."

"I just meant that you had to bend over—"

"I am fine outside *or* inside the mountain. It is my birthright."

I gave up.

As the basajaun muttered away, we entered the berm, the lighting once again dim. A sign pointed my team away right, and we walked into what could only be described as a locker room. There were flat benches and little cubbies, plus a big pile of rusty swords and various other weapons next to the door leading outside. The meadow, I'd noticed, had been stripped of grasses and flowers. Sand had taken its place, clearly having been brought in. It didn't look natural to the area. This kind of preparation didn't happen overnight...

Elliot had definitely planned all of this way in advance. But how far in advance? When had he hatched his plan to get me here?

"Really?" Ulric took a half-cleaved helmet out of a cubby and showed it to Broken Sue. "This yours?"

"Intimidation tactics," Austin said, stripping off his shirt. "I don't smell blood in here, or see it on any of those weapons. These are just props. They're not meant for people like us."

"Speak for yerself," Niamh said. "I think they're good craic. Look at this one." She held up a breastplate. The strap over the left shoulder was broken and the whole left side was bent in, suggesting the person in it had been crushed by something. "Or look." She grabbed a metal shin guard, twisted so badly that any leg inside of it would have been hanging on by a thread. "Here, Jessie, wear this one." She grabbed a woman's breast-plate, shining bronze, the breasts large and ending in points. "Go on, wear it. *Go on*, ye might as well."

I shook my head and plucked at my muumuu, nothing but a thin bit of fabric that could easily be pulled off before a change.

"Missed opportunity, that," Niamh said.

"I will." Cyra took hold of it and affixed it to her middle. "I'll try to boob-ram someone. That'll hurt worse than my fire."

Edgar stepped out from behind another set of cubbies with a bicycle helmet a size too big and catcher's gear. "Look, they have something like what I first wore when Jessie started learning. It almost fits."

Niamh stared at him blankly. "It's not funny when ye do it."

"It is." Cyra held her stomach and laughed. "It *is* funny when he does it! Hollace, you put something on, too."

"They couldn't possibly take this less seriously," I said to Austin.

"It won't detract from how they perform," he replied.

"Girl's plate or guy's plate?" Hollace asked.

Cyra held up a plate for the groin with a very detailed metal casing of male genitalia. "Take your pants off. See if it fits."

Hollace took it from her and stepped into it. "Don't know if I can run in this."

"No, no, pants off. There's a place to—"

"Miss Ironheart." A woman in a red coat stepped into the room. She blinked at Hollace, who had frozen halfway through pulling up his metal penis. "Please assemble your team and follow me. It is time to fight."

CHAPTER 19

SEBASTIAN RUBBED HIS hands together, sitting above the arena in a cushioned fold-out chair midway up the side of the plateau. A rock wall ran in front of him, keeping him from pitching over the side and falling ten feet to the grandstands, where the other mages and some of their people had filed in to watch. He'd made sure they were all invited.

"Your girl could get her ass handed to her right now, and you're excited?" Nessa shook her head and consulted her watch.

"She won't. You'll see."

"I didn't know you liked blood sport this much." She pushed forward and looked over the side. "I still don't see Burke."

"I'm sure he's skulking around the tunnels, trying to find my residence. He has no idea there are two separate tunnel systems."

"He's a fool. You shouldn't have bothered to bring him."

"And rob me of the fun of watching him try to kill me? Poppycock."

"He doesn't have any hope of even getting near you. You know that."

"Not unless I let him stumble into me, no. Which I will, just for giggles. But I want to see this competition first. I want everyone to see it. After these games, Jacinta will no longer be a pitiful Jane with a bunch of animals. She will be recognized as the most powerful mage in the world, with the second most powerful mage at her back. She will be a rising star. These games won't only give her status—they'll give her connections."

"Won't it be a grand joke if you have done all this to help her, only to be killed by her in a few days."

"Not the kind of joke that would make me laugh, but certainly the kind of cosmic joke that would be par for the course with my life experience." He sucked in a breath. "Here we go. *Shh-shh.*"

"It was sweet the way the shifter stayed to dance with her last night," Nessa whispered as Jessie's crew was led out of the holding area. "Holy crap, are they *naked*?" Nessa leaned forward, squinting, then reached down to grab her binoculars.

"Sure, now you're interested," he murmured, using his own binoculars to check on Jessie. She looked nervous, with tight shoulders and fisted hands. He felt bad for her, continually being thrown in the deep end, but trial by fire was the only sort that worked in the magical world.

Her big alpha was as experienced with the nuances of body language as she was naïve, thankfully. He walked by her side but a step or two behind her, giving her the head position while making it clear he would not hesitate to protect her.

"This is like Christmas," Sebastian said, giddy. "You have no idea how powerful she is, Nessa. She learns fast, too."

"You've said, yes. I can't believe so many of them are walking out naked. And look at those others. They're actually wearing that ridiculous armor you put in there." She looked over the wall at the mages gathered below. When she sat back down, she said, "Some clearly think this is a joke, and others are disgusted."

Noah and his group of mages walked out next, led by another of Sebastian's people. They walked in a cluster. A couple of stragglers in the back seemed less sure of themselves—those were the smart ones—but most of the mages strutted right alongside Noah, who clearly thought this was a waste of his time. The group stopped at the other end of the meadow in their mages' robes, hands by their sides, silently broadcasting their assurance of victory.

"They have no idea what they just walked into," Sebastian murmured, looking at Noah's smug face through his binoculars.

"A bunch of naked guys, that's what they just walked into. Why did you put the magical ceiling so low over the arena if they fly?"

"I wanted to let the shifters shine on this one."

"You need to get over your love affair with shifters."

"I don't love them. I'm terrified of them. It's nice to feel a strong emotion again after Jala died, even if it is fear."

They fell silent as the two red-clad staffers met in the middle of the meadow. Kiki, the brunette with a very pleasant way about her, worked a spell to broadcast her voice.

"This tournament will continue until one party yields. At that time, the winner is decided. *Do not kill.* This is not a fight to the death. If you kill, you will be gravely penalized. When we leave the field, you may commence."

His people walked to the little protective alcove at the side of the field. The second they were gone, Noah blasted out a spell from way, *way* too far away. He wasn't nearly strong enough to make any impact with it. He clearly thought Jessie was nothing.

As expected, she brushed it away as though it were a

spider web and then started working her hands. Magic coalesced and took form, wrapping around her and her people.

"Is she trying to protect them all?" Nessa asked.

"She's the only mage on her team. If she wants them magically defended, she has to do it herself."

"That's going to put her at a severe disadvantage."

Noah and his people walked forward now, their robes rustling around their feet. Jessie's people still hadn't moved. Sebastian sat forward on the edge of his seat anxiously, wondering what was taking them so long.

"Good," Jessie said, her voice barely audible from where he sat. "Good, good. Go. I'll cover you."

"She's playing defense?" Nessa asked.

He shook his head slowly. It wasn't like her to stay out of the fight. Unless she was worried about her control. Perhaps she feared she'd accidentally kill someone.

"She needs training in a bad way," he said as the first gargoyle—still in human form—lowered to a crouch. He was the one with the colorful hair, but Sebastian was blanking on his name. Niamh reduced down into her little gremlin creature, black as night and with a mouthful of teeth. Blasts of light erupted from the shifters as the attacking mages bore down on them, shooting off paltry spells meant to toy with them, the spells barely missing. It was the equivalent of shooting bullets at someone's feet to scare them.

Two huge wolves emerged from the light, followed by an enormous silverback gorilla that quickened Sebastian's heart.

"Holy crap, Broken Sue turns into a bad mama ja-ma," Nessa said, her voice reduced to a whisper.

The huge polar bear was the last to emerge, down on all fours and no less massive for it. Nessa's jaw dropped.

"Here we go," Sebastian said.

Austin reared up on his hind legs, topping the basajaun in height by three feet, and let out a roar that thundered through the air. It soaked into Sebastian's blood, turning his bowels to jelly. He shivered even as Nessa did, but the display had only just begun. The basajaun was next, his great arms wide and his hair puffed up. The silverback followed, roaring as he beat his arms against his chest, white scars knifing through his leathery black skin. The wolves growled, heads down and hackles raised, working around the outside of the mage group, flanking them.

The little gremlin creature shot forward, skittering on hands and feet, fast and agile and creepy as hell. The shifters and basajaun surged forward next, all rage and raw power and incredible speed and force, cutting down the distance between them and the mages in no time.

The mages cowered on instinct. Confident and full of swagger one minute, they were stooped and frozen solid the next. Not all shifters were created equal, and they'd clearly never seen any like this.

Austin reached Noah before Noah even straightened up, but instead of engaging him, he plowed into the man directly next to him, clamping those great jaws on the man's shoulder before ripping to the side.

The mage screamed and tumbled like a rag doll, hitting the ground ten feet away and rolling. Blood smeared the sand. The basajaun got the mage on the other side of Noah, grabbing him by the feet, lifting, spinning, and then throwing him. The mage smashed into the barrier wall, what should have been an impossible distance for a throw like that, and crumpled into a heap.

"Don't kill!" Jessie yelled.

"Good God, Sebastian," Nessa said, her mouth still hanging open, staring.

The silverback took a shock of magic. It vibrated within the protective spell Jessie had placed on him, gaining power, and then shot back at the mage who'd fired it off, smacking him in the middle moments before the silverback was on him, knocking him to the ground and clubbing him.

Cyra took a hit and then turned. The spell shot off to the side rather than rebounding directly like the others. Sebastian had never seen that happen. The meaning became clear when she turned back and grabbed her attacker and another mage, hugging them to her strange armor. She hadn't wanted the return fire of the spell to spoil her fun. From their screams, it sounded like they were being tortured. And honestly...they were. Sebastian remembered what that phoenix could do.

"Sebastian," Nessa said, reaching out. "If you want them to live, you should stop this."

The pink-blue gargoyle rose into the sky, able to just barely navigate within the available space. The other gargoyles couldn't do much, their wing spans too mighty for them to take off. They tucked in their wings and crowded in around Jessie, on protective detail.

Noah got a spell off at Austin, only for it to hit his defenses and rebound, but it missed the mage.

"She changed the protection spell I taught her. Her creation is damn good, but it needs some tweaks," Sebastian said, wondering how it worked so efficiently. "Is it siphoning energy or power from Jessie?"

"How can you worry about magic right now?" Nessa stood. "What the hell am I doing?" She sat back down. "I feel like I should…run…or fight, maybe."

Austin ignored another bolt of magic coming for him, taking out two mages with a hard swing of his huge paw.

Jessie didn't ignore it, though.

A huge swell of power made Sebastian's eyes water, even from this distance. She put out her hands and readied a blistering spell that would kill Noah where he stood, Sebastian just knew it. She was reacting instinctively to seeing her intended mate in harm's way. She'd lost control.

"No, no, no!" Hollace dove into her, and her spell went wide, glancing off Noah's right shoulder.

The air concussed and Noah flew sideways, landing on the side of his face, his legs flying into the air over him. He crumpled and lay still. Even though the impact had been blunted by whatever defenses he'd erected, plus the fact that it had barely glanced off him, he still wasn't even close to a match for her.

Sebastian and Nessa stood. "Oh!"

"Yield, yield, yield, yield," a mage said as he sprinted away from the rampaging gorilla.

Another ran toward the stands, a woman who was pretty quick on her feet. The basajaun was faster, though. He swiped her from behind and sent her up into the air, over the first barrier and into someone's lap.

"The fight is done," Kiki called, not entering the field. "The fight is done!"

Jessie's people stopped moving, and Noah's people—those still standing—kept running, their flight reflex taking over.

Austin turned toward the crowd, toward Sebastian, and reared up again, releasing a roar full of rage and dominance and challenge. Sebastian could feel it in every fiber of his being. He reached for the back of his chair with a shaking hand and sat down slowly. Nessa took one step away, then another.

Austin lowered back down to all fours before changing back into his human form. He'd just issued a promise, and while Sebastian didn't know exactly how it translated, the effect had rattled his bones and made him rethink this whole endeavor.

"Okay, yeah," Nessa said, out of breath. "Sure, yeah, okay. You win. You were right. That is…"

"Terrifying, yes."

"It's not even a normal kind of terrifying. It's like it…" She touched her chest. "It's not rational, that fear."

"They're predators. It's primal."

"Yeah. Wow. Why am I more attracted to Broken Sue because of it?"

"I do not know. You're crazy."

"No argument there."

Jessie walked her people off the berm, and though Sebastian's attendant should've accompanied them, no one stepped forward to do it. Sebastian didn't blame them. He wouldn't want to, either.

"That is why I want the shifters on my side," Sebastian said.

"And the basajaun. Don't forget that crazy basajaun. Now I get why that guy froze in the hallway."

"And the basajaun. Jessie and her team of shifters are worth more than any other crew at this meeting. If the others can't see that yet, wait until I let her fly and remove the restriction against killing."

"Those shifters wouldn't have been so effective without Jessie's magical defense," Nessa said thoughtfully. "They still would've won, definitely, but they would've felt the hits. It wouldn't have been such a landslide. And if the mages had outnumbered them...well, I could see the battle going a very different way."

"Yes, and that is why shifters are under the thumb of mages right now. But Jessie—and I—teaming with them changes the score card. It'll make all the difference."

"I agree." She was quiet for a moment. "I think you should rethink the way you plan to meet her, Sebastian," Nessa said as she sat down again, her voice tight with nerves. She clearly hadn't taken the threat seriously before, seeing what everyone else did—a past Jane, a bunch of animals, plus a few dudes with capes. The reality was beyond what any sheltered mage—and there were a lot of those—could imagine.

"I can't," he replied. "It's been foretold. I will keep my end of the bargain, come what may."

CHAPTER 20

"WHEN IS THE next battle?" I dried my hair with a towel, wearing workout sweats and a hoodie. Most of my crew lounged in the common space, lazy this morning after dominating in the arena yesterday. Everyone was present except for Austin, who was in the shower, and Edgar, who was drinking some blood in his room so as not to gross everyone out. We'd just barely managed to follow the no-kill rule. I'd had to come back out and heal Noah, plus the guy the basajaun had thrown into a wall.

I'd also seen Elliot Graves up in the stands, and I could tell he was in the flesh. He was there, just out of reach. With everything going on, there was no way I could've gotten to him, not without him getting a good shot off at me first.

"This afternoon." Niamh sat on the couch with her feet up. "We goin'?"

"Yeah, I think we should, don't you? It's the two more powerful mages, right?" I slung the towel over my shoulder.

"I'll have that, miss." Mr. Tom took it from me. "Are you hungry? Do you want anything?"

"Order from the kitchen," Cyra called from her position near the fridge. "I like their cooks."

"I can make whatever they can make," Mr. Tom replied, puffing up.

"Yes, it just won't taste as good," she said.

"Ah, sure," Niamh answered me, beer in hand. "It'll just be spells, but we can go if you wan'ta."

"Maybe I can get some ideas for spells or something." I plopped down into a chair. "Or we can at least see how they fight."

"With spells," Niamh replied. "That's how they fight. They wave their hands around and largely stand in one place. It's right boring." She was annoyed she hadn't been able to do more in our fight—the other side had given in too fast.

"It's not boring when you don't have a mage at your back," Broken Sue growled. "Not everyone can withstand one of their spells. And even if they can, there's always a limit. Whether it's two or three, or more. At some point, it's too much."

"I knew a mage that was super scared of shifters," I said. "And everyone yesterday just froze. Were the mages you...dealt with not afraid?"

Broken Sue crossed his arms over his wide chest. "One on one, yes. Small groups, sure. But when they stood behind the mercenaries, no, they weren't scared. They had numbers and power. We had a few guarding many. They bulldozed us."

The room went silent for a beat, everyone clearly processing the pain behind Broken Sue's words, the raging memories that must be ripping him apart.

"You had to spare fighters to guard the vulnerable," Nathanial said, leaning against the wall with an apple in hand. "That was not a fair fight."

"Fair or not—"

A knock sounded at the door. I'd put up Elliot's ward, after searching it for hidden tricks and finding none, and it vibrated with an unnecessary warning. Mr. Tom came out of the laundry area and headed that way.

"Fair or not," Broken Sue began again, "they did more than just stand there slinging spells."

"Are ye sure, now?" Niamh narrowed her eyes. "They brought in mercenaries. Who was actually fighting?"

Broken Sue stilled, eyes on Niamh.

"Hiring mercenaries seems to be their go-to move when they're up against a wall," I said as Mr. Tom closed the door. He walked over and handed me a note on plain cream cardstock, which he'd already divested of its envelope in his usual way of helping himself to my mail.

"Money can buy you a victory," Ulric said, lounging on a chair, his leg thrown over the arm. "It can't buy you class, but it can buy you a victory."

"Ye know from experience," Niamh intoned.

"Nah, I don't have money or class." Ulric laughed. "Just wild hair, a bad attitude, and a tricky tongue."

I frowned as I read the note. "Elliot Graves needs to see us. Well…me and whoever I want for protection. A few of us. It's about tomorrow's battle against Mr. Bow Tie. Chambers."

"Why a few of us?" Niamh asked, sitting up.

I shrugged. "Just says to bring a few people if I want protection, although he says I won't need any. It'll be a quick chat about a rule change." I put the note down, my stomach swirling like I'd been caught cutting class. "He probably wants to caution me. We went a little overboard."

"You need to learn how to do that shadow soul thing or whatever it is," Hollace said.

"Who wants to come?" I put up my hand.

"Ah, sure." Niamh pushed herself up to standing. "I might as well. I'm bored sitting around here all the time."

"I don't know why," Mr. Tom said, pulling a bowler

hat and a pair of sunglasses from his disguise suitcase. "You're doing what you always do—sit on your butt and drink."

"No, no, don't ye get out that stuff a'tall. Ye look like a clown, so ye do."

"I don't want to stand out in places where I can't blend in," Mr. Tom said.

Niamh stared at him for a long beat. "Then why in the beejeebus are ye putting on that garb? Are ye out of yer mind or what? Of *course* ye stand out, ye donkey. Who in a dark tunnel wears a feckin' bowler hat and sunglasses? Ye've got to be takin' the piss altogether."

"We'll all go." Austin walked from the bedroom with tousled wet hair and a five o'clock shadow. He'd clearly overheard our conversation and decided not to primp. No watch lined his wrist, and he wore a simple T-shirt and jeans. "A Jane and some animals made laughing stocks of mages yesterday. That won't sit well."

I slipped my arm around his middle and gave him a quick squeeze. "Wise."

"Cyra, at the back," he said, pulling the door open for me. "Watch our six. Weakest in the middle. Shifters flanking."

Shivers ran down my arms and a strange feeling quaked in my middle. We started walking before I could decipher it. The banter and relaxed chatter from a moment ago had completely dried up, everyone now on their guard. Austin was entirely correct—we'd been noticed yesterday and might be a target today. No one wanted to be made a fool of by the butt of the joke.

"Where to?" Austin asked, and I handed over the note. Rather than take it, he read the message and then nodded. As we made our way to the meeting point, cutting through the repaired and empty lobby area (with a longing look through the new double door), and into the smaller, danker tunnels, he dropped his voice to address me privately. Or mostly privately. "You let the shifters upstage you yesterday."

"I didn't want to accidentally kill anyone. I almost did anyway."

"I know. And that made sense at the time. But we're at a meeting of mages. *You* need to shine. You need to show them the full extent of your power, your ferocity. I think Cyra was right: Elliot knows why you're here. He's keeping himself away from you. He's playing games with you, just like he was with that lesser-powered mage. You shouldn't play by his rules. I wonder if he *expects* you to break them. You certainly haven't come across as a rule follower in the past."

I took a deep breath. "I don't want to kill anyone."

"I know. But sometimes you don't have a choice if you want to survive. Try your best, but if the worst happens in this place, make no apologies. He should've known better than to let you loose on these people."

I nodded but made no comment. My anger toward Elliot Graves burned a little hotter because of the position he was forcing me into. I didn't want to hurt people. I didn't want to battle. I didn't want to be stuck in a cave dealing with the belittling buttheads. All of this was on him, solely, and I would not forget it.

"The other thing that has become clear is that he's treating you like an honored guest," Austin whispered as he glanced behind us. "Our rooms are much more spacious and high-ceilinged than one would expect in a tunnel, and judging by these other paths, the other suites aren't as nice."

"I know. That had occurred to me. Someone is bound—"

A flash preceded what felt like a heavy hand slapping me sideways. I hit the wall headfirst, and blackness dragged me under.

CHAPTER 21

MY VISION SWAM for a moment and my head pounded. Something wrapped around my body from my elbows to my knees, cutting into my skin and squeezing. Lifting me into the air at an angle. Hair cut off my vision, hanging in my face.

"She's awake, sir!"

I craned my neck, finding myself in a circular area covered in couches and chairs. A common room, half the size of ours but laid out in the same way, with the kitchen at the back and an archway that probably led to other rooms.

"Well, well."

The man from dinner, Chambers, walked up and stopped in front of me, his dress shoes shined up and his suit expensive, one hand in his pocket. He wore a smirk as calculated as that impeccable bow tie from the other night.

"We're not supposed to battle until tomorrow," I said, wheezing. I set to work healing myself immediately, checking on my team through the links. Austin was unconscious, but Niamh was awake and mad as hell. Mr. Tom mirrored her sentiment. Cyra seemed patient and Hollace equally so; they were probably waiting for the others to join them. None of them seemed worried about me. But then, why would they be? They could feel me, a little dazed, a bit confused, but otherwise fine, at the end of the tunnel they were in.

Edgar seemed groggy, so he would be good in a bit. That vampire was incredibly hard to keep down for long. Nathanial was coming along too, but Ulric and Jasper and the basajaun were lights out like Austin. All of them had been on the same side of the line and had clearly gotten the brunt of the spell.

I breathed slowly, keeping calm. They were just un-conscious. On my radar but without emotions. I didn't know when I'd learned the difference between sleeping and dead, but I felt it with an assurance that I didn't question.

That I *wouldn't* question.

I sent some healing energy through the links to speed things along. I didn't want to drain too much of my energy, since I'd likely have to fight my way out of this, but I needed to make sure everyone else was okay first.

"I don't think we're going to battle at all, are we?"

He motioned at me.

Feet came into my vision. Something tugged at me from behind. A rope, like what was wrapped around my body.

"Clever," I said through a grunt as the ropes jerked me to an upright position. "Can't magic my way out of a rope." I thought about that for a moment. "Or can I?"

Chambers crossed his arms over his chest, looking me over. Three other people were in the room, one who'd just stood me on my feet, and two others loitering by the far wall, probably security in case something happened.

"Where's everyone else?" I asked.

"Handling your shifters. I told you to bring a few people, not your whole posse, but no matter—they are handled."

It hadn't been Elliot who'd sent me that note at all. It had been Chambers. Thank God, because a situation like this with Elliot would've been much harder to navigate, I was certain.

I huffed out a laugh. "You think a few mages can handle Austin Steele, a phoenix, a basajaun, an alpha gargoyle, a *thunderbird*—Stop me when you realize what a terrible idea that is."

"That polar bear will get an offer he can't refuse. They all will."

"Austin can't be bought."

"Oh no? What if I guarantee his brother's safety? Word on the street is, Momar is through with that meddling shifter trying to organize. It's a big, strong pack, but with my help, he has a way to take them down. And he will." A vicious grin spread across Chambers's face. "*If* I help. I have some experience in those matters. I could just as easily choose not to, of course."

"What do you get out of it?" I gave him a shallow smile. "Me, right?"

"Obviously. The others are blind to how Elliot Graves works. They think he is bringing a lamb to the slaughter. That he wants a bit of fun with you before he teaches you a lesson for making such a ridiculous show of yourself. But he wouldn't give a plaything the largest suite of rooms. I have it on good authority that he spoiled you rotten with gifts, too. He gave you instructions on how to properly ward your rooms, since apparently you're too...naive? Stupid? I'll let you choose your own adjective. Regardless, he's pampering you."

"And you want to know why."

"I know why, and it's not the power, though I will admit you clearly have a lot of it. You don't know how to use it, however, and we all know Elliot doesn't take apprentices or partners, despite what he's said. No, he wants those shifters, doesn't he? He plans to organize them against Momar." He shook his head. "I've never totally understood why Momar hates them so much. Hire some people and they aren't hard to take down. But that bear you have is something else... That's what Graves wants, isn't it? The gorilla wasn't a subtle hint. He's calling me shortsighted for how I handled him. I will admit, it isn't a bad idea to use the shifters against Momar. Too bad it won't work."

I'd never stared so hard in my life.

The gorilla wasn't a subtle hint.

How I handled him...

"You killed Brochan's mate and children. You killed *children!*"

His eyes narrowed. "I killed poachers and animals."

Power boiled through and around me. "That doesn't even make sense. Number one, you were on their land. You're the poacher. Number two, poachers are people, animals are prey. You can't call them both. Just call it what it was—slaughter. Despicable slaughter that will be your death sentence."

He chuckled without humor. "And who will carry it out? You? Wrapped in rope with no use of your hands? Can't even put up a simple ward spell or wash away those crow's feet on your eyes? Sure. Or are you talking about the shifters? Because I'm all that stands between them and their annihilation."

Finally Austin clicked back onto my radar, and a wave of dizziness rode the link. The other unconscious members of the crew woke up soon thereafter.

I breathed a sigh of relief and refocused on the issue at hand.

I could kill this disgusting mage right now. I didn't need my hands—I'd learned some spells without them. I could kill every person in this room. I didn't care that I would be stranded, tied up in ropes without even Cheryl to saw myself out.

But I wouldn't.

Because Chambers wasn't my fight. He was Broken Sue's, and I wouldn't take that from him.

I shook my head as Austin snapped to focus, and a deep, aching pain pumped through the link. Not a pain of the flesh, but a pain of the soul. He was reacting to the fear of what might happen to me—to the anguish of possibly losing me—and I could feel it overcome his whole person.

My heart throbbed and then overflowed, the pure, unchecked, incredibly raw emotion bringing tears to my eyes. If I'd needed proof of how much he cared for me, I had it.

"No need to cry. You won't be hurt," Chambers

said, but I wasn't paying him any attention.

Shock and alarm radiated from the links. Frustration. Anger. I wondered what was happening. Whatever it was, it was happening to everyone.

"So your plan is to trade me to Elliot for…favor?" I asked, passing the time. "For some sort of back-scratching thing?"

"Yes. There you go. Not so stupid, then?"

"And you will give Austin a hollow offer to keep him at bay until you can kill him, and then try to…what, play Elliot and Momar off each other or something?"

Chambers's eyebrows pinched together. "A simplistic and juvenile grasp of the situation, but…you have the gist of it."

Rage sparked in a few of the links, but none felt so tumultuous as Austin's. From that alone, I knew he was being given the offer he supposedly couldn't refuse.

Once upon a time, I might have worried he'd take it. It sounded good on paper. He would want to protect his family. I was just his girlfriend, after all.

Once upon a time, I'd been young, without any self-confidence. Without any power or strength of my own. Without the drive to insist I be given the things I deserved.

I wasn't so young anymore. I might be naive when it

came to magic, but I was no longer naïve about love.

And I did love Austin. I loved him with all my heart. I trusted him with everything that I was. He would come for me, just as I would fight for him. He wouldn't take a ridiculous offer in the hopes it might be legit— he'd do battle, and once we were together again, we'd join forces to combat whatever came at his family.

No more holding back out of self-preservation. It was time to swing my leg over the saddle. It was time to accept what he already had—that we were meant to be bound together, body and soul.

First I needed to get out of this rope.

"You're an idiot," I said as Austin's rage built, dark and twisted, a nightmare bubbling up from down deep. He would lose himself to his beast. This time, he *wanted* to. "Holy hell, you are an idiot. He's pissed."

Excitement surged within me. Anticipation. The desire to meet Austin and fight by his side.

I scowled down at the ropes.

"You've turned me into a damsel," I murmured.

"Are you hearing a word I've been saying?" Chambers demanded.

The walls shuddered around me. The ground vibrated under my feet.

That wasn't Austin.

My eyes widened as I looked at Chambers, my focus

split between him and whatever was happening around us. "No, I haven't. You unleashed hell, do you know that? Listen, really quickly, because it's the last chance you'll get. If you try to hold something over Elliot's head, he'll just kill you. He has no qualms about it. I don't know why he's pampering me, but it probably isn't good. The others are almost certainly right about that. Second, your ego is out of control if you think you'd be able to pit Momar and Elliot against each other and not end up being smashed between them. You probably aren't smart enough, or rich enough, or…whatever enough to handle the kind of crap you're wading into."

Glasses shook on tables. A small rock fell from the ceiling. The three lackeys in the room looked around, wondering what was going on.

I also wondered what was going on. What was the basajaun doing to this mountain?

"Third, you do not understand shifters at all. *At all.* They are incredibly loyal. They have pack mentality. If you are in the pack, they will saw off a limb for you. They wouldn't leave a member of their pack out to dry. They aren't like mages. And you just so happened to mess with the baddest shifter in the world. His brother doesn't need you for safety. His brother needs *him.*"

Austin changed into his animal; I could feel it

through the link. Niamh shifted, and the gargoyles did the same. They couldn't use their wings, but their flyer forms had tougher hides and sharper claws.

Edgar came toward me fastest of all, slipping by whatever opposition waited in the halls in his swarm-of-bugs form.

I felt bad for standing here without doing anything, letting myself stay tied up. But I'd feel worse if I didn't let Broken Sue decide what he would do with the guy who had stolen his life. Besides, I knew Austin was coming for me. I knew he would deal with this situation. That he would also want to give Broken Sue a chance for revenge.

The ground rumbled. Little pebbles fell from the roof.

"Find out what is going on," Chambers told one of the guys at his back.

Power radiated through the walls.

A knock came at the door.

The attendant ran forward to get it. He cracked it open and peered out. That small space was all Edgar needed to slip by, materializing next to me before the mages could react, his eyes taking me in.

"Oh, good, you're not terribly hurt," he said. "The alpha is coming. The rest of our crew is with him."

Magic jetted through the air. Edgar puffed into his

insects and beelined for Chambers.

"No," I shouted, wishing I could throw out my hand. "He's Brochan's."

Edgar materialized inches from the mage, who staggered back in fright, a stream of magic going wide and crashing into the kitchen at the back.

"He's the one?" Edgar asked, stepping calmly to the side as another stream of harried magic zipped past. "Despicable. Yes, that's fitting."

Austin ran at me now, moving fast, full of consuming rage. Power pulsed in the air around me. It throbbed, wild and intense, and I couldn't tell if it was his or mine.

A great shadow blackened the doorstep. I could feel it—Austin's nearness pounding through me. The mages in the room must've been able to feel it too. All four of them snapped their heads toward the door, Edgar forgotten, the ground rumbling under their feet, power pulsing through the air.

The door exploded, ripping off its hinges and pulling completely free of the frame. Austin's roar filled the confined space, full of blistering rage, and then he was inside, impossibly large.

A mage shook free of his stupor and shot forth a stream of magic. It slashed across Austin, opening a gash and spilling blood down his dewy white coat. He didn't even flinch. He roared again as he rushed forward, grabbing the mage and chomping down on his head before ripping to the side.

Something inside of me roared in response. It scrabbled to get out. To feed on his power. To bask in his strength. To merge with him, giving him some of my own power and strength. He was showing me his beast, and mine was answering in kind. Magic shed from my body, colorful light drifting into the room.

Chambers put up his hands, but not to throw a spell. He was shielding his face from what Austin was doing to the other mage. Crimson splattered across his palms.

One of the mages in the back shook into action, hands shaking so badly that the spell he churned out withered and died on the vine. Austin wasted no time, shoving furniture out of the way, knocking over anything that hindered his movement. He grabbed up that mage and ended his efforts. The last ran out of the door. Austin turned toward him, but the basajaun's roar said he'd get there first. The mountain shook under my feet again.

"Don't bring the mountain down on us," I hollered, a backseat driver if ever there was one.

Austin lowered down to all fours, his predator's gaze on Chambers as he stalked around him in a circle, putting his body between me and danger.

"I c-can save you," Chambers said, his palms still up, his hands shaking. "I can k-keep Momar away from your brother. From y-your people."

"As *if*," Edgar said, unintentionally (I was pretty sure) sounding like a character out of a nineties movie.

Light and heat flashed in the room. Austin stood there in the flesh. "I would like to kill you for what you've done, but my mate is safe. I must defer to the one whose life you took."

The huge silverback gorilla filled the doorway, his arms and legs thick with muscle, his chest robust.

"No," the mage said, backing up, tripping over a chair and falling. "No! It wasn't me. It was my people. I didn't do anything!"

Austin turned, his eyes twin cobalt flames. He grabbed the rope attached to the bindings on my back. The other end was tied to a hook in the wall, and he ripped it out in one crisp gesture. "Send everyone back to the rooms," he barked.

"Yes, sir, colonel...ah...alpha." Edgar puffed into his insect form and zipped from the space.

"Edgar got in by knocking," I said, heat pooling in my middle. Power still pounded in my chest, filled the air, sizzled through my blood and bones.

Mate.

I wanted to give him his due. I was ready to merge our beasts.

Mate.

I didn't know what any of that meant, but the need was there, pulsing within me, insistent.

"I was giving orders," Austin said, and I could barely focus on the words. "He ignored them. His first inclination was to get to your side. He's nuts, but he's got his heart in the right place. I won't fault him for it."

And then he unwrapped me, blood trickling down his cut chest, and all I could do was stand there, buzzing. Aching. Desperate for him. Wanting his arms around me, his body inside mine, his heart beating in my chest.

Click.

It felt like a giant's hand punched through my chest, grabbed my very center—my life's essence—and squeezed.

Suddenly I couldn't breathe. I clutched my chest, and his heart gave one hard throb before settling into mine, our link deeper than my connection to Ivy House. Stronger than the roots of a mighty oak. Permanent.

MATE!

The world shifted, but it didn't go anywhere. Everything changed, but nothing did.

His eyes moved over me for a beat, and then suddenly I was in his arms and he was hurriedly walking through the halls. The basajaun froze when we neared him, a head in each of his huge hands, doing some sort of end-zone dance.

Cyra looked up from a pile of char, and I did not want to know what that had been. This crew was getting out of hand.

I'd deal with them later.

"What's happening?" But I didn't need to ask. I already knew.

CHAPTER 22

*M*ATE. *MATE. MATE. Mate. Mate.*

It was a pulse within me. It was an assurance. My beast had finally accepted Austin. And so had I.

"I lo—"

"No," he growled, reaching the end of the tunnel and cutting across the foyer. A man in a red coat paused as we passed, his eyes widening, clearly responding to a naked and bleeding man carrying a woman through the hallway like Tarzan. "Not here."

I tightened my hold around his neck and ran my lips down the shell of his ear. "I can't wait much longer."

"I know. I…" He shook his head, his breathing ragged. "Almost to our room. I didn't want us to claim each other in enemy territory, but…"

"It's happening."

"Yes," he growled, and he staggered into the wall, his knees nearly giving out.

I sucked in the fevered skin of his neck. "I lo—"

"No! Not here. Not yet, baby. Please. Not yet."

"Why not yet?" My voice was thick and sultry. "You saved me. You gave a blood price. You appeased the beast." I sucked in his earlobe. "I want to fu—"

"No, no, no—" He staggered again, crushing me to his chest, nearly going down. "I'm not going to make it," he murmured, barely loud enough to hear.

I laughed, emotion gushing through me. Power. Desire.

"Oh God," Austin breathed, reaching our front door and kicking it open. On the other side, he kicked it closed again. He pushed off the frame, his hand beneath my shirt, holding me up, cradling me. Panting, he settled next to it. "Do the ward. Hurry."

Passion built. Expectation. My core throbbed, and pleasure unfurled from every point of contact between us, driving me to the brink.

Breathing heavily, barely able to focus, I laid the ward. My people could come in but no one else.

"Good," I said, pulling his face up so I could suck in his bottom lip.

He groaned and staggered toward our room, pushing it closed with his backside and then ripping at my clothes, tearing off my shirt and shoving down my jeans and panties.

"Now," he said, stilling for a moment, his eyes

dazed and soaked with feeling and passion. His presence inside my chest was more comforting now than it had ever been.

This felt right. What was happening felt *right*.

"I love you, Austin," I said, and tears came to my eyes. "I trust you. I cherish you. My heart is safe in your hands. The other Ivy House heirs chose men who wanted to be more powerful. Men who wanted their woman to stoop lower so that they could stand taller. But you've always tried to build me up. Even when I don't feel I need it, you put me above yourself. I'm lucky to have you. I've always been lucky to have you. I love you."

He pulled me to him with a hand at the back of my neck, his kiss hard and insistent. When he let up, I had to catch my breath.

"I love you too," he said. "It's been a long road for me, finding you. Finding my mate. But it was worth it, because I appreciate you so much more. I appreciate what you mean to my life. You're the light in my darkness. You're my hope in a bleak world. You're the reason I strive to reach to my true potential. You make me a better man, Jacinta Ironheart. With you in my life, there is nothing holding me back."

A tear slipped down my cheek, and I ran my thumb across his stubble. "Mate."

"Your beast has chosen. Shall we…consummate the pairing?"

"Is that how it goes?"

"I honestly have no idea. That's not something I ever wanted to ask my brother."

I laughed as he walked me back to the bed, and then that thing down deep—my gargoyle—growled for him. I craved him like I hadn't craved anyone ever in my life.

"Austin—"

I didn't need to say anything more. He settled between my legs and found my center, entering me slowly but quickly speeding up. I clutched his back, swiveling my hips up to meet him. Our bodies clashed together again and again, the bed rocking beneath us. Our fevered breathing filling the room. Magic flowered and rolled around us, vibrated between us, sank down deep.

I groaned, pushed higher. Striving harder. Filled over and over, not able to get enough but almost too much. Too hard. Too good. Too—

I cried out with the release, shaking beneath him. He quaked above me, digging his face into my neck, nipping me softly.

"Why didn't you fight earlier?" he asked as he slow-ly plunged into me, starting up again. "Why didn't you do any magic?"

"I realized who he was, and since I can only really

do defensive spells or kill shots without my hands—nothing with finesse—I figured I'd wait for you. He wasn't planning to kill me. I knew you'd reach me before anything happened."

He swore softly and rammed into me, making me squeak in surprise and then moan in utter delight.

"There is a deep and primal…satisfaction in hearing that your mate knew you'd come for her. That she had no fear because she believed in your abilities. It's…" He drew back and rammed into me again. "This is damned bad timing for the bond to click into place." I groaned, tightening around him. "Focus is going to be hard to come by."

"Hmm." My eyes fluttered shut, my body on fire, his ministrations sending me to the next level.

He chuckled darkly and worked faster. I held on for dear life.

"My mate," he said softly, and I shattered.

This time around, I knew I was doing it right. I loved myself, and I loved him, and I loved us together. We were two individuals who were more together than the sum of our parts. It was the kind of love I'd always wanted. He wasn't a perfect man, but he was perfect for me.

The journey leading here had been long, but I'd learned so much from it, and from the mistakes I'd made along the way. I'd found myself. And now I could share myself with another, and delight in him sharing himself with me.

✧　✧　✧

MR. TOM FELT goosebumps as a pulse of power lightly concussed the air. Nathanial shifted in his seat. Ulric uncrossed his left ankle from his knee and shifted to the opposite configuration, right over left. Jasper paced in the back by the kitchen. Edgar sat in the corner, doggedly working on the latest monstrosity of a doily.

"Why are ye all so jumpy?" Niamh asked, flicking through a magazine on the couch. "Ye got fleas?"

"The female gargoyle has found her mate," Mr. Tom said, turning a page in the book he was looking at but not necessarily reading. Those pulses from the miss were messing with his focus. "Would've been nice if she'd chosen an alpha gargoyle, or even looked around a little more before settling on someone, but alas, we'll take what we can get."

"Why is that making yis so jumpy?" Niamh stopped flicking pages. "Ye knew she was going to settle on him. It's the best thing she could've done, really. Ivy House agrees that he's the best bet for her protection, or didn't ye notice that he was given the number one spot?" She turned a page. "Ye can see the number one spot, can't ye? From all the way over at number nine?"

"Big words from someone who keeps sliding down in the order of importance," he replied.

"Don't ye worry." She flicked a page, not looking down at it. "Ye'll act as a doorstop."

"What's happening doesn't really translate to modern times," Ulric said, clasping his fingers.

Kace walked out of the archway leading to the rooms. Everyone else was holed up in their little cells, taking a break after their impromptu battle and the flash burning party that had followed it. Cyra had tried to make the massacre look like an accident, only her pyrotechnics had made it look like arson. They'd decided to give up and flee, especially since they weren't sure they'd found all the pieces of Chambers after Broken Sue was done with him. It hadn't been a pretty scene.

"You all talking about them mating?" Kace asked, heading straight for the fridge. The shifters all ate like they had holes in their stomachs. "This isn't a great place to do it—not that they had much choice."

"This is the perfect place to do it," Nathanial said as another pulse of power made them all squirm again.

"When ye explained all this a month ago, it seemed pretty simple." Niamh closed her magazine. "Like a shifter mating."

"On the surface, yes, it is like a shifter mating." Ulric nodded. "But there are some fundamental differences that I, myself, didn't realize until it started happening."

"Like what, then?" Niamh asked.

"She's sending out pulses of power every so often. Calling us to her. Or sending us to the skies. Or urging us to join with our brethren and unite around her. Every ten minutes, it seems like, I'm getting a different directive, more and more intense, probably because I'm not doing any of it."

"I don't think she understands what she's doing," Nathanial said, "but she's bringing her cairn together. She's organizing her protection while she delights in her mating dance, which is more or less like a shifter, only much more violent."

"She's like a praying mantis?" Kace asked as Edgar sighed in satisfaction. He held the lopsided doily up to examine it.

"Not so much sexually violent," Ulric said, "though I'd bet there would be a bit of that."

"The shaking of the walls and light fixtures proves that, I should think," Niamh said dryly. "That bit wasn't the basajaun."

The basajaun had called upon the mountain earlier to claim its vengeance, whatever that meant. It was a mountain, for heaven's sake. What could it possibly do, besides collapse and kill them all?

Turned out, it could shake and roll and drop a few pebbles. Basically, theatrics. Mr. Tom hadn't understood the point, other than to freak out their captors, and the basajaun could have just roared to achieve that much. Mages these days seemed a very fragile sort. Quite different from the ones he'd battled back before flushable toilets.

It was probably for the best, since mages currently dominated the magical world and kept bothering Ivy House and the miss. All the better if they were cowards.

"The violence portion was why she waited so long for him to prove himself," Ulric said. "Gargoyles have always been on the front lines. They are strong and sure and powerful, and she must be their alpha. Which means she must be capable of handling violence. And, if necessary, thwarting it. Her beast wanted proof that her mate would do the same."

"You don't think an alpha shifter knows about being on the front lines and handling and thwarting violence?" Kace laughed and shook his head. "No gargoyle is going up against Austin Steele and winning, I'll tell you that much."

"Well, clearly one gargoyle is, ye donkey." Niamh went back to her magazine. "She's in there right now, going up against him. Surely enjoying herself while she does."

"I wondered if she was hesitating because she worried about repeating the pattern of the past heirs," Edgar said, standing and backing farther into the corner. It was very creepy in an endearing sort of way.

"I wondered that meself," Niamh murmured. "Did she give him that protector's magic yet? Do we know?"

"He couldn't harness her magic." Ulric leaned forward again as another pulse of magic moved through the air. "He's not a mage."

"He couldn't harness the bulk of her magic, but the protector's magic can be used by anyone, including someone non-magical," Edgar said from his corner, still analyzing his handiwork. "The magic will customize to the recipient."

"I wonder what that will look like with a shifter," Ulric said, frowning.

"But he does get that protector's magic, doesn't he?" Mr. Tom asked.

"I guess we'll see soon enough," Ulric said.

"I wonder if he were to harness that magic," Edgar said, scratching his head. "Could he use it to kill her?"

"Glass half-full, aren't ye, boy?" Niamh said.

Ulric and Nathanial exchanged a look.

"He could've killed her ten times over by now," Niamh said into the silence, not concerned. She was correct. "He could kill her with or without that magic. She's given him ten opportunities since breakfast, and he's a man that would know how to make it permanent. But he won't, because he's loyal to her, and that's that. More magic will just make him better at his job."

"He doesn't know about the magic, does he?" Kace asked. "Not that I am trying to get into the alpha's business."

"He wanted to go blindly into the gargoyle mating ritual." Mr. Tom turned a page, going back a page to read something he'd missed, then realized he'd missed all of it and just closed the book. "He wanted to experience it as it came. It sure made things awkward after he saved the day and then carried her through the halls in that...state."

"He's been in that *state* loads of times," Niamh drawled. "He's well aware that if he turns around too fast, with the size of that willy standing on end, he's liable to take out a building."

"Saving her was part of the ritual?" Kace's brows pinched together.

"I've always heard that when female gargoyles are locking in a mate, they wait for the male to prove his ability," Ulric explained. "What better way than to bust into an enemy stronghold and save her, huh? She was right on the cusp—if he'd known more about the dance, he would've known that would set her off."

"Not like it would've changed anything." Kace walked closer and plopped into a cushy sage chair.

"Oh. Here you go." Edgar bustled forward, his doily outstretched. "Here, this will help." He took away the malformed doily currently graffitiing the arm of the chair and exchanged it for the newly finished monstrosity, three sizes bigger than a normal one. "This one is better."

"Than what?" Ulric asked in bewilderment, watching.

Kace somehow ignored the disastrously crocheted item. "She handled things the right way. She stepped back so Broken Sue could confront his demons—"

"Are we all calling him Broken Sue now?" Edgar asked. "I worried that he might take offense and rip my arms off if I called him that without any of the enemy around."

"It's a good name." Niamh nodded. "He wouldn't rip off your arms because you offended him, though. That would be his reaction to the way ye always lope around like a gobshite."

"Yes. I can see that," he replied, retreating to his corner.

"Speaking of Brochan, how's he doing?" Mr. Tom asked. "Does he need something to eat?"

"He's got whiskey. He'll be grand." Niamh leaned forward and tossed the magazine onto the nearest coffee table. "Hard not to believe fate played a role in sending him here, eh? After wandering around the country, he found himself in the one place where he could confront the person that tore down his life."

"Maybe the basajaun was right about those stars," Ulric murmured.

"Whatever the reason, he's a damn good addition to the pack." Kace leaned back. "He's fierce, experienced, and smart. He's got great control."

"Worried you'll lose yer job?" Niamh gave him a wicked grin.

"I'm not worried about anything," Kace answered seriously. He spread his arm over the back of his chair, and Mr. Tom wondered if that was because it was the only place not littered with Edgar's failed attempts at craftwork. "Whatever is best for the pack."

Goosebumps spread across Mr. Tom's skin again as another pulse rolled through the suite, this one more powerful than the last. Ulric and Nathanial both shifted, as if to move to standing, then pushed out a simultaneous breath and leaned back.

"It probably makes it worse that we're under a mountain," Jasper said from the back.

"Amen." Ulric ran his fingers through his hair.

"Tomorrow is the battle, though. She should be able to let off some steam. Maybe it'll also shift some of her focus off the mating dance."

"The only problem is, Cyra torched everyone we were supposed to fight tomorrow," Edgar said. "We can't even drive sticks through them and prop them up to give the illusion they're alive."

The room paused and looked at Edgar. There was that endearing creepiness he did so well.

"Well." Mr. Tom rose as a shock of hunger pierced him through the link. The miss was coming up for air and needed some sustenance. Time for an early dinner. "Either we will face the winner of today's battle, or we will face an angry Elliot Graves. Either way, we'll do battle, and we'll be one step closer to our goal. Our time in this mountain is almost done."

CHAPTER 23

I EMERGED FROM the room in my muumuu and leaned against the wall before breathing a sigh.

"I feel good," I said to the room at large.

"You look good." Austin stopped beside me, taking a moment to slide his hand across my back and hook it around my hip. He pulled me nearer and kissed my temple before heading to the kitchen.

I smiled and breathed another sigh of utter relaxation.

Which was odd, because I had gotten virtually no sleep last night (having reveled in Austin), and the Chambers thing had gone down less than twenty-four hours ago. We'd gotten a note from Elliot himself this time, changing our opponent for today's battle from Chambers to the winner of yesterday, since "*a freak cave firestorm seems to have taken out Chambers and his crew—beware those strange phenomena.*"

Obviously that meant Elliot was just letting us off the hook. Which was disconcerting in itself—what was his motive? What else did he have planned for me?

And then there was the fact that Kingsley might be in trouble, and we'd obviously join him, heading to his aid.

But man, none of it was sticking in my mind. It was like everything that didn't directly relate to Austin and mating was not important.

This bubble would pop very soon, I knew. But for this one last moment, I intended to savor it.

"How's everyone?" I asked, smiling at Ulric as he walked by. He nodded, his eyes bloodshot and sporting dark bags. "Good?"

Jasper paced at the back of the room. He paused for a second, shivered, and continued pacing.

"Morning. Sleep well?" Kace stood to our left with a cup of coffee. He had on gray sweats and nothing else, but then again, I suspected he'd be losing the sweats before the battle.

"Not at all." My smile burned brighter, and I took a cup of water from Mr. Tom. Smiling down at the contents, I said, "I hardly slept at all and it was wonderful. Mr. Tom, why do I have a glass of water in my hand and not a cup of coffee?"

"Battle is only an hour away. I thought you should hydrate."

"Huh." I drank the water and handed the cup back.

"I don't trust this good mood," Niamh said from the couch, squinting at me. "Is it the sex or the mating or what?"

"Yes, miss, listen to the Paddy," Mr. Tom said, heading back to the kitchen area. "It's wise to be cautious of happiness. You don't want it to sneak up on you and take you unawares."

"*I* don't, that's fer sure," Niamh said. "And I especially don't want some grinning fool sneaking up on me and doing God knows what."

"Like telling a joke?" Ulric asked, running his hands down his face. "Or laughing? Making you less grumpy, perhaps?"

"Making you likable?" Mr. Tom asked.

"All of the above, yes," Niamh said. "Never trust someone high on life. They aren't in touch with reality."

Ulric spat out a laugh.

Austin came back from the kitchen, stopping beside Broken Sue. The former alpha sat at the counter, his arms folded, staring at nothing. Austin bent and murmured something to him, resting a hand on his shoulder. Broken Sue blinked and leaned back, his eyes haunted. But he nodded, and when Austin walked away, he straightened up just a little bit more.

My heart swelled. Warm fuzzies tickled me. Purplish-pink magic shed from my skin before drifting into the air.

Austin glanced up, and his gaze stuck to me, his body going tight and fluid all at the same time. He started toward me with a killer's grace.

Arousal wound through me. The craving for him intensified—sated a moment ago, it now felt like we'd been apart for a solid year.

"Ah crap, no." Niamh stood up in a hurry. "If I want to be happy and relaxed, I'll drink a cider and take the piss out of *Mr. Tom*, thank ye very much," she said, rolling her shoulders.

"Fantastic," Mr. Tom said dryly.

"Jessie's affecting everyone's mood now, not just the gargoyles," Ulric said, heaving a sigh. "This is a nice one."

"Speak for yerself. I don't need some purple-shedding past Jane to force her feelings on me," Niamh said.

"Watch what you say about my mate," Austin growled, his power pulsing in the room, most everyone snapping to attention, including Niamh (before she scowled and swore). A shiver arrested me.

"Do not play with fire right now, Niamh," Kace said out of the side of his mouth.

I laughed, of all things. I was as Froot Loops as Edgar, high on this feeling. Sore and languid and coiled and desperate.

As soon as Austin was within reach, I grabbed him and forced him back into the room, no embarrassment at this (pretty extreme) display of hunger. I slammed the door and ripped down his sweats before grabbing his neck. His kiss was aggressive and bruising and sexy as hell. He pushed up my muumuu and hiked my leg onto his hip, bent, and thrust upward, stealing my breath.

"*Yes,*" I groaned, throwing my other leg over his hip and wrapping around him. "Hard. Really, *really* hard."

He spun me and rammed my back into the wall before hammering into me, his body crashing into mine, his tongue in my mouth, his hands on my breasts. I gyrated to his rhythm, felt the wall quiver around us, the light fixture shake in its casing.

I yanked his hair, straining against him, already so high but wanting more. Wanting his body harder. More aggressively.

He tore me away from the wall, not bothering with the short trip to the bed, and sank onto the floor. Hands on my shoulders, he pulled me down on top of him as he thrust upward, filling me completely, erasing my thoughts. Control spun away.

I yanked his hair again as I fell on top of him, claiming his lips. He growled into my mouth, still thrusting like a demon, deliciously bruising. Hitting all the right spots, as hard as I could handle.

I slammed my body repeatedly on top of him as he thrust upward, then arched back and cried out my orgasm, almost inhuman, all-encompassing, the best high I'd ever had—and that was saying something, because I'd had a lot of bests last night. He shook beneath me, growling out his release.

Breathing heavily, I laughed like a madwoman.

"I'm losing my mind, I think," I said afterward, lying on top of him, not at all caring that we were on the floor.

He wrapped his arms around my back and heaved a sigh of contentment. "Mating. Best just to go with it. This is why we'd usually head out into the woods for the week and just...be together."

"Yes, but if you're in the woods away from people, you can't fight. I feel like kicking some ass and then screwing you into oblivion as the victory lap."

A smile spread across his face. "Quite the change from when we first got here. The battling, I mean."

"I know. I'm sure it'll wear off, but...you said to go with it."

"Yes, I did." He squeezed me a little tighter. "Damn it, I'm turned on again. You are a literal dream come true. Yes. Let's battle. First a quickie against each other until one of us submits, and then against the enemy with our pack."

✧ ✧ ✧

TAKE TWO.

"Okay." I gave a thumbs-up to nobody as I again walked out and leaned against the wall.

"Feel any surlier?" Niamh asked, now back by the kitchen.

"A little happy magic might do you good, *ye olde crone*," Mr. Tom said.

"Is that supposed to be my accent?" Niamh turned to him as he filled another glass of water.

"Mine was less shrill, I know. I'll work on it." He sniffed.

"No, Mr. Tom, coffee this time. Time to get my game face on." I held out my finger as Austin exited the room, silently telling him to get away. His proximity got me every time.

"Ah, good, she's seeing some sense." Niamh wandered my way, in her sweats like everyone else. They were all ready and waiting, eyes on me, faces blank.

"So." I took a deep breath and noticed all the younger gargoyles shivered. "What?"

"Time for battle," Nathanial said gruffly.

Excitement rolled through me. A smile blossomed

on my face and anticipation flowered in my middle.

"Yes, it is." I accepted a steaming mug from Mr. Tom. "Here's the thing: that low magical ceiling isn't fair to the gargoyles. I'm going to try to break it."

"No need," the basajaun said, munching on a banana. "The mountain will help."

"What, by doing a little rumble?" Mr. Tom asked.

"It was just warming up," the basajaun replied.

I remembered that rumble. The vibrations beneath my feet had been subdued but unmistakable. I also remembered what Elliot Graves had said after I hit the wall of a tunnel with my magic. He'd seemed genuinely nervous about the prospect of bringing the ceiling down.

Austin stared at me from across the way, and I could feel the coiled darkness within him. He was battle-hardened and ready to claim the victory we were owed.

My smile was back. My manic cackle. My departure from rational thoughts.

"Just go with it."

It was the first time Ivy House had spoken to me in these tunnels. She'd clearly followed our progress through the links.

"This is your destiny. Seize it." It was a battle cry if I'd ever heard one. She was egging me on.

"Go for it," I said to the basajaun, and Austin nodded. "No more playing by Elliot Graves's rules. If he won't come out to me, he will go down with the ship."

"Yes!" the basajaun roared, fired up. The shifters shed their clothes, including Austin, and changed, adding to the chorus. The gargoyles and Niamh turned into their other forms, joining in.

Edger yelled, "Whoopie!"

If vampires roared, he'd clearly forgotten how.

Magic pulsing through me, feeling the call of battle in my bones, I headed for the door. "Let's go."

"*Change,*" Ivy House said.

"*I might need to talk to—*"

"*You are a female gargoyle and the heir. You have given in to your beast. You are, even now, calling your cairn. Change, and show them that you are no mage. Own what you are: a creature with magic. An animal, if they so choose, that is more than they can ever be. Show them. Change.*"

I stripped off my muumuu and shifted like the others had. My claws tapped on the ground as I walked toward the foyer. My wings fluttered behind me. It felt wrong to be trapped in this mountain. Wrong to be away from the sky.

"Wake up the mountain," I said to the basajaun, which came out a garbled mess.

Nathanial repeated it, much better at speaking in his gargoyle form. Really, I had no idea how he'd understood me. Very handy, that guy.

The ground beneath my feet vibrated, and somewhere deep within the rock, I swore I heard a moan.

The path to the battlefield was the same, but we traveled it so much differently this time. Adrenaline coursed through us, one and all. Fire pumped in our middles. The excited shifters were breathing in hard pants, and the wings of the gargoyles fluttered like mine.

The sunlight cut across my face as we emerged outside, but I didn't raise my hands to it. I looked up at the magic keeping us enclosed, keeping us on the ground, and a strange pulse blasted out from my middle. Nathanial roared, followed by Jasper, Ulric, and Mr. Tom. The basajaun took up the call, followed by the shifters. The mountain groaned louder, its rumbling intensifying.

"Whoopie!"

I shook my head. There had to be a cooler thing for Edgar to shout.

As we descended the steps, I paused and pointed. The magical roof of the makeshift colosseum had been altered. It was a huge dome now. Plenty of room for even Hollace to fly.

Elliot Graves clearly wanted to meet with me in the flesh. There could be no other explanation. He'd allowed me all of my resources, and given the strength I had on my team, no one would be able to defeat me.

How could I ever have doubted?

"*You were a Jane,*" Ivy House said, and I wondered if I'd thought that at her instead of just to myself. "*You are now a gargoyle. You are donning your mantle and owning your place as Ivy House heir. Banging that alpha has done as much good for you as pining after you has done for him. You're welcome for forcing him into it at every turn.*"

When she started singing "Matchmaker, Matchmaker," I cut her off. Couldn't she stick with the battle cries and call it a day?

The setup was the same in the locker room, down to the attendant in the red coat. Her eyes widened when she saw me. They drifted down my body, snagging on my wings as I fluttered them.

"Hel-lo?" I ground out, trying to be as clear as possible.

She started. "What are you?"

"A female gargoyle," Cyra said. "Cool, right?"

"I thought you'd be as ugly as the men—" The woman cut herself off, as though realizing her words might cause offense, about-faced, and walked from the room. Apparently that meant we were supposed to follow her.

The sand in the arena was the same, but for some droplets of blood here and there. The blue sky above called to me, and as I followed the woman to our position, I looked up.

Forms of all different colors and sizes soared in the sky, gargoyles all, some just outside of the dome and some far beyond it. Thirty, at least, more than had flown from town to await our call.

Even as I stood and watched, in rapture, wanting to lift into the sky and soar with them, two more flew over from the closest peak, coming toward us and joining the others.

"*Joining your cairn. You will lead them, as Austin leads his pack,*" Ivy House said, and this time I didn't understand how she knew what was going on. I wondered if there were more secrets she had yet to share, and if I'd have to figure them out the hard way.

Rufus and his mages waited on the other side of the field, staring up at the circling gargoyles with their hands as makeshift visors against the sun. He'd clearly won the battle against Maverick, something I'd missed because of mating.

When we walked toward them, they lowered their gazes. Even from the distance, their body language gave away their shock. They'd probably expected us to shift after the match began, like we had last time.

A voice boomed out from higher in the viewing area. Elliot's.

"Greetings, all." He stood in front of a chair, tucked behind a rock barrier, here in the flesh, just like the other day. His warding spell offered him safety—supposedly—and so did the distraction in front of us.

I hadn't gone for him the other day because of the way the fight had ended. Because I hadn't wanted to risk messing with his spell, knowing he could take a shot at me while I tried. Because I hadn't wanted to make a fool of myself in front of the other mages if I failed.

But the time for self-doubt was over. I needed to take advantage of this bubble of amazingness. He might be able to get a shot off, but I'd spent the last month practicing how to defend my crew and work magic at the same time. I could handle it, knock that spell down, and go after him.

His tenure of rigging the game was over. His constant influence in my life was at an end.

It was time to say goodbye once and for all to Elliot Graves.

CHAPTER 24

"A SLIGHT CHANGE to our contest of champions today," Sebastian said, trying to ignore the butterflies in his stomach and the nervous sweats, made worse when Jessie flapped her wings in a gorgeous aura of color and rose into the sky. "It seems a freak accident has befallen our dear Chambers. His whole crew has been wiped out. We are not investigating because, frankly, I don't care. So, in light of his inability to protect himself from whatever may have gotten to him..." Sebastian let a beat of silence linger. It would make them curious. The rumors that it had been Jessie were already spreading. It would only help her, and her not claiming it would add to her mysterious power. "We have our final competition today. While I ask that you please don't kill each other, because networking after this competition might be in our—all of our—best interests, I will not penalize you for doing so. Accidents happen. Try not to—I repeat, *try not to* kill your opponents—but I will not penalize you if you do."

Rufus didn't seem to hear him, hands slack at his sides, staring up at Jessie...who was staring straight at Sebastian.

"You need to go." Nessa shoved at him as he took his seat. "You need to leave. She's not here for them. She's here for *you*."

"I know." He shrugged her off, watching the female gargoyle hover in the sky. His gaze drifted further upward, to the swirling gargoyles staring down on them. "It's exactly as Jala envisioned it."

"Which means you don't have long. Give up on this, Sebastian. I had no idea what you were getting yourself into. You were right, okay? The shifters, her—Oh holy hell."

The great thunderbird rose into the sky. Thunder pealed, shaking the ground beneath them.

He braced his hands on his knees. The thunder died away. The shaking grew more pronounced.

"Oh no," Nessa breathed, and it was obvious she recognized it too. The prophecy was upon them.

"We can't run," he said, holding on to his courage, remembering the days when he hadn't been afraid of much of anything. Clearly that was only because mages weren't scary. He'd been missing out on a large part of the magical world. If he lived through this, he'd remedy who held the power, and it wouldn't be the corrupt organizations that had their fists wrapped around it now. "We can't tell anyone to run. Those who survive will be our allies."

"But—"

"*We can't run.*" Sebastian took a steadying breath, Jessie still staring right at him.

The biggest gargoyle snapped his huge wings to the sides, the sound sending a shiver through Sebastian's body. The great beast rose into the sky, and it struck Sebastian that he hadn't ever been in a place to really appreciate their dexterity in flight. While the thunderbird was massive and powerful, these creatures turned on a dime and dove and attacked at a breakneck pace.

Jessie turned toward the opponent, who was just now starting to rapidly fire spells.

They were so outmatched that it wasn't funny.

Jessie didn't bother to fling the incoming spells away. Each member was equipped with a defensive spell, and the energy from the onslaught of spells soaked into the shield, seemingly spreading to her team, making them more powerful.

"That shouldn't be possible." Sebastian sat forward, the danger forgotten. "Is it the link she has? Is Ivy House acting as the go-between, transferring power?"

"The big alpha gets her power, right?" Nessa said.

Sebastian shook his head as Jessie lazily fired a spell down at Rufus. She was far away from him. If another mage had attempted a shot like that, it would have lost potency by the time it hit its target. But Rufus went flying through his band of young mages. If not for the distance, Jessie's spell would've probably ended his life. Maybe that was why she was staying so far away.

"The protector magic is different, and it doesn't look like he has it yet. Or knows he has it. He's not using it, at any rate."

The great polar bear rushed in and swiped at someone, but didn't connect the way he had in the last battle.

"He's taking it easy on them," Nessa said, riveted, just like Sebastian was.

Jessie dove, and all four male gargoyles quickly dove with her, covering her on all sides.

"She's not a great flyer," Nessa whispered, biting her nails.

Jessie sent out a thick ribbon of a spell. Before it got to Rufus, it fractured into spears and slammed into each and every mage on the other team.

"Oh!" Nessa jerked back in her seat. "Did you see that?" The mountain rumbled under them, shaking now, like an earthquake. "Oh God, Sebastian. Crap. Go!"

"Not yet," he said, heart in his throat, shaking all over. "It's going to be okay. It's going to work out."

Because it had to. Because it was either that or it would be the end of him.

Jessie's wings snapped open, stopping her up short.

The largest gargoyle did the same before grabbing her around the middle and pumping his great wings, jetting into the sky.

The phoenix swooped down in bird form, sending a streak of fire into the air. She didn't spray the enemy or catch their spells, like she'd done in the battle with Kinsella. She merely *dripped* on them.

It was plenty.

They screamed and ducked, diving away, clutching themselves and rolling on the ground.

The thunderbird swooped in next. A peal of thunder froze everyone before lightning zigzagged around him, catching people with its tiny filaments. But it was nothing compared to the defenses he'd shown in that initial fight with the gargoyles. He was holding back, too.

"What are they..." Sebastian looked up as the mountain lurched. The big gargoyle—Nathanial—was flying Jessie toward the top of the dome with powerful pumps of his wings. She was going to break through his spell.

"Sebastian." Nessa pointed.

The basajaun had hung back, which was not like him. He was kneeling now, his palms pressed to the ground.

Nessa reached out and grabbed Sebastian's hand.

"Here we go," Sebastian said quietly.

CHAPTER 25

I HELD BETWEEN my palms an intense ball of pure energy and power, pulled from everyone's defenses. Nathanial flew me up to the dome, knowing I needed speed and that my smaller wings couldn't do that job. The gargoyles above us circled the dome, waiting to join us, eager to fight—I felt it clouding the air.

I answered with a pulse of power, not quite sure how or what it meant, but it felt as natural as breathing. I was meant to lead. It had taken giving in totally to my beast in the mating to feel it. To know it.

I liked it.

Somewhere below, I heard the basajaun roar. The rumbling of the mountain grew louder, more violent. A deep, subatomic groan spoke of large, probably horrible things about to happen.

I needed to make sure my people didn't get caught up in that. Thankfully, I'd summoned enough gargoyles that we could transport all of our non-fliers to safety, much as the shifters might hate it.

When I neared the magical dome, I closed my eyes, drawing magic from my very core. Light flared against my eyelids, and I felt the heat between my palms as I hurled the ball with all my strength. A pulse of raw power rocketed out from the point of impact.

I felt the magical dome bend, stretch...and then shatter. Magic released in a heady wave.

Sky clear, gargoyles dove in around us, circling, waiting for what came next. Waiting for me to lead.

I pushed away from Nathanial, and he let me go immediately. I put out my hands to clear the gargoyles in my way and dove down to join the rest of the team. Isabelle and Kace circled the last two standing mages, flinging spells that only added to the strength of our defenses. They had courage but not much power, which was more than I could say for Rufus, who was hightailing it across the field toward the locker rooms, followed by five of his people, Edgar whooping and hollering behind them.

A few more mages lay on the ground, either curled up and hoping for this all to go away or (hopefully) playing dead. My team had showed their merit, and the mages had shown that they didn't usually do a lot of actual battling. My early experiences in the magical world had clearly been unique. They gave me an advantage. Regardless, the fight with Rufus was over.

The fight with Elliot had just begun.

Something told me that Elliot wouldn't roll over and play dead quite so easily as the others. He had a list of faces on his wall. He was an outlaw. You didn't get that status by playing nice.

The chairs in the small stands rocked. People jumped to their feet, hands out, looking at the ground, looking around, probably wondering if it was an earthquake. Elliot had already stood, hands out for balance, staring at me. I couldn't read his expression, but he knew it was *on*. He had to.

He'd wanted to test me, to see what I was really made of, and he was about to find out.

I flapped my wings as hard as I could, pushing forward with as much speed as I could muster. The ground gave a mighty heave and the basajaun roared. The standing mages toppled over. The shifters braced or stumbled. Everyone in the stands was thrown onto their sides or forward. Elliot somehow remained standing, still staring at me, seemingly unmoved by the scene around him.

Dirt and rock slid down from the peak in front of me. A dust plume rose into the sky just beyond the stands, and beyond that the ground caved in, crushing the network of tunnels within it. I realized with horror that we'd left all our stuff in our rooms. Hopefully the basajaun had worked out some kind of compromise with the mountain.

The people in the stands staggered, running toward us to escape the collapsing mountain behind them. I swooped down toward Elliot, hands held out in front of me to deliver the first spell, but he disappeared.

I kept going, not believing my eyes, cursing myself for not bringing a revealing spell. Nearly there, I sent a jet of magic at the spot he'd inhabited, then fired off more magic all around it, trying to hit anything still there. The mountain heaved. More areas caved in, probably the second series of tunnels the basajaun had mentioned. Anyone in them was lost to the rubble and rock, a thought that might have made me feel guiltier if an anguished roar hadn't risen behind me. A moment later, Austin went offline. Unconscious, not dead.

Heart in my throat, I snapped my wings taut and angled, wrapping myself in a tight defense spell so I could safely look back.

Bile rose. Austin was gone.

Elliot forgotten, everything beyond Austin forgotten, I banked fast and dove for Broken Sue, who was slapping at the ground and roaring. As soon as I landed, I changed into my human form so I could talk, not worried about nudity for once.

"What happened?" I demanded amid the deep

rumble of the mountain's shifting. It was quieting now, settling.

Austin's distance grew. He was being carried away, not toward the collapsed tunnels but in the other direction, still unconscious. I sent a thread of healing in case it had been blunt-force trauma of some kind.

"*What happened?*" I yelled, fear climbing into my throat. Black rage such as I had never known rose within me, seething, pressing for release.

"Elliot appeared right next to him," Cyra said, newly changed into her human form and running over. "I saw it. He appeared right next to the alpha, the alpha collapsed, and they both disappeared."

I swore, remembering when Elliot had made that delivery truck disappear. I still had no idea how he'd done it.

The Ivy House link between Austin and me went dead. My gut churned as I tried, and failed, to bring it back online. Fear ate at me.

But I knew he was still alive, because we had another link, a deeper one, that was alive and well. Our mating bond, newly forged and continually strengthening. His heart pulsed with mine in my chest, strong and sure.

"Shifters, change," I ordered, a pulse of magic pulling the gargoyles to the ground. I had no idea how I was doing all of this, but I'd figure it out later, once Austin was safe. "Change into your human form. The gargoyles will carry you with us."

Niamh landed beside me in her nightmare alicorn form, her crystalline horn bloodied and her golden hoofs stamping at the ground. Edgar, returned from chasing the mages, jumped onto her back.

Isabelle, the first to change, turned to Jasper as he touched down. "Give me a lift?"

He hopped, his wings fluttering, and she jogged over. He scooped her up in a princess hold and swiftly rose into the sky.

Kace changed and then shook his head at Mr. Tom, who'd stepped forward. "I'd prefer someone I don't know. This is going to be awkward."

"Only if you let it," Cyra replied.

"Oh, I intend to let it," Kace muttered as a large male I didn't know grabbed him by the chest and pushed into the sky. "Holy sh—"

Broken Sue, face a mask of rage, stalked up to me, his body all scars and muscle, his beast owning his powerful movements. "Do not let him kill your mate, Jessie Ironheart. It is a soul-crushing pain that I wouldn't wish on anyone. Unlike me, you have the power to save your mate. *Save him.*"

I nodded, unable to speak, overwhelmed by both his

pain and mine. He walked to the nearest gargoyle, a big, scarred creature that kind of matched him, and held out an arm. The male swooped him up like a bride, neither of the guys caring or reacting, and pumped his wings. They shot up into the sky.

Cyra joined them, and Hollace and the other flyers were already up there. I prepared to change again, but Nathanial landed next to me.

"Yeah. Good call." I jogged to him, turned, and stuck out my arms like a child. "I'd just slow everyone down."

"It does nnnot lo-ok bad on you, I-ron-heart." He grabbed me and shot skyward, faster than any of the others. "You we-re not ma-dde for aer-eeal warfare. You pro-tect with ma-gic."

"Let's hope so." I pointed in the direction Austin was still traveling, moving fast. Elliot had to be flying somehow. There was no other way he could be moving so fast, not without a road.

Nathanial pumped his wings and carried us forward, faster than the others, and everyone else spread out behind us. The wind whipped at my face, and I realized flight was more comfortable in my gargoyle form. Too late now. I'd change once we landed.

"There," I shouted over the rushing wind, my eyes watering, Austin's heart beating true and mine on the verge of breaking. I let the black rage in my chest seethe and boil, the aggression blotting out some of my fear. I would get him back. He'd saved me yesterday. It was my turn.

And I would make Elliot Graves regret the day he'd shown up in my life.

Austin stopped moving, and I could feel he was being lowered. We were gaining on him fast, gargoyles blotting out the sky as they carried my fighting unit over a smaller peak and beyond. I monitored Austin's movements and worked at the Ivy House link, trying to get it back online.

"*Why won't it respond?*" I asked Ivy House.

"*Magic, somehow. A vulnerability?*"

I could feel the uncertainty in her tone.

It didn't matter. Even if Elliot had severed it for good, it wouldn't matter. We had our mating link, deeper than magic.

Closer now, nearly there, I spotted a flat spot on a big outcropping of a mountain, open to the sky. A helicopter waited, its rotors still spinning. The maw of an open cave could be seen beyond it.

"How in the hell?" I murmured.

There were too many questions to process—how had Elliot managed to get Austin into that bird? How had he silenced the chopper? How powerful was this guy?

The most important of all—was he still toying with me?

I gestured for Nathanial to descend, and he squeezed me to his chest and dove at a stomach-losing pace. On the side area beside the helicopter, he snapped out his wings, slamming on the brakes, and gently lowered to a stop. Despite the fact that we'd practiced these maneuvers—a lot—my stomach rolled. I wasn't sure if I would ever get used to that.

Austin's progress had stopped, inside yet another mountain. Elliot was cutting off my aerial artillery.

Hollace dropped the basajaun before rising higher into the air and changing form. With people already gathered on the small platform beside the chopper, he was too big to land.

A gargoyle swooped toward him before I could point and shout, grabbing him up and depositing him next to us.

"What do you want me to do, Jessie Ironheart?" the basajaun asked as he caught up.

"What can you do? Can you feel his positioning within the mountain or anything?"

"When I get inside, I should have a better idea. It's hard to make a first acquaintance on the surface."

"Then let's get inside." I turned back to everyone,

the platform filled up and gargoyles still in the sky. "Keep on your guard. We don't know what we're walking into."

I stayed in my human form, checked to make sure the helicopter was empty, and then jogged to the large opening in the side of the rock face. The air changed as soon as I passed through, much colder than it should've been. I pulled magical warmth over myself as my eyes adjusted to the darker interior.

The tunnel had concrete sides and was similar in size to the one leading to our rooms. Service lights were on one side, giving off enough of a glow for me to see a few steps in front of me but not enough to illuminate the way ahead. I suspected that was by design.

The basajaun didn't follow, and I glanced back to see what was keeping him.

A rockface greeted me. Rough and dark, it gave zero indication that it had ever been anything else.

I backtracked and put my hand against it. It felt exactly as it looked.

Scowling, I pulled at my magic—

"That's not going to work."

I jumped and spun, pulling my defenses tightly around me, recognizing Elliot's smug voice and looking for the source. A momentary bout of vertigo dizzied me. The tunnel from a moment ago had changed. Smaller but just as dim, this one had electric-blue and butter-yellow flowers crawling up the sides. As I watched, they moved softly, swaying in a magical breeze.

I blinked and rubbed at my eyes, holding on to that well of black rage.

Instead of asking where I was, or what was going on, as I desperately wanted to, I took the situation in stride, walking forward with clear purpose. Austin's presence pulsed straight ahead, a hundred yards or so.

"Do you want to cover up?"

A little table appeared on my right. A garment lay folded on the flat surface.

Right now, I didn't care about my nudity. Nor did I care about the likelihood that I was trapped down here with a manipulative mage and no backup. I only cared about Austin's safety.

Without comment, I continued walking onward, working closer to Austin.

"Are you at all nervous?" the floating voice asked.

No comment. I was done playing his games.

"Do you think your power is greater than mine?" he asked. "It was your team that won those battles—all of them. I should know, I've been watching. But now you are alone."

I was never alone. I had Austin in my heart, and my links to the Ivy House crew remained fully functional.

They were all frustrated and angry and trying to find a way in. The basajaun was calm, probably because he was trying to make nice with the mountain, however that worked. They might not be physically present, but they were still with me. They wouldn't give up on me.

Rage burning bright, determination fueling me, I strode on, getting closer. The tunnel was long and unchanging, the lights spaced a consistent five feet apart.

"So much for pleasantries," the voice said. An opening glowed up ahead, bright lemon light spilling into the shadowy passage. "Let's get to business, shall we?"

The slice of light was shaped like a half-moon on top and straight at the bottom. I couldn't tell if it was a doorway or a bend leading to another tunnel with much better lighting.

"I want a trade," Elliot said. "You for him."

No. There would be no trade. There would be a dead mage and a safe shifter.

The opening grew in size as I neared it. Above, the basajaun stayed stationary while the others spread out farther, searching. If they found an opening, it would still be a chore to get through the tunnels without a map, unless they were all as straightforward as this one. My hope for reinforcements probably rested on the basajaun making friends with an inanimate object.

"Say yes, and I will put him outside with the rest of your crew. You'll feel him out there. You'll know he's safe. You know I don't have the forces to take them on. I just want to talk to you, Jacinta. I want to have a conversation with you. You'll be perfectly safe too."

I squinted when I reached the opening and slunk to the side, peering in. The space opened up into a large chamber with a sparkling chandelier hanging down over a dark, polished wood floor. Couches and chairs lined the sides, not unlike the setup of our common room, only it was much bigger, with more gaming tables and a few arcade games.

"I have something you need, Jessie," Elliot said, and his voice stopped echoing, now coming directly from the source. "I have training that will be very valuable to you. I've spent these long years learning more about magic than anyone would ever dream of knowing, waiting for you to be ready."

Then I saw him. At the side of the room, a metal cage hung from a chain. Austin lay inside in his human form, sprawled out. His chest rose and fell, but his breathing was too shallow for comfort.

My world tilted. My beast came roaring out, consuming me.

My wings snapped out, and then I was running into the large room. I sensed him before I saw him, off to the side, standing in front of a stone dais.

"I only want to talk!" He held out his hands, but I was already opening fire.

The magic I shot at him, one jolt after another, was simple but full of power.

He deflected the first two shots and danced to the side, the third slicing into his shield. He swore and then fired a shot back at me. It hit my shield but didn't soak into it as it should've. As everyone else's did. This one stuck and then festered, starting to unravel my defenses.

I had to kill him before he could get my magical shield off me. I had to beat him with power before he crushed me with experience.

I kept at him. All of my practice had prepared me for this moment. All of those long hours I'd spent battling my team had given me the ability to fight for my freedom.

A blistering spell crunched into his defensive shield, but he quickly erected another. I tore that one away too, slicing through his shoulder with my follow-up spell. He jogged to the side, making me turn. He fired back. My defensive spell started to smoke. I dropped more power into it and fired another spell at him, this one complex and intricate, taken from the second of Ivy House's training books.

"Damn it, you've gotten so much better," he ground

out, still moving, hitting me with spells intent on breaking through my defense. Spells that *were* breaking through my defenses. He almost had me. "You learn magic so damn fast. You're a natural, Jessie. I wish I could take more credit. Also, I wish I was powerful enough to combat these spells."

Doubling down, summoning my power, I rocked him with a blunt-force spell. It slammed into him and knocked him back against the wall. I was on him in a moment, tearing at him with claws and slicing at his shield with magic.

"Think it through," he said, his voice shaking, the smug arrogance gone. "Think it through."

He sounded exactly like Sebastian when we'd taken on the phoenix. His tone, cadence, timbre.

I pummeled him with another spell, cracking through his defenses and leaving him wide open. His shoulders dropped and his face fell. He was beaten and he knew it.

"We didn't have much time together," he said, "but I'm proud of what we accomplished. I would've liked to be your mentor and your friend, please know that," he whispered. The tension fled from him and then he closed his eyes, finding peace and ready to die.

CHAPTER 26

MY WORLD CAME to a grinding halt.

The tone...the cadence...the words...

I stood over him, poised to kill. Ready with the spell.

The tone...

The cadence...

The words...

I straightened, confused. Elliot Graves lay prone at my feet, hands down, eyes closed, face peaceful. He would accept his fate.

I staggered backward a few paces, turning back into my human form, memories flitting through my mind. Pairing up Sebastian's voice with what I'd just heard. Considering the fact that both he and Elliot shared an obvious (and rare) appreciation for shifters. Thinking through how he'd set up this whole thing to make me stand out.

"But you killed him," I said softly, my mind whirling, my gut saying one thing, and my logic saying another. "You killed Sebastian."

His right lid peeled open to reveal a pale blue eye, followed by his left. He didn't move any other part of his body. "I killed Kinsella because you can't be in bad standing with the Mages' Guild. Not yet. I put the glamor you know as Sebastian over Kinsella's face. Sebastian isn't dead. I am the mage you knew. Elliot Graves is my stage name."

I shook my head. "Fat chance. If that's the case, why did you want to trade me for Austin?"

"I needed to get you down here so we could talk. But when that big shifter wakes up, it won't take him long to get out of that cage, and I do *not* want to be on the other side of his wrath."

I stared down at him, horribly conflicted, knowing this was a trick. Elliot Graves was great at manipulation.

But now that the idea was in my mind, it blossomed. Elliot and Sebastian, Sebastian and Elliot. Several of his tics were the same.

"If you're Sebastian, how did you act around the shifters? How did you stand?"

He huffed out a laugh and closed his eyes. "You're so freaking clever, Jacinta. If I had cracked someone's mind open for their secrets, there's no way I would have thought to ask that question." A smile drifted up his face, a little crooked, and my heart beat faster. "How did I stand? I hunched, unable to help it at first because I kept wondering what I would do if one of them attacked me, delighted by my fear, and then on purpose to make sure no one thought I was challenging them." He licked his lips and opened his eyes again. "I have a lot to tell you, Jacinta. I have a lot to explain."

"Elliot Graves has a lot to explain."

"Yes. But so does Sebastian. Two halves of the same coin. I meant what I said last month. I will never hurt you, Jessie. I want to be your instructor. You need one. I would be a great one. We worked insanely well together."

"You'd never hurt me? You just tried to kill me!"

"I challenged you, and that was ordained. I knew I wouldn't hurt you. I just didn't know if our...contest, if you will...would result in my death, or a nice, long chat. I still don't know."

"Where did you set up your lab as Sebastian?"

"My table and camping stove, you mean? Do you still have those? I'd like them back if you do. That stove had a really good control of the flame. I've gotten the same brand, but it doesn't work as well. Or maybe it's that crystal room." He hesitated. "I'd like to work in there again. Within Ivy House. I have so many ideas for some of those spells."

"I don't..." I took another step back. I didn't know what to say. What to do. I freaking believed him! It wasn't his words so much, either. It was the way he was talking. The down-to-earth, chill vibe. The unassuming look in his eyes—when they were open.

But all of that was so different from the Elliot Graves I'd met in this place. The smug, arrogant guy who'd been dogging my steps.

"Please, Jessie, let me explain," he said. "Let me tell you my history. You can lock me in that cage if you want. For God's sake, let your mate out. I approve, by the way. I thought he would be perfect for you even before you mated. He's perfect for an heir. The only reason I brought him here like this was so I could get the chance to talk to you without ending up like Chambers. You can let him out and put me in. Whatever will give me some time."

He sat up, his hands clasped in his lap. Eyes wary, he stood, moving just as slowly. "I'll just go let him out, okay? Will that work?"

"Why don't you just wake him up? You can sit in the chair, and he can sit beside you…"

"I'd rather not. I think I'd be safer in a cage."

I let out my breath. It was the kind of thing Sebastian would have said.

"Open it, wake him up, and sit in the chair." I pointed at one in the back corner.

"You drive a hard bargain."

With a snap of his fingers, the cage sprang open. Another wave of his hands and Austin jolted to consciousness, his eyes blinking open, rage immediately surging through him. Elliot practically sprinted to the corner and quickly sat.

"Please don't let him kill me," he said. There was no disgust or condemnation in his tone—just the fear of someone who deeply respected what shifters could do.

Austin practically jumped out of the cage and stalked toward me, his fingers wrapping around my upper arm. Assured I was okay, he turned and stared Elliot down.

"I heard everything that was said just now," Austin said. "He spoke to me on the way here, too. I couldn't answer, but I heard."

"Yes. It's quite a simple spell, really," Elliot replied. "You just need the power to pull it off. Listen, Jessie, I built in some assurances. I let Edgar have some of my blood—I assume vampires can identify people by blood? It never even occurred to me to ask." He shook his head. "Now I feel dumb. Hopefully that's an assurance. I made a certain type of magical flowers for the basajaun using the potion I made for Edgar. I have them growing just..." He pointed to a bookshelf at the far side of the room. It was probably one of those secret doors. "I also told Ivy House everything. You can ask her when you get back. She knew who I was the whole time. She tends to think like I do—we don't always take the nicest approach, but we try to do what's right. You can also ask your shifter there. I should smell the same. I knew he'd identify me right away if I was ever in his vicinity, so I made sure I wasn't until now. Also…I knew you'd try to kill me, so it was best for me to appear to you as that really uncomfortable hologram."

I turned and looked at Austin while sending a message to Ivy House. "*Did you—*"

"*Yep,*" she answered before I could finish. She could definitely hear my conversations outside of Ivy House somehow. When I wasn't busy being blindsided, I'd get to the bottom of that.

"*You knew who he was, and you didn't say anything?*" I asked, outraged.

"Different cologne, but…" Austin wrapped his arm around my hip, his touch grounding. "I think he's telling the truth, Jess."

"*You need to be pushed,*" Ivy House told me. "*You need to be prodded. I swear, you are the most timid wild child I've ever met. It's like you lock all your good qualities up inside, and it takes a battle or taunting to bring them roaring out. He helped me even before I knew who he was. He helped you. Listen to him. If, when he's done, you don't like what you've heard, kill him. It's pretty simple. You really shouldn't hold grudges in the magical world. Things change too fast for that."*

I walked slowly to the little chair opposite Elliot and pulled it back a little farther. Austin pulled up another and we sat.

"So." Elliot ran his hand down his face. "How about I start at the beginning?"

"Probably wise."

"I had a twin sister. Both of us had great magical talent, but hers was as a *Seer*. It was…a burden to her. She had visions all the time. She knew what was going to happen tomorrow, or five years from now, or after her death. Good and bad things. Horrible things, sometimes. She knew our parents would die in a car accident. She knew our uncle would be physically abusive. Of course, we tried to prevent those things from coming to pass, to change the stars, but the end result was always the same. She finally realized that when she saw a vision, it represented the path of least resistance to an end result that would happen no matter what. It was best just to go with it.

"When we were in our late teens, the visions started coming faster and becoming more vivid. They were so encompassing that she started to lose track of reality. She wouldn't know the difference between a vision, a waking dream, or something happening in the present.

Her mind started to slip, unable to deal with it. Finally, she had a series of visions about *you*. How you came to accept the Ivy House magic. How you blossomed into the mage you are today. She guided me through the role I was to play in your rise to power, including the things I would need to construct, like the tunnels your basajaun destroyed—don't worry, my people moved in the second you left your quarters so as to move your things—and the meadow flowers on the tunnel walls. I knew what the Ivy House crystals looked like before I'd ever set foot in that room. She also told me spells I would need to track down and figure out. Books I could find about Ivy House. Things like that. She told me my path, and begged I follow it, even though it would require a grave sacrifice."

"And what sacrifice was that?" I asked.

"When I was forty, I walked away from an empire and became a hermit inside of a mountain. Or I might have ushered in my own death. That's up to you."

I squinted at his face.

He nodded. "I have an amazing potion for youthfulness." He gave me a small smile but didn't ask if I wanted the recipe, which I was thankful for. "I sent a pretty useless mage and his right-hand man to apprehend you when you first got to O'Briens. Remember him?"

Yes, I remembered him. A man in a poncy cape had tried to grab me, but Austin, Niamh, Mr. Tom, and Edgar had shown up and saved the day.

"You needed a push," he said, as though reading my mind. "I was that push. Not just with the caped fool, of course. I sent people into Ivy House after you. I had them loiter on the property. You fulfilled your destiny and took the magic. You were always going to. I just helped you along." He shrugged. "Next I put out a bid for someone to kidnap you and put you in that cave. I offered just enough to bring in some decent people. Some were cleverer than others, I must admit." He paused for a moment. "I never intended to retrieve you. You were going to be in that cave as long as you needed to be in order to escape. That was the push. You needed to figure out how to fly. Turned out, it didn't take you any time at all. That's when I knew Ivy House had chosen well."

He smiled again, his eyes crinkling at the corners.

"No," I said, remembering the pain I'd gone through, the pain *Austin* had gone through, trying to get out of that blasted cave.

"Moving along." His lips tightened. "The issue with the competing forces—the one that came at you from the front of the house? Those sort of…barbarian people? What was up with them? I only got a glimpse as they traveled to your town, but hello, cosplay, am I right?" He rubbed his face. "They were ridiculous. That wasn't in the cards, actually. I got wind of them heading out there to check you out, wanting to know your relationship to me. It was bound to happen. I had to scramble a little, but I figured it was time to get the basajaun active, and for you to start working on some of Ivy House's key vulnerabilities. Also, you know, to meet an adversary who would give you a pause." He rubbed his chin. "It took you a while to find that deer. That guy doesn't even like flowers. Didn't you stop to wonder why a man was eating flowers? Just because he changes into a deer, doesn't mean he eats like a deer."

Austin and I both tensed, and I exchanged a glance with him. Yes, we should've realized that. We hadn't. Too much had been going on.

"What do you mean, get the basajaun active?" I said, adrenaline going through me. I knew Elliot had always been a step ahead, but not just how big that step really was.

"The basajaun was always meant to be part of your journey. Fun fact, my dear friend Burke, who has been sniffing around the tunnels for the past few days, had finally found the entrance to my residence. I'm not quite sure what he planned to do there. Hide under my bed and try to kill me in my sleep? Look for incriminating evidence? Check my browser history? We'll never know. Unless he has hidden powers we don't know about, he got squished in the fallout from the basajaun's cave-in. I'm not sure if I should add him to my wall, though. Technically, he wasn't my kill... Ah, sure, I might as well, as Niamh would say."

"How did you...get him active? Did you tell him to help me in the cave?"

"Good Lord, no! That was a shock. But then, if he was destined to be part of your journey, it makes sense he'd feel an immediate rapport with you. No, I simply gave him a reason to join your fight. I told my man and his merry band of helpers to head over the basajaun's mountain. The vision said it would anger him." He spread his hands. "I wasn't sure how at first, but now I realize it takes very little to anger him. So..."

"You sent shifters to die," Austin said with a growl.

Elliot held up a finger. "No. I sent the deer shifter to keep an eye on you, and then to get your attention when those barbarians were sniffing around. That fool Marcos collected a bunch of passive shifters and drove them to you for a distraction. Good riddance, huh? I hoped you'd take him off my hands. I won't ask where he's buried."

"You're telling me that you had no hand in that?" I asked.

"I sent the mage with the directive to kidnap you using the potions that make Ivy House vulnerable. The rest was his creation. I don't tend to micromanage. In that situation, I wish I had."

"What if he'd kidnapped me?"

"Your alpha probably would've tracked him down and killed him horribly. Or the basajaun would've. If all else failed, I would've…figured something out along the way. I wasn't too worried, though. You always rise to the occasion."

"Kinsella?"

"Another fool. He was not my design, and it was a real treat to tear off my illusion and give him the justice he'd eluded for so long. What a wanker."

"That wasn't part of the vision?"

"No. Not directly. But I knew I needed to extract myself from the situation and figure out a way to lure you here. He provided…" Elliot chuckled and shook his head. "That whole thing was perfect. Talk about fate. You handled it all beautifully, and now here you are. Owning your gargoyle, falling in love, contemplating killing a double-crossing scoundrel. I deserve it, I get that. I wasn't fully honest with you at Ivy House. Shifters *do* fascinate me, and they made me feel fear for the first time since my sister died. There was something enlivening about it…I was truthful about that. But the real reason I stayed there was you. To train you. To fulfill the vision. That's not something I could say."

"Were you even summoned?"

"Yes, but I knew I would be. It was part of the vision. Listen, Jessie, here's what it comes down to. So often powerful people will hide evil deeds behind empty promises. I decided early on that I'd wear what I am on my sleeve. I'm weird, I do things oddly, I don't play into the mage hype, and I'm rotten in plenty of ways. The thing with my sister, with my upbringing, messed me up quite a bit. But I promised myself that I wouldn't hide what I was behind a crooked smile." He paused. "Yes, I recognize the irony. I know that when I accidentally smile in that illusion mask, it comes out crooked. You have to be really careful not to make any facial expressions in that thing or the mask slips. That or you look weird." He waved his hand. "But you know I mean figuratively crooked."

"What's your point?" I said, trying to wrap my brain around all this and decide if he was lying, or if he was telling the truth and I was still mad as hell anyway.

"I also decided that if I was ever fortunate enough to get to work with you, I'd be the bad guy so you wouldn't have to make the hard decisions. To take out mages like Kinsella. Or to organize extravagant meetings with people neither of us have any intention of working with so they can see your power, prestige, and potential. I decided that I would set the stage so that you may shine."

"Why?" I asked. "Why would you forgo the audience? You seem to love holding court."

He frowned at me. "I didn't say I would forgo an audience. I said I'd be the bad guy. It's much more fun."

CHAPTER 27

I SAT AND stared at Elliot, mulling over what he'd said. So much of it had struck a chord. The more I thought about it, the less I doubted him. His story checked out, as crazy as that might be.

But it was hard to let go of the hate. It was hard not to blame him for all the hell I'd been through.

"What do you think?" I asked Austin, turning my head a little.

He shook his head. "This isn't something I can direct you on. Either you trust him or you don't. I'll back you whatever you choose."

"Including sitting on my chairs without a towel under your naked butts," Elliot said softly.

I quirked an eyebrow at him.

He shrugged and looked away. "Common courtesy."

This wasn't the time to laugh, but I wanted to.

"You're positive he smells like Sebastian?" I asked Austin.

"Yes. But given his powers as a mage, it's probably wise to get a second opinion."

"*He's Sebastian. Here's your second opinion,*" Ivy House said.

"*I'm not so inclined to trust you. Or talk to you right now.*"

"*I sided with Austin when you two had your spat. I was right then, and I'm right now. I look forward to eventually telling you* I told you so."

"By all means." Elliot waved his hand. "Let them through."

I stared hard at him.

"You didn't think I'd be totally alone here, did you?" He frowned at me. "You trust too much, Jessie Ironheart. Your shifter does, too. Never trust a mage. *Never.*"

"And yet you are sitting here, asking me to trust you…"

"Okay, well, yes, I can see where that would be confusing." He rubbed his chin. "I'm not a typical mage, though. Also, I've taken you on as an apprentice. In mage-land, that means that I will only help you achieve, because your successes will reflect favorably on me."

"Until the student outstrips the teacher and the teacher gets jealous and tries to kill the student."

"You've watched too many movies." He crossed his

ankle over his knee. "In case you are wondering, my longtime friend and second-in-command has been watching us. She is taking down the spells and letting your people in as we speak. She could have come in and tried to prevent you from killing me. She didn't. We've always known my death was a possibility, and she has helped me orchestrate all of this. That should tell you how serious we are about what we've been doing. What we've done."

"So let's say…" I felt my people rush forward. Elliot hadn't been lying—someone else had taken down the spell and let them in. "Let's say I forgive you for making my life hell. Then what?"

"I'll ask for the privilege of training you."

"Where? Here?"

"Of course not." He held out his hands. "There is no here. Your basajaun destroyed it. I have very little left other than a couple of guest rooms and this common area."

"I highly doubt that."

He grinned. "Okay, fair enough. I do have a great many other places I can go in the world. But none of them are home. I haven't had a real home since I stepped back from the magical world and started preparing for you. We could train wherever you prefer, although I assume that would be on Ivy House soil, where you are best protected."

"Not so sure about that anymore," I muttered.

"You rose in the magical world after your sister died?" Austin asked.

"Yes," Elliot answered.

"Why? Why not just start preparing then? Why climb to the top, with all the sweat and tears that must've taken, only to step down?"

"Climbing to the top *was* preparing," Elliot responded. "I established myself as a key power. I created a network. Everyone knew my name. *You* knew my name, which made it easier for me to tamper in your lives. To get people to come to this meetup. It's easy for me to get an audience with whoever I want. Stepping back doesn't mean disappearing when you've reigned as mob king. Your return will always be feared. As it should be. Also…I like holding court, as Jessie said."

"If you moved to our town and started training me, wouldn't the people who've been watching you show up and try to kill you?" I asked, monitoring my people above me. They hadn't been magically transported part of the way like I had been, which meant it would take them longer to reach us.

"Yes. And now you, too. Beating Kinsella put you on the map in a big way. Showing your might here has officially made you a talking point. You are still an enigma, I think, but a powerful one. Welcome to the big leagues."

"So you've painted a target on my back."

"No. I've scrolled a marquee above your head that says, 'Do not tread lightly.' Without that marquee, what you're about to do next would've put a target on your back, and your life would've been a lot harder, trust me. A lot more dangerous."

"What do you mean, what I'm about to do next?"

"First things first. Let's make sure you trust who I am." Elliot uncrossed his leg. "And if you want to put on some sweats, that would be fine too. I stole some of those purple ones Mr. Tom orders. They are just…" He motioned at a table across the way, and it was the first time I noticed the neatly folded articles of clothing on it. "Whatever makes you comfortable. I will point out that *I* am not comfortable, because your big shifter keeps…animating certain parts of his anatomy, and it is incredibly distracting. I'm not used to casual nudity, and I am less used to casual nudity when it's a man who keeps getting aroused for no reason that I can discern."

"It's the mating," Austin replied. "I'm drawn to how she is handling you."

"Oh, great. That's lovely." Elliot looked away. "Not at all terrifying. God, this is awkward."

My people came through the door, Niamh first with

a surly expression, followed by Mr. Tom. At the back was Broken Sue with his arm out and looped around his hip, straining as though he were carrying something like a bag of sand.

Elliot noticed, and his lips tweaked up into a smile. "I told you, Nessa! Didn't I tell you that simply being invisible wouldn't work with these shifters? Now look, Broken Sue has caught you."

"It isn't the nicest of holds," came a disembodied female voice, "but the muscle I am squished up against isn't unpleasant. He has a lovely, earthy smell. I could definitely be in worse places."

"Here, what's goin' on, Jessie?" Niamh demanded, walking over to us. Broken Sue didn't drop his cargo. "Why isn't he dead?"

"He claims he's Sebastian," I answered, turning and finding Edgar, already drifting toward one of the corners. "Edgar, I need you."

"Oh, how nice. I love to be needed." He loped toward me.

"I'll never get used to how that vampire runs," Elliot muttered.

"Elliot says that you bit Sebastian. Can you tell a person by the taste of their blood?" I asked.

"Yes, of course. Mostly."

I lifted my eyebrows, losing confidence. "Okay, well,

can you bite him, then?"

Kace walked forward from the flank of my crew. "Alpha, I smelled Sebastian when he was in town. Should I verify?"

"How do we know this isn't mind control?" Niamh asked. "Sebastian told me that he could control minds if he wanted."

"I said I could control moods, not minds," Elliot said. "I cannot implant ideas into people's minds. If my scent didn't match, or my blood, I could make you feel okay with that, but I couldn't erase your knowledge of the discrepancy."

"All due respect, miss," Mr. Tom said as the basajaun found the nearest wall and put his hand on it. "How do we know he isn't lying?"

"Ivy House says he is Sebastian as well," I replied.

"Yes, miss, and that *is* interesting, but she is also old and bored and cunning, and she'll slit a proverbial throat to help you get ahead. I do love that house, but she is rooting for Austin Steele, and I must say one final time that a gargoyle would be just a bit more fitting, don't you think?"

"He's never going to let that go," Austin murmured, and he didn't seem mad. But then, how could you be with Mr. Tom? There simply was no point.

"The house's goal is to keep Jessie alive," Niamh

said. "What's that ye say, Jessie? Ivy House approves of Sebastian?"

"I don't know that she—"

"*I approve of him,*" Ivy House cut in.

I gritted my teeth. "Turns out she can hear my conversations no matter how far I am from Ivy House, so that's something you might not have known, and also, yes, she apparently does."

"Well, then." Niamh looked around the room. "That's fine. Do ye have any whiskey? I could do with a pint. Or maybe a bottle. This situation has made bags of the day, so it has."

"So, shall I…" Edgar stopped just beside and a little behind Elliot, hands at his sides, looking down at the mage's neck.

Elliot breathed deeply, his gaze rooted to mine, his expression saying he was not comfortable with Edgar standing there. Which was understandable, really.

"Yes." I motioned Edgar on.

"I also have those flowers for the basajaun, if he can taste the difference," Elliot said, his voice strained. He held up his hand. "Oh, wait, this is going to put me out."

Edgar's bite caused his victims to temporarily lose consciousness.

"That's okay. I need time to think anyway." I nodded at Edgar, and he moved with amazing speed, clamping down on Elliot's neck.

Elliot gave a shriek, and then he slouched, his limbs relaxing. Edgar gulped twice before straightening up.

"Ah, yes." He pulled on Elliot's sleeve and then bent again to dab his mouth. "I remember that taste. Very spicy. Magic will do that. I've feasted on many mages. He is the spiciest of them all. He gave me terrible heartburn. Does anyone have any Tums?"

I blew out a breath, remembering all of the time I'd spent with Sebastian, remembering his patience, his easy communication, his eagerness to help.

"Elliot Graves knows an awful lot about shifters," I finally said, standing up.

"I was thinking the same thing." Austin joined me. "What will you do?"

"I don't know. Let's go home. We'll talk about it on the way, since it's pretty clear this affects you and your pack, too."

"I have your stuff," came the disembodied voice from earlier. "We have a plane standing by for you. Also, there is something you should know regardless of the decision you make. I can either tell you while hanging from a very strong arm that doesn't seem to feel my weight, or you can have Broken Sue put me down so I can take a revealing potion first."

This situation straddled Austin's domain and mine, but I didn't have to work through the nuances of who should do what—the details were crystal-clear to me, as if we'd been doing this forever. Broken Sue was his pack, so Austin needed to make the command, but the woman—Nessa—was appealing to me about Elliot, which made it my decision. Perhaps mating had opened up these new insights, or maybe they'd unfurled for me because I'd finally unleashed my gargoyle. Whatever the case, the simple equality between Austin and me made my heart sing. We were bringing our two factions together, and one day we'd build something even greater.

I'd made a good decision with him.

I also wanted to rush him to someplace quiet and rip his clothes off. Would this craving ever cease? Did I want it to?

After a deep breath, I glanced at Austin.

"Drop her," Austin barked.

Broken Sue pulled his arm away. The sound of the body hitting the floor made Edgar start laughing.

"Not as pleasant as being carried," Nessa murmured. A moment later, a middle-aged woman with curly brown hair, severe cheekbones, and high-arching black brows nodded at me as she tucked an empty vial into the back pocket of her jeans. "Hello, everyone. I won't bother asking if you want a seat…or some sweats. This won't take but a minute, and then we'll get you some transportation. The jet is standing by to take you home." She pointed at me. "Do you remember what Chambers said to you before Broken Sue ripped him into pieces?"

"Momar intends to go after Austin's brother's pack. How do you know?"

"We have cameras all over this place. Don't worry, Sebastian turned off the ones in your rooms. You had privacy. No one else did. For every camera they found, there were two they didn't." She turned a finger to Austin, and I felt a sinking in my gut. We hadn't even checked for cameras. Hadn't even thought about it. "And you remember the deal his people tried to make with you?"

"I wasn't really listening," he said gruffly. "I was no-ticing all their weaknesses. Jess mentioned something about this yesterday evening, but…" He tensed, and I knew he'd just held back one of those twitches that were making Elliot so nervous. "I wasn't in a logical place."

"Yes, the mating." Nessa squinted. "Sebastian knows more about that than I do. I confess, I don't really get it. Regardless, you better get in your right mind quickly. Momar has his sights set on your brother. This is what Sebastian was going to tell you before the vampire ate him. Momar won't advance quickly, because your brother is the biggest fish he's ever gone after. By far. Word is, he's collecting mages to help advance his cause, and he'll get them because Kingsley hasn't been quiet about pushing back on the Mages' Guild's influence in the magical world. Momar means to hit him with an overwhelming force." Broken Sue tensed. Nessa noticed it and nodded at him. "Yes, that's their jam, as you know. They don't fight fair. They buy grunts to do the dirty fighting and then follow behind with spells. That's why they didn't know how to combat you guys in the colosseum. In a fight with equal numbers, the shifters will clearly dominate. But that's not how mages fight in real life."

"What kind of numbers are you talking?" Austin asked.

Nessa studied him for a moment. "We don't know exactly. We're working on it. We have some time. A couple months. Maybe a few. After that, Kingsley is going to have his hands full."

Austin nodded but didn't comment. I studied his face for a long moment, knowing we'd help, obviously. That wasn't a question. We'd need more guns. More firepower. We were no strangers to fighting against large odds, but Momar was a growing power in the magical world, and he had access to a huge swell of people who hated shifters, would not balk at helping to take them out, and would fight as dirty as possible.

"I can pull in the gargoyles," I said softly, touching Austin's arm. "Nathanial can command them."

"Yes," Nathanial said, standing taller.

"And if anyone can bring the various alpha shifters together, you can," I told Austin. He'd already been talking about it before we knew about Momar's next intended victim.

"Not in three months," he replied.

"Sebastian can help," Nessa said. "We are owed favors everywhere. He can't bring in the shifters, but he can get you an audience with some big players."

"Other alphas are working with Elliot Graves?" Austin asked.

"Obviously not. A good mage deals in secrets and backdoor discussions. Our network, which Sebastian controls, can get you the meetings. And after this, we'll have some powerful mages who will either stand with us, or stand aside and not interfere."

"Why would you want to help my brother?" Austin asked.

"Me? I don't, particularly," she said without flinching. "If he wants to reclaim his mantle from Momar, there are safer ways of doing it. Shady dealings and double crossings. The mage way. But Sebastian fought beside your brother, I believe, against the phoenix."

Cyra nodded. "He is noble, that tiger."

"Sebastian talks about Kingsley with the utmost respect," Nessa went on. "He also wants to help Miss Ironheart. She'll want to help you. You will, without a doubt, help your brother. So Sebastian is connected to this cause. Even if you don't consent to his friendship or his teaching, Jessie—may I call you Jessie?—he will try to help you. He promised as much when he took you on as an apprentice. Those pledges aren't ironclad among mages, but it was to him." She spread her hands and stepped back. "Look, you can figure all that out for yourself. You'll see what you're up against pretty quickly. Jessie has a crapload of power, but she doesn't know dick. She needs a teacher, and you won't find another mage as powerful and knowledgeable as Sebastian who doesn't want to use you. It was his sister's dying wish that he follow this journey to the end of his life. A smart woman would realize what that means."

"A smart woman can deliver a manipulative speech in the guise of sisterly love," Hollace said.

Nessa laughed. "If she'd killed Sebastian, I would've died trying to avenge him, hopefully taking her down with me." Austin tensed, and power pulsed through the room. Nessa rubbed her arms. "Yeah, yeah, the bear is protective. I get it. Listen, think it over. And if you decide not to allow him into your life, can you leave behind that jewelry we gave you in the basket? That stuff was amazing. I'll take it, no problem."

"Let's go." Austin turned and strode for the door.

"I'll arrange transportation to the jet—"

"Don't bother," Austin cut in. "Jess, can your people fly us?"

"Yep."

Kace softly groaned.

"Okay, well," Nessa called after us. "I guess I'll just mail your stuff to you?"

"Sir, if I may?" Broken Sue murmured as we walked through the tunnel.

"Go," Austin said.

"I know that your inclination is to keep the situation with your brother a shifter matter. In times of danger, especially with our families, we feel like we can only rely on those we trust. We stick with our own. I felt the same way, and I lost everything. Your mate is the doorway to survival, for all of us. Even if you get all of the shifters to stand together, it still won't be enough, not against the kind of might these mages will throw together. They don't fight even remotely fair. They go after the vulnerable, and they use the mercenaries they bring in like pawns. Lives to be thrown away. They have no loyalty themselves, and so they do not adhere to the normal principles of warfare. If you want to truly help your brother—help us all—you will heed that woman's words. You will trust your mate to bolster your pack with people you otherwise wouldn't have access to. To fight beside you with magic. I think you two were brought together for a reason. That is only my opinion, but that's the way I see it."

"The stars are guiding us," the basajaun said. "This mountain is quiet. Peaceful. It does not want violence. This meeting was important. I will call on the elders. The basajaunak will join this fight." Austin glanced back, shock riding the link. "Edgar, we will need more flowers," the basajaun continued. "Maybe some of those violent ones. That was tasty."

"My mother is the biggest busybody in the history of the world," Ulric chimed in. "She knows gargoyles from all over. You want to talk about a network? My mother has a network. I've told her that she isn't allowed to tell anyone outside of the parish there's a new female gargoyle—I was waiting until Jessie was a little more up to speed—but say the word and she can make sure the biggest cairns in the world hear about you, Jessie. If there is a big battle on the horizon, they'll want in because the status of fighting beside a female gargoyle will be passed down their family lines. We can get enough forces to fill the sky."

"I told my mom," Jasper murmured. "My village knows, but…"

"And that's it, right? Yeah. My mom is not a normal gargoyle's wife. She doesn't keep business in the cairn. This is the only time I will brag about that fact."

I slipped my hand in Austin's and grabbed the muumuu that was still on the little table as we passed by. "Kingsley will be okay. We'll make sure of it."

He didn't say anything as we continued, but I could feel the turmoil roiling within him.

CHAPTER 28

AUSTIN HAD BEEN quiet the whole plane ride home, us having used the plane waiting there instead of calling in another. It had been stuffed with snack foods and drinks, but by that point, I hadn't been hungry. Austin had stared out the window, his emotions troubled. It wasn't just worry. There was a certain prickly protectiveness that suggested Broken Sue had gotten it right. Austin wanted to react to danger the shifter way—banding together with those most trusted and fighting. They reached for loyalty and togetherness to get them through hard times.

I guessed I sided with the mages in how I handled things—I would reach for whatever would help us win.

In the limo on the way back, just the two of us, I said, "I'm going to say yes to Elliot."

Austin didn't comment, holding my hand, staring out the window.

"I'm going to have him teach me," I continued, wanting to soothe his worry. "I'll be pissed for a while,

I'm not saying I won't, but…I believe him. I hate to say it, but I believe him. And even if I didn't…we need him. Your brother needs him. I'll walk into the belly of the beast and come out on fire if I have to, but I will show up in your brother's town ready to unleash hell. I'll make you proud to have mated me."

He met my eyes. "Nothing could make me prouder to have mated you. You're perfect as you are. Don't do this for me, or my brother. Do it for you. You need to trust your teacher."

I leaned against him and rested my head on his shoulder. "I just have to get used to the fact that he seriously tricked me. I had *zero* idea. Absolutely no inclination. That guy is good."

"He is. I wasn't sure about him at first, but he seemed genuine when he was at Ivy House. He only wanted the best for you, and he helped protect you. That wasn't an act."

"Yeah."

He was quiet for a moment. Then he breathed out a sigh and said, "Brochan is right. Every fiber of my being is telling me to push away from all these extra people and join my family with just you and my pack. That we'd be enough to face this thing."

"And your logic tells you?"

"That if we do it that way, we'll all die."

"That's why you called in Kingsley when Kinsella came," I said, finally understanding.

"I wasn't thinking about it at the time, but probably, yes. Call in family when things get too big to handle."

"Well…I mean, you *are* calling in family. Extended family. You're bringing in me, and I'm bringing all my gargoyles and my Ivy House crew. The basajaun is bringing in his family—"

"I can't believe that. That would be…incredible."

"Yeah. So you have him. And Ulric's mother will apparently make my gargoyle influence bigger, so we have that. And Elliot and his hookups—some families are just really big. But they're still family."

He huffed out a laugh and shook his head, putting his arm around me and pulling me in. "I know." Another quiet beat. "How will you punish Sebastian for lying to you?"

I laughed as we pulled up to the house. The driver came around and opened my door.

"I'm not sure. I have to think of something vile. Maybe Niamh can help me with a practical joke. I don't even know how I'll—"

The words died on my lips. Right there on the stoop, holding a long stick topped with a filled kerchief, sat Elliot Graves. He stood as I walked up the path.

"After your battles, I always have the last say," he

said, the stick resting on his shoulder.

"How'd you get here before us?" I asked.

He gave me a smile. "Magic. Do you have a couple hours so I can fill you in on my plans? I'll tell you everything. We can knock Momar to his knees and signal to the world that you"—he put his hand to the side of his mouth—"and I…aren't to be messed with, and neither are shifters. The shifters can organize and force the Mages' Guild to start playing by the rules. I have complete confidence we can pull it off, Jessie, but only if I start training you now. There is no time to lose. When you set foot on that battlefield, you need to own your title as sorceress."

I gave him a lofty stare. Austin waited behind me, and I could sense the rest of my people climbing out of the limos. Ivy House was, thankfully, quiet.

"Fine, Elliot—"

"No." He put his hand on his chest. "My birth name is Sebastian. Please, Elliot Graves was a stage name I made up for a different, more ruthless person. Sebastian was what people called me when I was just a weird nerd who liked to play with magic and geek out with Star Wars. I'd like to be your friend again, Jessie. I know I tarnished your trust, but I really did want to stay and train with you. I was happy doing magic in the bowels of Ivy House, or helping Edgar with his flowers. If it was a different world, and I didn't have the name I do, I'd even love to join your team. I am comfortable here. I feel like I can finally be myself."

And just like that, the ice within me melted. I never had been very good at holding grudges.

"Okay. Sebastian. But we won't just bring Momar to his knees. We will tear him off his perch and make an example of him. You do not threaten my friends and live to tell the tale."

The door swung open as I neared it.

Sebastian fell in behind Austin, following us. "Are you ready, alpha? It's time to climb atop your own perch. The female gargoyle and the most ruthless shifter the world has ever known."

"I'm already on that perch," he replied. "The enemy will find out the hard way."

"Okay, but…remember, I'm supposed to be the bad guy," Sebastian said. "Don't steal all my thunder."

As I settled into a chair in the front sitting room, heaving a sigh of relief to be home, Ivy House said, "*I told you so.*"

THE END

About the Author

K.F. Breene is a Wall Street Journal, USA Today, Washington Post, Amazon Most Sold Charts and #1 Kindle Store bestselling author of paranormal romance, urban fantasy and fantasy novels. With over four million books sold, when she's not penning stories about magic and what goes bump in the night, she's sipping wine and planning shenanigans. She lives in Northern California with her husband, two children, and out of work treadmill.

Sign up for her newsletter to hear about the latest news and receive free bonus content.

www.kfbreene.com

CPSIA information can be obtained
at www.ICGtesting.com
Printed in the USA
LVHW111131060822
725316LV00001B/27

9 781734 624694